Readers Love Z. ALLORA

Rocking Thin Ice

"What secrets lie on the surface, who really *is* that person that the cameras want us to see…these two are so completely opposite in every way possible, but the two of them together is nothing more than magical."

—Diverse Reader

The Great Wall

"There is plenty of heartache, drama, desperate people taking desperate measures, and of course beautiful boys and rock stars."

—MM Good Book Reviews

The Temple of Heaven

"…if you're looking for a read that has cultural and psychological depth, multilayered characters, a wonderful plot, and a love that will not be denied, then you will probably like this novel as much as I do."

—Rainbow Book Reviews

Illusions & Dreams

"There erotic elements are subtle, but well done, and there's quite a bit of humor to balance out the tears and the fears…in the end, what you have here is a story of four lovers, finding each other and finding themselves."

—Beauty in Ruins Reviews

By Z. ALLORA

Bent Not Broken
The Craving
Illusions & Dreams
The Librarian's Rake
The Longest Night
Not Another Boy Band
Rocking Thin Ice

ENTWINED DREAMS
Lock and Key
Secured and Free

JUST BL
Just Acting
Just Pretending

MADE IN CHINA
The Great Wall
The Temple of Heaven

Published by DREAMSPINNER PRESS
www.dreamspinnerpress.com

Z. Allora

JUST PRETENDING

Published by
DREAMSPINNER PRESS
8219 Woodville Hwy #1245
Woodville, FL 32362 USA
www.dreamspinnerpress.com

This is a work of fiction. Names, characters, places, and incidents either are the product of author imagination or are used fictitiously, and any resemblance to actual persons, living or dead, business establishments, events, or locales is entirely coincidental.

Just Pretending
© 2026 Z. Allora

Cover Art
© 2026 Andrei Bat
https://99designs.com/profiles/bandrei
Cover content is for illustrative purposes only and any person depicted on the cover is a model.

All rights reserved. This book is licensed to the original purchaser only. Duplication or distribution via any means is illegal and a violation of international copyright law, subject to criminal prosecution and upon conviction, fines, and/or imprisonment. Any eBook format cannot be legally loaned or given to others. No part of this book may be reproduced or transmitted in any form or by any means, electronic or mechanical, including photocopying, recording, or by any information storage and retrieval system, without the written permission of the Publisher, except where permitted by law. To request permission and all other inquiries, contact Dreamspinner Press, 8219 Woodville Hwy #1245, Woodville FL 32362 USA, or www.dreamspinnerpress.com.

Any unauthorized use of this publication to train generative artificial intelligence (AI) is expressly prohibited.

Trade Paperback ISBN: 9781641088831
Digital ISBN: 9781641088824
Trade Paperback published April 2026
v. 1.0

This is dedicated to all the BL actors and actresses who have founded new production houses to give us amazing stories.

Acknowledgments

I want to thank Dreamspinner for the opportunity to share my stories.

Big hugs to my talented alpha reader, Amaya. She assisted me in untangling my squirrel speak.

Huge thanks to Andi and her incredible team for making my words tell the story I want to share. She helps my words sparkle.

As always to the love of my life; without you by my side, I would have never believed in happy endings. Thank you for the last thirty-eight years of love, happiness, and romance.

And to you, dear reader, for accepting my invitation to go to Thailand with me to explore the BL industry through *Just Pretending*.

AUTHOR'S NOTE

Dear Reader,

This series is a love letter to the Thai BL industry. *Just Pretending* is my way of correcting reality so I can give the characters the happy ending I need them to have.

I'm not glossing over the cruelty and pain this industry has caused people, because unfortunately these types of abuses happen globally in the entertainment industry. No matter the language we speak, there are people who take advantage of the innocence that is always in the background.

However in recent years the fandom has witnessed production houses change their policies and protections for their artists. Sometimes actors create their own opportunities by writing screenplays, investing in productions, or setting up their own companies. The people I dedicated this book to did just that, producing television programs and managing talent, partly because of negative experiences they faced with management and production companies.

In the past ten years, I've followed many painful scandals that ruined or almost ruined careers and have sunk some of my favorite acting couples (meaning no second season).

The industry has a long way to go, but I will stay the course because I believe in the Thai BL industry and that love always wins (at least when I'm writing it does).

Many hugs,
Z. Allora

CHAPTER 1

"WHERE IS everyone?" Dusit Sitwat glanced up from the latest social media post that rang his notifications. The bar was empty. He grabbed on to the bar top to stop himself from meeting the floor.

The bartender threw a hand out to help keep him on the stool. "Careful there. It's closing time. Everyone's gone home."

"Home." Dusit sighed. Such an incredible idea—a safe place to call your own, but one that seemed out of reach living in Bangkok.

"Thanks." He should really know the guy's name. He'd been coming in here for a few months. No one knew him, but he found the familiar faces more comfortable to get drunk around. "Everyone's gone?" Dusit was alone again.

"Sleeping it off. Exactly what you should be doing. Can I call you a taxi?" The bartender tossed the bar cloth in a bin.

Dusit waved him off. "Nah, it's okay. I can walk."

The music changed from something easily ignored to something familiar. The angelic voice reached out to him.

"Let me sit for a minute." Dusit laid his head on the bar and crooned the words. The lyrics stirred his heart with the best memories of his life, followed by gut-wrenching pain.

He drank the shot in front of him.

"Oh shit," the bartender said. "Sorry. Let me find the remote and turn this off. I know how you hate this song."

Was this guy that good that he'd noticed? "Why do you think that?"

"I gauged your reaction." The bartender shrugged. "And you told me several times you hate hearing this song."

"Sorry." Dusit hoped he hadn't rambled or raged much.

"Where is—ah. Found it." The bartender pulled out the remote from inside a drawer and pointed the clicker at the stereo system.

"Don't. Don't." Maybe he had no right to demand anything, but this near stranger honored the request.

"Sure, man. Whatever you want." The bartender put the remote away.

Whether Dusit heard this song or not, it had embedded itself in his heart years ago and would forever play on an endless loop. "So, you like this song?"

"It's an excellent song, and my sisters love it." The bartender grabbed a fresh cloth and began wiping down the liquor bottles.

Dusit sighed and set his empty glass on the coaster. "You know, I wasn't even a singer or an actor when I had moved to Bangkok."

"Where from?" The bartender continued to straighten up behind the bar.

"Chiang Mai. I got a job at a production studio, working in their maintenance department." The job was mostly indoors, and it paid well.

The bartender paused and tilted his head, which was all the invitation Dusit needed to continue.

Shrugging, he admitted the truth. "It was crazy. I had been passing by to change a light bulb at the end of the hall."

"Passing by where?" The guy leaned on the bar, listening intently the way bartenders did.

"The recording studio. This woman—the singer's mother, it turned out—asked me to stand in for the other singer, who couldn't make it."

Dusit's words might have been a bit slurred, but from the look on the bartender's face, he was making himself clear enough. The man seemed interested.

"Whose mother?" the bartender asked.

"*His*." Pain ripped through Dusit, wrapped in regret as it did whenever he so much as thought the name, let alone tried to say it out loud.

"Oh, okay." None of the judgment his vague words usually received sounded in the bartender's voice.

Dusit wanted someone to believe him. "I tried telling her I didn't sing except for a little karaoke. You know what she said?"

The bartender leaned toward him. "No clue."

"She laughed at me and told me she expected little. I would be a placeholder for someone better." That summed up the story of his life. "Sorry, I'm rambling."

"I don't mind. Talk to me. I'm all ears." The bartender tossed a fresh towel on the bar and started freeing the shiny surface of wet circles left behind by patrons. "You were a maintenance worker, and they wanted you to stand in as a singer? What did you do?"

Ah, the bartender was clearly invested now. Good. Dusit knew his story seemed unreal—and maybe it was. At least it sometimes seemed that way to him, and retelling it might be the only way he could convince himself it all happened. "I followed her into the studio. That was the first time I laid eyes on him."

"Him?"

Dusit could still feel the desire, enthrallment, longing, wrapped up with feeling unworthy of such an angel. "He was so shy he didn't even look at me when he handed me the page of lyrics. And when he finally glanced up at me while we were singing, he had the biggest eyes, and I lost my heart to him."

The confession hurt, but maybe the ache was good. Hurt reminded him that everything they had been to each other had been real.

"Who?"

"Him. My heart…." Dusit swallowed hard. "Gamon Chaisit."

"Wait." The bartender pointed to the speaker. "Gamon Chaisit? Actor? Model? This singer? The one with two number-one hits?"

Best person in the entire world. Dusit grunted, "Yeah."

When Dusit entered the recording studio, they hadn't spoken to each other. The first words they exchanged were the lyrics of the song.

"My sisters love that guy," the bartender said.

So do I.

"Did you sing this duet with him?"

Recording that song made everything seem possible. He had felt the world opening and welcoming him. Instead of answering, Dusit sang the lyrics along with the stereo. "I love you. Don't break my heart. I love you…."

The excitement that had plowed through him whenever he'd caught Gamon's gaze overwhelmed him. Singing the words of the song was much like an admission of love that was as true the first time he sang the words as it was now. He had held on to Gamon's gaze throughout all the various takes of the recording. From that first moment on, being with each other was magical, or at least that's how Dusit felt until everything evaporated.

Once he started singing along in the bar, there was no way not to continue through to the end.

The bartender stopped wiping down the bar and peered at him as the song concluded on a high note. "So *this* is Gamon Chaisit, and that's you singing?"

Dusit glanced around for an escape. His drunken ramble had ripped away his privacy, and the exit door seemed too far away.

"Wait, you're Dusit Sitwat. After that reality show a couple of years ago—"

"I had my fifteen minutes." Dusit ran a hand over the stubble that didn't always work to hide who he was.

How he wished he could forget all the mistakes he'd made between singing that song and now.

Every time he woke up alone, the hurt and betrayal of Gamon disappearing from his life slashed through him. And every morning since, he'd never gotten used to waking up alone in an empty bed. But Gamon was no longer reachable. That was something his heart still didn't understand.

Gamon's mother had told him in no uncertain terms the relationship between him and her son was over. He'd waited for Gamon to reach out and tell him what was going on.

HE WAITED and waited, because he longed to hear what had gone wrong from Gamon himself, and then he'd try again. But she always answered and continued to let him know her son had moved on to better things.

Dusit was left with no recourse. Gamon never reached out to him, and that spoke to how little Gamon had valued what they had.

Gamon had done what many Thai entertainers have done—did a series simply as a stepping-stone to his singing career, which was going rather well. Dusit had been another stone Gamon used to continue down the path to success. If given a chance, Dusit would do whatever it took to have one more chance to sing even one more song with him….

Why was he moving?

He opened his eyes. Ah, so he'd closed his eyes. Why was there motion?

The bartender tapped his shoulder. "Man, I'm locking up. You okay?"

"I don't know. That last shot really got me. Even if I can't have him, I should at least clean up my—" Time to find another bar.

Dusit stood.

Everything spun.

Ow! His ass hit the floor. He needed to rest before he got back to his feet.

CHAPTER 2

GAMON CHAISIT'S cell phone buzzed again.

A quick glance said it was the usual evening call from his ex-manager. That's what he categorized his mother as, and until she apologized and let him live his life, he'd dodge calls and visits from her.

He'd never imagined she'd betray him the way she had. It has been two months since he'd found out how she'd blown up his life five years ago.

Maybe his reaction was harsh, but he needed to stand on his own without her wishes and needs affecting every decision he made. This separation and the strict boundary might allow him to heal and have a relationship with her in the future.

Perhaps. But currently she refused to listen to him, so he wouldn't answer her calls. Parent or not, she'd caused him too many regrets.

Gamon craned his neck left and then right, providing a satisfying crack.

He grinned as he read Achara's email. They'd been friends for years. If there was tea to be spilled, especially on which actor was dating their co-star or who had a girlfriend, she made sure he was in the loop. After spending a little time away from the Y-series fan culture, he resented how actors and actresses needed to hide their relationships for fear of becoming unpopular.

Achara gave advice but never took it. Still, she concluded the email by telling him he was right and agreeing that her new doctor was trying to get a date with her by making her come in for extra hormone checks.

"I told you so," Gamon said to the empty room.

Achara always had fascinating adventures to share with him.

He sent a quick note back, including his new condo address, and now that he was back in Bangkok, he promised to get together with her soon. It had been exhausting finishing out his contracts in France while still taking on parts in Thailand.

Now he refocused on answering his fan email.

Gamon responded to one of the usual questions he got with yes. He originally wanted to be a singer, but acting was where he found the freedom to be himself. What he didn't say was how grateful he was that acting gave him his one true love, for however short a time the relationship lasted. He'd known pure love.

The next email touched him with the sincerity of the sweet words, but he didn't need to click the link to the video to know it was a fan-made video made up of clips from years ago. He'd seen every one of them numerous times.

He sighed.

There had to be some way to make himself stop yearning for the past. Not for the first time, he promised himself he'd start checking out some dating apps, or at least a hookup app, to get back out there. No one was near him to control his every move; he needed to try.

"Yeah, like that ever worked." He talked to the empty room, but he had to release his doubt about the idea.

Gamon had attempted a few dates after he stopped his mother from setting him up with women, but he didn't enjoy any of them. He'd gone on three dates in the last three years—not an impressive average—and the dates all ended before they even started.

He couldn't help himself. Taking a deep breath, he clicked the link the fan attached.

His eyes got blurry as he watched the clip. The fan-made video pieced together snippets from *Don't Break My Heart* and fan meets to show the chemistry and love between him and Dusit.

God, how could he have lost the best thing that ever happened to him?

The video ended with a searing kiss that Gamon still felt to this day.

He opened yet another email begging for him to consider *Don't Break My Heart 2*. The fans were unaware that he had very little say in whether that Y-series drama would ever be made.

Gamon had read the novels that the Y-series was based on, and if he was in control, he'd jump at the chance. That way even if there was no hope for his happy ending, at least his character could have one.

Embedded in the email was another link. Apparently he was a masochist, because he opened the link.

Dusit's beautiful face filled the screen. Then the camera panned back to reveal Gamon and an interviewer. There was no way he could have hidden the love he had for Dusit. His adoration shone through every part of him until he glowed with affection.

He paused the video and studied Dusit's body language and his expression. Gamon would have bet everything he owned that Dusit had felt the same way he did… but here he was alone. Gamon lost everything he never really had.

His love for Dusit still burned bright in his heart and mind. His body ached for Dusit. The video morphed into the two of them singing *Don't Break My Heart's* theme song at a fan meet.

His mind dragged him back to the beginning.

THE DAY he and Dusit met was the first day they had sung together, and it always struck him as destiny. The recording session started with upset and chaos, mostly because of his mother's demands on his would-be co-star.

Gamon had been terrified because he didn't want to act, but his mother convinced him to take the part so they could showcase his singing talent. He was excited to sing the original theme song, but the producer informed him his co-star had resigned from the series.

His mother demanded, "Why did that little sandfly back out of the entire project?"

The producer shrugged. "He didn't think it would be an easy working relationship."

His mother had picked the actor apart, and now they were without a co-star and someone to sing the duet with. "Was that the only reason?"

The producer sighed. "The actor's manager said he was uncomfortable with some of the NC scenes."

Gamon's mother grimaced. "NC scenes? What are those?"

Pasting on a smile, the producer explained, "NC is shorthand for not-for-children scenes."

She placed her hand over her heart and stared at Gamon like he'd done something wrong. "What scenes are my Gamon doing that aren't for children?"

"There are a couple of scenes that are a bit spicy." The producer spoke slowly, as if that would help her understand.

"How spicy?" she asked, horrified, as if she hadn't read the script.

"Some kissing scenes." The producer was fibbing, because from what Gamon had read, it was much more than kissing.

"So this actor is refusing his part. Fine. Find someone else who is okay with NC scenes." Gamon's mother's voice sharpened as she made her demands as if that wasn't what the entire production house was scrambling to do.

Time and money both wasted.

Gamon didn't understand why anyone would take such a role and assume they could change it into something else. Unfortunately that wasn't the last time he'd seen blatant homophobia in the industry.

The producer was furiously texting as he spoke. "Casting is looking for a replacement, but we've got this sound studio today only, so we need to do this song today. Even if it's Gamon's part."

And then a beautiful man sauntered past the glass walls of the sound studio. Gamon stared so hard, he dropped the sheet music.

Pointing at the man, his mother asked, "What about him?"

The producer waved her off. "I believe he works in maintenance and is not an actor."

His mother shot into the hallway and shouted, "Hey, you. Can you sing?"

"Me?" Dusit looked down in that sweet way of his and said, "A little."

AS THE video in front of Gamon continued to play, anyone would say Dusit understated his voice.

He looked at the sheet music only for a couple of minutes before signaling his readiness.

Their first take gave Gamon chills, and the second run-through made him fall in love with Dusit right there in that recording studio. Everything and everyone vanished, and the only one who existed was Dusit, with his soft smile and his sparkling brown eyes that lit with affection as he sang the lyrics.

Gamon touched his heart as he remembered the pain caused by his mother's assurance that Dusit was probably just pretending to be interested in him to get the abandoned role.

Staring at his computer, he decided no, he wouldn't write off what they shared on- or off-screen. Their love had been real and deep.

No! Don't look back. You must look forward… but back is where he wanted to go. Back to when he got stolen moments away from his mother to spend with Dusit. The private jokes and little touches for only him to savor.

But there was no way back. Too much time had slipped past before he found out how his mother had ripped them apart.

There was no closure between him and Dusit. Dusit simply left without a goodbye, vanishing after a night they'd spent together.

Or so he'd thought for years. But a couple of months ago, during one of his mother's tirades to a producer, he overheard her spill the truth. She threatened the production house that she'd cut them out of Gamon's life the same way she had Dusit.

First he was shocked, then confused, and now he was seething with anger.

Over the last couple of years, Gamon only heard snippets of how Dusit was doing through their mutual friends, but even that bit of information trickled to nothing.

Thirsty for the tiniest bit about Dusit, Gamon clicked through his social media platforms again. He only found a drought. The most recent posts were from three years ago.

Sometimes Gamon wanted to find him and make sure Dusit was okay. They could never get back what they'd lost. That was long gone, but.... He wanted to apologize for what his mother had taken from them both.

CHAPTER 3

DUSIT LAY still as voices seeped into his brain. He kept his eyes closed.

One seemed familiar, but another was a female voice. With any luck, they would grow tired of watching him pretend to sleep and he could slip out from wherever he was.

Perhaps he should feel more disturbed when waking up in a strange place, but that was commonplace for Dusit. This time it was soft and not a sticky bar floor, or worse, an alley behind a bar.

"Are you sure it's him?" a quiet voice asked.

"That's what he said. He was drunk, but I couldn't leave him on the floor of my bar." The guy was probably the bartender.

The man had no knowledge that Dusit was no stranger to sleeping on bar floors.

A high-pitched squeal was followed by thudding footsteps that stopped a meter from him. "Oh my! What is Dusit Sitwat doing on our sofa?"

"He passed out at the bar, so I brought him home last night," said the bartender.

Bringing home a stranger was risky. Either the man was brave or stupid.

"That was ten hours ago. Shouldn't we try to wake him? He must be thirsty," the woman said with much less squeal, much more concern, but the same amount of excitement.

A fan would make his escape more difficult, and there were probably pictures on various social media platforms of him sleeping it off. Again, not for the first time, but irritating when someone worried his mother by putting his antics on display.

"How do you even know it is him?" another voice chimed in.

"I'd recognize him anywhere, and even if that failed, look at his tattoo." Acknowledging his *Don't Break My Heart* tattoo identified her as a definite fan. "There were rumors he and Gamon Chaisit got couple tattoos."

Dusit laid a hand on his chest and tried to swallow all the memories that pounded in his heart and threatened to surface at her words.

The bartender cleared his throat. "I don't know about that, but I think we should wake him up. He's got to be hungry."

"No, he's been through too much these last few years. Let him sleep." His fan was trying to protect him. Fans could be a very kind group of people… if you gave them what they wanted.

"What do you mean?" the bartender asked.

Yeah, what did she mean? Dusit always felt amazed by how many people knew about his life.

"After *Don't Break My Heart the Series* ended, he and Gamon broke up. He spiraled after that and lost all his brand ambassador deals. People started spreading a rumor that he got kicked off a reality show for being drunk and argumentative.

"I wasn't argumentative." Drunk, probably, but he couldn't let anyone talk rudely about Gamon. Dusit needed to open his eyes. "I simply corrected misinformation someone spewed."

Then he did open his eyes—ouch! He shut them immediately. When he dared peek through mostly closed eyes, bright light and three faces appeared before him. The bartender, a smiling young woman, and a frowning teenager stared at him.

Struggling to sit up, Dusit accepted a bottle of water from the young woman as the teenager glared, arms folded over her chest. "Thank you."

He drank all the water as they studied him like he was teaching a method-acting class on how to act hungover.

The bartender patted him on the shoulder. "My sisters are going to make some breakfast. Want some?"

He stood and glanced around for a door leading to the outside. "I don't want to bother you. I should head—"

The bartender handed him a towel and some clean clothing he had under one arm. "These should fit you. Bathroom is through that door."

Dusit wanted to argue. He should flee this family gathering, but a hot shower would feel amazing.

After the shower, he felt the most refreshed he'd been in years and followed his nose out to the dining room.

They'd laid out skewers of chicken and pork, omelets over rice with sweet chili sauce, and even khao tom, his favorite comfort soup, on the table. How long had he been in the shower? "This is a feast."

The woman smiled. "We didn't know what you liked, so—"

"My sister fangirled and made you everything we had in the fridge," the bartender said, smirking at his very pink-faced sister.

She shook her head. "I did not. I—"

"I'm Charong Rattana," he interrupted. "This is my sister Chatchada. She goes to Chulalongkorn University."

Chatchada smiled at him. "I'm studying pharmaceutical science—I want to work in research. I'm a big fan. Please call me Chat."

Dusit smiled, trying to avoid his regret at not continuing his own studies in engineering. But his folks needed the money to move out of the night market and into a shop of their own. Maybe if he had continued….

"I'm the youngest and most forgotten." The teenager's arms remained crossed over her chest like she was erecting a wall.

Charong snorted. "Right. Our parents, who are starting a chain of family restaurants in Europe, call their very forgotten child twice a day."

"What? They need advice. It's not to talk to me." She glared at Dusit as if she expected him to deny this information.

Charong chuckled and gestured to the not-forgotten teen. "This is Chatrasuda. She attends the NIST International High School."

"Smart family," Dusit muttered. Fancy, top-notch schools, comfortable home, and nice people. He was out of his element.

"The name is Lyric," Chatrasuda—Lyric—advised him while adjusting the school uniform she wore over biker shorts.

He remembered how to be polite. "Got it. I'm—"

Chat grinned and said, "You're Dusit Sitwat from Chiang Rai, but you moved to Bangkok about six years ago. You were working at the production studio in the maintenance department when Gamon Chaisit asked you to sing with him, and then you became one of the best BL actors ever."

"Actually, it was his mother, who is his manager, who found me." He'd been a warm body… a placeholder until the director saw the spark between them.

Chat wrinkled her nose. "At the time, yes, but that manager partnership has sunk."

"What?" News to him. Gamon listened to everything his mother said and did everything she commanded him to do. "She's no longer his manager? When did that change? Why did that change?"

"There was a quiet switch in management a few months ago. Right before he moved back to Bangkok," Chat said and then waved her hand toward the table. "Please sit and eat breakfast."

Gamon was in Bangkok? And had parted ways with his mother? Dusit had seen nothing like that on Gamon's social media… not that he looked more than once or twice a day.

Suddenly his stomach unknotted, and his extreme hunger registered as he inhaled the scent of grilled meat and the sweet chili sauce. He sat and shoveled an omelet into his mouth, barely chewed twice before swallowing. Perhaps he'd missed a few meals. That happened when he was drinking. "So good."

Chat, who didn't stop smiling at him, put several skewers on his plate. "Please enjoy."

"Thank you." He ate at a slower pace and tasted the delicious sugary tang of the chili sauce.

Charong pointed at Lyric. "Remember to take out your earrings. I don't want you in trouble again at school."

Lyric huffed and rolled her eyes but then removed the three silver hoops and one long dangling one from her left ear. "So dumb."

Leaning in, Chat asked, "Where have you been for the past few years?"

"Working construction and odd jobs." And on the floors of bars. He worked enough to send money home and to keep him in beer.

"But you will go back to acting for the second season of *Don't Break My Heart*, right?"

Dusit frowned, hating to disappoint her. "It's been five years. I doubt they will do another season, and if they do, I'm sure they can find someone far more skilled than me."

"Nope." Chat gasped and frowned at him. "It's still the best series out there."

"Used to be...," he mumbled. The Y-series content was much better now. More realistic and with a clear push toward equality. He didn't keep up much, but that's what people were saying on the various platforms.

"No, you and Gamon were incredible."

Dusit didn't mean for the sound of an injured deer to come out of his mouth, but he couldn't press his lips together tight enough to stop it.

"Oh, I—"

Charong gave his sister a look, which thankfully stopped Chat's backpedaling. "Hey, man. I don't know your situation, but if you work in construction—"

"Yeah, it's been on and off." He had plenty to be ashamed of, but sending money to his family by working with his hands wasn't one of them.

"I need help in the bar. Doesn't pay much, but it's air-conditioned, and you keep all your tips. And there's a room in the back you can stay in rent-free if you'd like."

Chat vibrated in her seat. "Yes, that would be great. Charong redid the bathroom last year, and I decorated it in white tiles like the home-decorating shows."

Dusit chuckled. He used to watch those shows with his mother. "Does it have a soaking tub?"

"Yes! See, I told you that tub was a selling point," Chat said gleefully, using his joke against her brother in what must have been an old argument.

Shaking his head and waving a hand in front of him, Dusit said, "No, I didn't mean—"

"No worries, man," Charong said, grinning. "Job is yours if you want it. Usually five till ten Tuesday through Thursday, and Friday and Saturday from seven until close."

Charong seemed like a nice guy, so Dusit asked, "What would the job entail?"

"Bussing tables, bartending, cleaning the bathrooms, and sometimes helping me if a fight breaks out."

Looking around the table at the happy family, Dusit knew the setup came with too many potential ties, but the job was plush compared to the work he had been doing. "Okay, but I don't know how long I'll stay."

Charong grinned. "No long-term commitment needed. I'm not clingy."

Chat bounced in her seat. "Eeeeee! Wait, does that mean you're returning to acting?"

Did it?

No, never again. But he wanted to be upfront about keeping his options open. If a better job came along, he'd have to take it. "Doubtful," he said.

AT THE end of his third week, Dusit took a seat at the bar and sipped at the glass of sparkling water Charong handed him.

"Busy night." Charong counted out a healthy stack of baht and handed the pile over to Dusit.

"Yeah." Dusit folded the wad of money and shoved it into his pocket. He'd wire money home tomorrow.

"So what are you doing with your money?"

Not spending it on booze, hard as that had been at times, especially surrounded by so much temptation. But he had always managed to stay barely this side of full-on alcoholism, drying out between binges when he needed to work, and he certainly wasn't going to repay Charong's kindness by taking advantage of him. "Sending money home, and I've got an appointment to get a tattoo removed."

He needed to move on, and the constant reminder of not being good enough for Gamon wasn't helping.

"Interesting. I hear taking it off doesn't hurt as much as the inking did." Charong patted him on the arm and gave him a pleased smile. "You seem better."

"I am. Not drinking, eating regularly, thanks to your sister, and I've even started running in the mornings." Hell, being able to exercise because he wasn't too sore from construction work was a novelty.

"Good. I'm glad." Charong continued straightening behind the bar.

It was good to have a friend and people who cared about him. They showed him he mattered.

A DAY LATER, Dusit looked around the all-white room as he lay there waiting for the doctor. He glared at the *Don't Break My Heart* logo tattoo scrolled on his bicep, surrounded by a colorful rainbow heart. He had gotten it the night of the first table read for the series. This tattoo held so much meaning.

Several actors had gone to get the same tattoo, and he'd gone along. It was a milestone he'd never imagined, let alone achieved. Acting had come naturally to him. But now he wished he could forget. This was one small step in the direction of moving forward.

A guy in a white coat swooped in. "Sawasdee krub. I'll be the doctor performing the removal. Is this it?"

Dusit *wai*ed back at the doctor. "Yes."

"Do you have other tattoos?" After Dusit confirmed he did, the doctor asked, "May I see?"

He pulled open the medical robe he was wearing to reveal his chest.

The doctor ran his gloved fingers over the name inked over Dusit's heart.

"Do you want this one removed too?"

An unexpected sob caught in Dusit's throat, and he placed a protective hand over the name. "No, never." Maybe it was wrong, but it was the only answer he could give.

He had gotten Gamon's name inked over his heart, but he never got to show him the tattoo, because that next day was when Gamon's mother made it clear Gamon had no interest in continuing any kind of relationship with him.

Rubbing his heart didn't ease the ache, but he'd never remove Gamon's name, and even if he did, it wouldn't matter. He would always carry Gamon etched into his heart, with or without the ink.

"Okay. So you want this one removed? The *Don't Break My Heart*. It's artistically done." The doctor traced the heart around the words with his gloved finger.

Dusit needed to do this. He should move on, but removing this tattoo would be removing part of himself.

He couldn't do this. Dusit shot off the table. "I'm sorry, I've changed my mind."

"Are you sure? You will lose a fourth of your deposit," the doctor reminded him.

"I'm sure." He couldn't get rid of this part of his past because he didn't want to let go.

Dusit tossed the robe on the bed and pulled on his T-shirt.

THE NEXT day Dusit said, "Thank you, Chat, for a lovely breakfast, but you shouldn't be late for school." Most days they insisted he have breakfast with their family.

"I've got afternoon classes today." Chat smiled at him.

Lyric rolled her eyes at her sister and grabbed the plates to carry them into the kitchen.

"You can leave them. Your brother and I will do them." He playfully punched Charong in the arm to stop him from bitching. "Your sisters cook delicious food, so we should clean. That's what my mother taught me."

Charong hid his grin and offered him a sad face instead. "Fine. I just—"

Dusit's cell phone buzzed. He glanced at the screen before swiping Do Not Accept.

Charong peered down at the lit screen. "Looks like you're getting another call."

"Yeah, it's been my agent's office calling." He turned the phone over. "Ex-agent. My contract must be up by now."

"Why don't you answer it? Maybe he's got a job for you, or an audition." Charong drank his tea.

Dusit had burned too many bridges. "The last time the office called, they wanted me to show up to an audition where the part was already slated for another actor." Not that he would ever work with anyone other than Gamon. Still, it had been nice to see Rose.

Charong squinted at him. "Why would they want you to do that?"

"He's trying to salvage my career or something, but that ship has sailed. So I don't know what he wants." And Dusit tried hard not to care.

The phone buzzed again.

Pointing, Charong said, "You could answer the call—if for no other reason than to stop getting calls constantly."

Dusit hesitated, but when he turned the phone over, the call wasn't from his agent's office.

This caller deserved an answer, if only for the sheer number of times he had pulled Dusit off the floor. "Rose, sawasdee krub."

"A miracle! You're alive," Rose teased him.

Dusit scoffed, "All rumors."

"I'm calling from Kanawat Anwar's office."

That was odd. "Why are you calling from my agent's office?"

"I'm working with him. I've got news. Are you sitting down?"

Dusit pulled the phone away from his ear to frown at the screen. He sighed and braced himself. "I told you when Anwar sent me on that pretend audition that I was done with acting."

He'd done the audition for Rose's last series to show people he wasn't the screw-up they believed him to be, and… he hadn't expected to see Gamon, but he had hoped.

"I think you might reconsider." Rose sounded pleased with himself.

Dusit didn't want to play guessing games. "Why?"

"They want to make *Don't Break My Heart 2*."

Getting gut-punched and kicked in the teeth at the same time might have described how he felt at that moment. He exhaled hard, and a tremor tore through him. "No. That can't be."

"Yes." Rose chuckled.

This made no sense. "After so long?"

"Yes." Rose spoke slower.

He turned away from Charong to hide his hurt and jealousy. "Who will play the leads?"

"Obviously you and Gamon." Rose's tone suggested Dusit was foolish to even ask the question.

Chaos broke out in Dusit's brain while happy screaming took over his heart. "That's as crazy as it is impossible."

Gamon wanted nothing to do with him. Right?

Dusit was having trouble catching his breath, because regardless of how impossible the situation was, his damned heart was triple-timing it.

"I'm getting my life together, Rose." He didn't need to be knocked off track. The disappointment he would feel when Gamon declined the role was too painful to imagine. It was better to not even go there.

"But Dusit—"

"I've got to go, Rose." Dusit ended the call before hope got the better of him.

Chapter 4

When Gamon's phone buzzed, he set his drink on the table and grabbed it.

His new agent was calling.

After the drama with his mother as his agent and manager, why had Gamon made the mistake of signing with an agent who was a friend? He should keep his private and professional lives separate.

The problem was, Gamon found it impossible to say no to Rose. The actor had recently started working with Kanawat Anwar's agency, and he only worked with a couple of actors. Rose had always been a good friend, so Gamon decided to use whatever clout he still had in the industry to help make Rose legit. No question Rose would have Gamon's best interests at heart.

Gamon decided to let the call go to voicemail.

Each time Rose talked to him, part of the conversation revolved around options for a new role. Rose was like a parent looking for a marriage match, but he didn't push.

In the last couple of months, Rose had booked him modeling jobs, a brand ambassador deal, and several minor roles in Thailand, allowing him to move back from France. He had played a coffee shop owner, a best friend, and even a car mechanic. That role had been fun, except for trying to get the oil out of his hair and from under his nails. Acting in those parts was a reminder to Gamon of how much he missed the entire process… and Dusit.

He longed for Dusit with every breath he took, but being on the film set heightened the loss. The expectation of running lines with Dusit or finding a private location so they could be together played havoc with his heart.

His phone beeped with Rose's message, and Gamon listened to it. "I have some interesting news," Rose said. "Call me back."

Was he going to start trying to push Gamon into another ship? How could Gamon agree to someone else? He couldn't work with anyone else. Crazy, but that would feel like an infidelity his heart wouldn't allow.

He'd been with a few men since Dusit. Originally he'd hoped that it was his lack of experience that made him so hung up on Dusit. Though the sex was a simple physical release to ease the pain momentarily, he'd experienced nothing close to what he'd had with Dusit.

His phone buzzed with another call. Rose again.

Gamon pressed his lips together but smiled despite himself at Rose's persistence. He sat at his dining room table and answered, "Hello, Rose."

"I'm glad I called back. Remember when I told you I'd find you a series that you'd want to do?" Rose asked with more excitement than usual.

Gamon sighed. "Thank you, but you know—"

"That you won't take a lead without playing opposite Dusit Sitwat, right?"

"Correct." He tried to pretend that the idea that would never happen didn't break his heart all over again.

"And that's why I'm calling you about *this* lead role," Rose said and then was quiet, acknowledging Gamon's requirements with the utmost patience.

The silence allowed Gamon to process Rose's words. No, that *couldn't* be what he meant.

"What? You can't be serious." Gamon tried to catch his breath. No way would Dusit say yes to working with him again.

"I am."

"You can't—"

"You'd be playing opposite Dusit Sitwat in season two of *Don't Break My Heart the Series*."

The snow globe of his world tipped. Gamon was glad he was sitting. "Really?"

"They want to do a second season of *Don't Break My Heart the Series.* You'll be playing opposite Dusit… and yes, I do mean Dusit Sitwat."

Shaking his head, Gamon couldn't fathom the possibility. "Dusit? My Dusit is going to act again… with me?"

"Your Dusit?" Rose's tone suggested he had caught Gamon's possessiveness about Dusit and was smiling.

"Rose…. Are you sure? That… he'll consider it?" Gamon must be dreaming.

"Your Dusit will be in the series."

There had to be a catch. "He agreed?"

"Kanawat is allowing me to represent Dusit." Rose hesitated. "I wouldn't bring this to you if I didn't think he would."

There it was, and the other shoe hit him right in the head. "So he hasn't agreed yet."

"Technically, no. But he will. I understand where he is on this," Rose reassured him with confidence.

Petting his chest, Gamon tried to imagine what would make Dusit come back to acting. Surely he'd never agree. But Gamon asked, "Is he doing okay?"

"Better than he's been in a long time."

Gamon's heart calmed, though the thought of Dusit doing okay seemed unlikely. Gamon had seen little information about Dusit in a while, but what had been said of him before that was alarming. "Really?"

"Yeah, he's got himself together."

Gamon was skeptical. He had been worried about Dusit for some time. "But he's still drinking, right?"

"He's no longer using alcohol to self-medicate."

"Self-medicate?"

Rose chuckled. "Recently I went to some classes on rebranding. Even though it sounds like spin, many people don't deal with their issues properly, so they use drugs, alcohol, food, or sex to make themselves feel better temporarily. Actors are no different."

That made sense. "Hmm."

"They call that self-medicating."

Maybe he could view what he'd done as self-medicating with sex. "So, he's stopped medicating with alcohol?"

"Yeah, and he's working. He looks good."

"You saw him?" Gamon didn't demand Dusit's address on the spot because he was afraid—afraid of seeing him, of not seeing him, of seeing him and Dusit not wanting to see *him*. Why would Dusit want to see him after Gamon's mother broke up their relationship and made it appear as if that was Gamon's choice?

"Not personally, but I know where he is. I tracked him down when he wouldn't stay on the phone long enough to have a complete conversation."

"Where is he?" Gamon couldn't keep the desperate need out of his voice.

"He's in Bangkok, working in a friend's bar." Rose said it calmly, like this wasn't big news.

"A bar?" Wait, if he used alcohol to—

"He's not drinking, though." Rose sounded confident.

Gamon wanted to believe that was true. "How do you know?"

"Someone I know has seen him and said he looks healthy."

Sounded like stalking to Gamon. "Someone you know?"

Rose cleared his throat. "The Kanawat Anwar Agency doesn't play games."

"Meaning?"

"Kanawat employs people to… vet people without notice."

"People who track down actors and spy on them?" It sounded a little cloak-and-dagger, but Gamon would put nothing past people in the entertainment industry. They would protect their bottom line.

"I thought you might want to know—"

"How is he? Really? Is he okay?" How could he be? He was alone—or maybe….

"My friend chatted with the owner of the bar, who seems to be good friends with Dusit. The owner praised him for not drinking. When he was there, the owner's sister came in with food for both Dusit and Rose. My friend says he looks healthy."

Some unknown anxiety Gamon had been carrying for a long time lifted. This was incredible news but…. "But he hasn't agreed to do the series?"

"He will. Only if you want…." Rose dangled everything in front of Gamon.

Gamon felt like he was shooting a scene with no script. He was too terrified to hope but too weak not to grab any opportunity to see Dusit. "Doing the series with him is something I definitely want."

"Good." Rose cleared his throat again. "I should tell you there's a catch. A small one, really."

He needed to see Dusit. Even if it was only through working with him again. The consequences didn't seem important. "As long as Dusit is in, I don't care. I want to do the second season."

Rose chuckled. "Don't you want to hear the catch?"

"Sure," Gamon said, because that was the correct response, but he would do the series regardless. "Tell me."

"The director and investors want your first interaction with Dusit to be shooting the initial scene in the series. It is where the characters first meet again." Rose's tone held the apology the shameless words didn't. "Fans would know this was the first time the two of you would be seeing each other."

To have that moment captured for all to witness seemed horrifying. How could he manage himself properly? "What? Not even a table read?"

"No, not before the first scene. Though I understand how big this moment might be for both of you." Few people knew for sure of Gamon's short-lived romance with Dusit, but many guessed. Rose apparently was one of them.

"Kanawat helped me with this and lived up to his reputation as a killer agent. He negotiated a closed set, with a skeleton crew and the two of you. It's only for the first interaction. After that it'll be back to normal."

Nothing had been normal in a long time. Gamon got lost on the paths of what-ifs of seeing Dusit again.

What that interaction would be was anyone's guess.

Gamon's fantasy of a loving welcome where they would hug and kiss and melt into how they used to be would remain in his imagination.

No, he needed to be realistic.

Would Dusit be mad, cold, and angry? Or worse, indifferent? "This is only for our reunion?"

"Right, only for the first scene, and then you would have the typical workshops, the table read, etc."

"Is Prem Li the director?"

"Yes," Rose confirmed.

Gamon needed to wrap his head around this entire conversation. "Why?"

"Why what?"

Gamon knew the money men wanted to see his heart ripped out and for his and Dusit's misery to be played out on film. But he wanted to hear that admitted out loud. "Why would the investors want such a thing?"

After a moment of silence, Rose sighed. "The investors think it's viral gold. Prem Li's hands were tied. He was originally against it but finally agreed when the investors threatened the series funding."

"Viral gold." Gamon's reconnection with the love of his life was simply a way to build an audience.

Rose *tsk*ed. "Come on, Gamon. You've been around. This is simply business. Every decision is based on money."

"I know it's a business, not a charity." His mother had said it enough times to keep that in the forefront of his mind. "Isn't this a bit much?"

Rose was silent. Had he ended the call? Did he lose his chance?

Gamon cleared his throat. "Rose, are you still there?"

"I think it's an outrageous stunt, but investors expect a return on their investment."

"And it will work." That wasn't a question. Gamon understood all too well how drama around a series cranked up the viewership.

"Absolutely, and the investors have glossed over their financial objectives and justified filming this way by claiming it is for the fans. They deserve to see this significant moment between their two beloved actors."

"Deserve?" Gamon had spent the entire first part of his twenties giving the fans what they believed they deserved. "This should be kept private."

"I know." Rose's conviction was in his voice. "The investors feel this isn't too much to ask for the risk they are taking."

"Right. They think Dusit Sitwat is an abusive drunk." That description was far from the truth, and it hurt Gamon's heart. "And without agreeing to this, there is no season two?"

"Correct."

Gamon had no choice. There was no way he'd give up this chance to reconnect with Dusit. "I need to do this."

"Can you confirm you haven't seen or heard from him?"

"How could I? I've been in France most of the past five years. He's not on social media. I'm not a stalker." Though if Rose had given him any information about where Dusit worked, Gamon would have been there within the hour.

"Okay. Good. Keep it that way. These investors are a skittish bunch who are dipping their toes in Thailand's Y-series industry." Investors saw baht in the soft power of BLs but weren't completely on board with trusting this relatively new genre.

"Got it. It's not like I'd show up at where he was working. Where did you say that was?"

"I didn't." Rose chuckled.

Gamon couldn't help but try. "I know you didn't. Don't you trust me?"

Rose snorted. "It's not that I don't trust you, but let's say now I have a better understanding of what it is to love someone."

"Rose." Gamon sighed.

"Look, you've got many people longing for this to happen, including my boyfriend's sister and mother, so don't blow it. I'll schedule this as soon as possible."

There was still one huge obstacle in the way of this series. "You really think he'll say yes?"

"Not only do I understand what it is to love someone, but what someone will do for the one he loves."

Was he implying Dusit still loved him? He couldn't and possibly never had.

"I won't do anything to jeopardize this from now on." How could he? *Don't Break My Heart* was their series, and to once again play his role with his one and only…? He wouldn't tempt fate. "I'll do whatever it takes to make this happen."

Even if it ripped out his heart.

CHAPTER 5

ROSE THONGSI strolled into the bar.

Shit! Dusit wanted to duck behind the bar, but it was too late. Rose's intense gaze had pinned him.

Strutting over to Dusit, Rose placed his hands on the bar. "Can we talk?"

"How did you find me?" Dumb question. "Aw, right, Anwar has people everywhere. Rose, I told you yesterday I'm no longer working as an actor."

"But I think you will."

"Why would you think that?" Dusit came out from behind the bar, started flipping the chairs back onto the freshly-mopped floor, and didn't look in Rose's direction.

Charong must have heard Rose's request, because he said, "Dusit, why don't you take a few minutes and see your friend?"

Glaring at Charong did nothing. Apparently having two sisters made him immune to meaningful scowls.

Dusit trudged to a nearby table and signaled for Rose to join him.

Rose followed.

"Can I get you something?" Charong shouted across the empty bar.

"Beer?"

"Sounds good."

After Rose's agreement, Dusit called out, "Beer and my usual."

Dusit gestured for Rose to sit. Then he spun his chair around and sat as well.

Rose said nothing. He kept looking around the bar, and then he studied Dusit.

"Thanks," Dusit told Charong when he set the beverages on the table. He tried not to feel guilty for not helping to close the bar.

Rose gave Charong a wink as if they were on the same side and had bonded. Two against one wasn't fair.

Turning his gaze onto Dusit, Rose grinned.

Dusit sighed as his walls came down.

Rose Thongsi was a person with whom no matter how long between visits, Dusit could fall right back into step with as if no time had passed. They were brothers of the heart.

Sipping his cola while Rose took a gulp of beer, Dusit said, "So you don't give up."

Rose studied him with a grin. "You're looking better than the last time I saw you."

"Thanks for picking me up from that bar last year… and all the other times." Dusit wasn't proud of all he'd done the past few years, but he wasn't in denial about it either.

Rose took a sip of beer and then said, "Before that, I saw you at the audition for *My Reality*."

"Ah, yes. I was auditioning for your man's part." Dusit couldn't help but be a jackass.

"Ha, yeah. Not for nothing, but I'm glad you didn't get the part." As if casting hadn't already had someone in mind.

Dusit's laughter barked out of him. "Me too. Could you see us doing NC scenes?"

"Right. Us doing not-for-children scenes would have been difficult since people have accused the two of us of acting like children on set."

Smiling at his friend, Dusit accessed fond memories of acting. "Yeah, and trying to kiss you would have been—"

"Weird. Yeah. And the whole Rose/Dusit or Dusit/Rose would have proposed an issue."

With a smirk Dusit said, "Nah, it would definitely be Dusit/Rose."

"Our ghost ship has sunk." Rose chuckled and put his beer on the table. "What have you been up to?"

"After the fake audition, I have vague memories of being helped off the floor by you and your man." That seemed like a lifetime ago.

"Yeah, but even before that, you dropped out of contact for a while." Rose was being polite.

Shrugging, Dusit glanced across the bar. What could he say without sounding pathetic? "Oh, you mean after that reality show? Well, once they removed me from the show, trying to forget was easier. Now tell me, why are you here?"

"You ended our call before I could explain—"

"Rose, I'm not interested in rumors." Why had Rose showed up at the bar? Dusit had finally settled down into a regular life.

Rose rested an elbow on the table and grinned at him.

Well, hell, this man's smile had to be made from pure magic, because he could get anything he wanted. "Don't smile at me like that."

"Like what?" Rose was a good actor; innocence was rolling off him in waves.

"You know what! All I'm saying is the world owes Nok Ayutthaya much gratitude for taming you and your get-whatever-you-want smile out of circulation."

Sighing, Rose swirled the beer in his bottle. "You are not wrong."

Dusit took a sip of his cola. He needed to be real with Rose. "Look, I can't get my hopes up for rumors and dreams. I need to survive in the real world."

"It's not a rumor. I told you—I'm working with Kanawat Anwar's agency. Since you aren't answering his calls and you hung up on me, I figured I'd pay you a visit."

"How did you even find me?"

Rose tilted his head and stared off to the right for a moment. "If I say social media, would you believe me?"

Fan posts? Maybe. Chatchada? Nah, she wouldn't rat him out. Probably the same people the agency employed to spin stories were also used to collect information, people, talent, etc. "Whatever."

Rose punched him in the arm. "Admit you had fun doing that audition, didn't you?"

"Fun? Is that what you call getting all fancied up for a fake audition? A good time?" The only reason Dusit had done such a foolish thing didn't pan out. He'd studied for the part of the best friend just in case the impossible had happened.

"Hearing the fans screaming your name? Working on a script? Or maybe you thought a certain someone might be there also."

"I don't know what you're talking about," Dusit mumbled.

"Are you telling me you weren't hoping to work with Gamon?" Rose could be diplomatic and careful with his words, but he never extended that courtesy to old friends like Dusit. With him Rose was always direct and to the point.

Dusit tried to open his mouth, but his heart wouldn't let him.

Leaning in, Rose asked, "Are you going to lie to me about not wanting to see him?"

"I didn't say that." For the first few years, that possibly had been one of the few reasons Dusit even bothered to get out of bed.

"You can't move on, not even after all these years," Rose said, giving words to Dusit's truth. "This hope you've done nothing to make a reality has locked you into inaction."

The words reopened everything Dusit had tried to stitch together. "Well, that's a judgy way to see my life. Look, I'm taking care of myself. I'm fine."

"Finally," Rose said. "I can see you've got a decent job. You've stopped drinking, and you're eating regularly. But I will not say barely functioning is fine."

"It's all I have. Surviving is on the right side of fine," Dusit pointed out, "and I've saved enough for my parents to move into a shop so they will be out of the heat and rain. The weather is too much at their age."

"That's great. You're a dutiful son." Rose patted him on the shoulder. "But how about you? What do you want?"

"I'm taking care of my parents, and I'm doing all right. What else can I expect?" Even Dusit had to admit he was disappointed by the low expectations his words conveyed.

"To be happy." Rose studied him way too closely.

"Yeah, look what that got me." Dusit had *been* happy.

"You're a talented actor." Rose stated it as a fact.

Scoffing, Dusit grumbled, "Right."

"I know you never studied acting, but you are a natural. You're more than good looks. You're smart, funny, and your kindness comes across on screen."

Back in his performing days, Dusit had gotten a lot of buzz for his acting ability, but it never made sense to him. Acting was easy. He didn't understand the difficulty some people had with it. All he did was let go of everything he was and learn the character, and then become the character.

"Part of the reason people still talk about *Don't Break My Heart* as one of the most beloved Y-series of all time is because of your acting and the chemistry you have with Gamon."

Every moment he had been with Gamon on- and off-screen had been a miracle and now should stay as a cherished memory.

"Had. The chemistry we *had* on-screen." He couldn't deny the truth. "It was an excellent series."

"The series deserves a happy ending on-screen."

And Dusit had wanted his and Gamon's happily ever after off-screen. He'd wanted to make good on his promise to keep Gamon feeling safe and happy always. There was nothing on earth he craved more than holding Gamon in his arms again.

But you can't always get what you want.

"The series ends with a phone call that can be seen as them reconnecting," Dusit said, then looked away so Rose couldn't see how he'd give up everything to get a phone call from Gamon. It was more than he could hope for with....

Rose tapped the table and then pointed at him. "Many of the fans read the novel, and they see that phone call as a goodbye, not a reunion."

"And that's what it was for the series. There is no need for a second season." Dusit couldn't give his words conviction because he knew they were false.

"Except *Don't Break My Heart the Series* season two is the offer on the table." Rose articulated each word in that way of his that made people listen and forced them to consider his words.

"What?" If this was legit, he'd not only get to see Gamon again, but work with him again as well. Workshopping, practicing, researching, shooting, dinners.... Was Dusit so pathetic that he'd even settle for just acting... as long as it was with Gamon?

"An offer is on the table," Rose restated, slower.

Dusit stalled for time and tried to pretend his brain wasn't melting. "So you're working with Kanawat Anwar now?"

Rose's eyes narrowed at the change of subject, but he replied, "Yes. Still doing some meetups with fans and a few cameos with Nok. I've got a few clients now too."

His grin was one of pure happiness and made Dusit incredibly jealous. "Sounds like you're in a good place."

"Being with Nok has allowed me things I never thought were possible. I've even reconnected with my brothers. For the first time I'm enjoying my life."

"I'm glad. You deserve it." Before Rose could regain control of the conversation and take it to places Dusit wasn't ready to go, he asked, "How do you like working with Kanawat?"

"Oh, I like it, but I can't say I'm working *with* Kanawat. One works *for* him, because he sets the direction and pace and micromanages everything, but he's a wonderful mentor and protects his clients."

"That was always my experience." In the BL industry, it was rare for an agent to have the respectable reputation Kanawat Anwar had.

"He helped me out of a bind as an actor, and now working for him in this capacity has proven to me how much he cares and how good he is at what he does."

Was that what this was about? Dusit's contract had to be up. "Are you asking me to sign with you?"

Rose studied him for a moment and then shrugged. "Since I started, I usually work with the newbies, but yeah, if you want to sign with me, I won't say no."

"So in order to work on the series, I'd have to sign with Kanawat's agency again?" Usually how it worked, but somehow that felt wrong.

"Actually you don't. Kanawat doesn't operate like that."

"One of the few." The horror stories of how agencies and management companies manipulated the actors and controlled far too much of the industry were well known.

"True, but that's why I'm with him. He was working in my best interests well before I signed with him. He's old school. Kanawat believes in doing things the right way, not for personal gain. Probably why so many of us signed with him."

Enough avoidance; back to the matter at hand. Dusit asked the most basic question. "Why did Kanawat really send you to find me?"

"You weren't answering his calls, and you answered mine."

And probably, Dusit thought, he wanted the plausible deniability of not knowing if Rose had to scrape Dusit off a barroom floor.

Dusit prepared himself to say no so he could set aside his impossible wishes and dreams. "Well, here we are. What's the deal?"

"Season two of *Don't Break My Heart* is hiring the crew. Casting wants to gather the actors." Rose took a sip of his beer.

Ah, there was no way they wanted him. They needed to appease the fans. "This will be an audition."

"No, they simply want to meet with you to make sure—"

"That I won't show up drunk to the set." That tracked.

Rose shrugged but didn't deny the truth. "You seem better."

"I am." Dusit looked him in the eyes. He wanted to make sure Rose understood this was for real.

"We've never talked about it, but I heard what happened on the reality show. I know none of that was your fault."

"Though getting plastered was no one's doing but my own." Dusit would take responsibility. "If I had been more in control, people wouldn't have been able to push my buttons so easily."

Rose grimaced, and his fist tightened on the bottle of beer. "That jackass baited you about Gamon."

"True, and there was no way I was going to listen to him bad-mouth Gamon." Not that it mattered. The production house had simply edited him out of the show.

"I know." Rose studied him and then asked, "What happened back then between you two?"

Dusit didn't need a diagram to know who Rose was asking about. "One minute Gamon was in love with me, promising me forever, and then I was kicked out of the apartment."

Rose's mouth dropped open, and he leaned back. "What did Gamon say?"

Pain ripped through Dusit, tearing at the never-healing scars. "Nothing."

"What?" Rose arched his eyebrow. "He must have said something."

"I'm telling you, I haven't spoken to him since." The hurt slicing through him was almost as strong as the day it happened. Probably every bit as strong—he was just used to the stabbing pain.

"Haven't you tried to get in touch with him?"

Dusit laughed bitterly. "Of course. Again and again."

"And?"

"Only spoke to his mother. He probably had her run interference so he didn't have to deal with me." But even as the words left his mouth, they felt untrue. Gamon was too nice to want to hurt anyone… even him.

"His mother told you what? That he didn't want to see you anymore?"

"She made it clear Gamon wanted to move on, and I'd be holding him back from his singing career. It was important for his well-being that I step away."

Rose leaned forward and tilted his head. "And you did?"

"Of course not. Not immediately. I attempted to call him, but he had already disconnected his phone. I tried emailing." Dusit swallowed the fact he'd even gone on one of Gamon's live streams and begged but was blocked from all his accounts within seconds.

Rose toyed with his drink. "I remember soon after your series ended, Gamon went abroad to host a musical show."

Dusit swallowed hard, but he couldn't avoid the hurt. "He did."

At the time, it felt like Gamon had escaped beyond Dusit's reach, but maybe that was his poor headspace. He hadn't had the means to follow, so he believed there was nothing he could do. "Gamon stayed out of Thailand. I'm sure by then I was a distant memory."

Rose pressed his lips together, remaining silent.

"What? You've got something to say?" Dusit wanted to know.

"I doubt either of you will ever be a distant memory for the other."

That was the case for Dusit, but he could only wish Gamon hadn't completely forgotten him. Everything in him craved to be with the man, even as nothing more than co-stars. He was ready to deal with the impossible. "So this is a genuine opportunity?"

Rose stared him dead in the eyes. "Yes."

How could Dusit pass up the possibility of working with Gamon again?

"You haven't been in touch with Gamon at all?" Rose asked and stared at him as he finished his beer.

"I've never seen or heard from him since that evening." If you didn't count social media stalking. There seemed to be a slash dug into his heart for each day of those days, months, and years he'd not seen his Gamon.

Rose sighed. "Okay. Good."

"Good?" Dusit squinted at Rose. Something was obviously up. What was it now? "Tell me."

Rose picked at the label on his beer bottle and refused to look at him. "The director wants to shoot the first scene before workshops and without a table read."

How would that be possible? "Why wouldn't we start with a workshop, or at least a table read?"

"The investors want the director to catch the first time you see Gamon on film… exactly like your character would see his character after their on-screen separation," Rose told him.

"They what?" That was sadistic, cruel, and okay, probably brilliant. It would take an actor far better than him to portray all the emotions that would flood him at that moment. Without a doubt, Gamon's presence for the first time in years would display his feelings more truly than any he could pretend to.

Rose glanced away and shifted in his seat. "To capture those first moments and to release that information would reach well beyond the fans of the show. The stunt would catch people's attention even outside the Y-series audience and BL industry."

"It's all about the money." Everything was always about baht.

"The entertainment business isn't a charity," Rose agreed. "But… the director is Prem Li." Rose said the director's name like it should mean something significant to Dusit.

"He directed *Don't Break My Heart*. And?"

"I guess you're not aware, but Prem Li's recent work always supports the LGBT community and brings awareness to various issues. He's more than simply a bottom-line guy."

"No, he's a sadistic bastard with a social conscience. Great." How could anyone suggest such a private personal moment be captured on film? But it was only a problem for him, right?

Rose chuckled. "You're not wrong, but if the goal is to draw attention to the issues of inequality for LGBT people in Thailand, highlighting the reason the characters were unfairly separated will do that. The buzz will hit the mainstream and be hard to ignore."

"Lovely." So Dusit's pain would be used for a social purpose. Was that supposed to make him feel better about it?

Rose spun the empty beer bottle. "I can't imagine how unsettling the reality will be for both of you, but—"

"How would that even work? Wouldn't we run into each other on set?"

"From what I understand, there will be a door between you. And many people will keep you apart."

That sounded like a lot of effort. Dusit's heart started beating faster. Could this be a way? "Gamon will never do this."

"Yes, he will."

Even if he might, there was another obstacle. "His mother—"

"Is no longer managing him."

Chat had been right. "Oh?"

"I don't know the details, but they had a falling out about something she did."

"And he's agreed to do season two?" Dusit couldn't imagine it.

"Yup." Rose's eyes sparkled, signaling his victory.

This might be the stupidest thing he'd ever done, but he asked, "When do I meet casting?"

"Tomorrow." Rose leaned in. "You're really going to do this?"

"You'll represent me?" Dusit was sure he'd need everyone he could muster to support him through this.

"You know it." Rose patted him on the shoulder as he stood. "I'll email you the contract."

Dusit didn't have a choice. He'd do anything to see Gamon again, but to actually work with him…. "I'll sign it. You tell me where and when."

CHAPTER 6

GAMON PACED back and forth in the room he'd been ushered into at the studio. He wiped his hands on the insides of his jacket pockets. Today was the day he would see Dusit again and film the first scene of *Don't Break My Heart 2*. He was torn between terror and excitement. Whatever happened, it would be a momentous day.

"May I get you anything, sir?" an intern asked in a meek voice.

He'd almost forgotten. "May I have a Sprite?"

"A Sprite?"

Gamon gave her a small smile. There would not be a kiss scene, but Dusit might be in proximity. They always drank Sprite before a kiss scene because it was their favorite soda. Would he even remember?

The intern returned with the soda.

He took a sip, then held the soda in his mouth for a moment. "Mmm."

The refreshing sweet taste made the memory of sharing a can of soda with Dusit and then kissing everywhere come rushing back. Their characters were affectionate, and Gamon loved it.

"Good?"

"I haven't had one in almost five years." Why would he?

Soon a familiar makeup artist halted Gamon's anxious patrol and dabbed his forehead with powder, then whispered, "He's still a looker."

"Who?" Dumb question.

She smirked at him as if she could tell how much he longed to storm through that door and see Dusit for himself.

"You know, and you'll be fine." She adjusted the front of his hair so a piece fell artfully over his forehead.

"Thanks," he muttered as she stepped back. He'd just pretend she was correct.

The scene called for him to head into an interview, not knowing he'd be seeing the love of his life for the first time in years. He'd have to call on all his acting skills to pull off nonchalance.

He needed to do something with his hands, so he shoved them in his pockets again.

Whatever had possessed him? How could he have agreed to greet Dusit this way—and on film? They should have met alone so he could get answers. Instead they would meet, and everything that was unresolved between them would be forever recorded on film.

His stomach tied itself in knots of fear and excitement.

Stepping into a blank canvas only knowing a few lines of dialogue didn't faze him, but being face-to-face with Dusit….

The director hadn't even allowed him to know Dusit's lines, only his own. His sole direction was to go with his feelings.

Gamon circled the room again. He had to move, even if he was going nowhere fast. That could be commentary on his life for the last few years.

If the director had been anyone other than Prem Li, no way would he have agreed—oh, who was he kidding?

He would have done whatever they asked of him for the chance to see Dusit again. He'd have said yes to anything.

Fellow actors had called him with jealous congratulations because surely this avant-garde approach to film-making would guarantee the series' success.

He stopped patrolling and stared at the door as if he could see through the wood. Dusit was on the other side.

Gamon exhaled hard.

After all this time, did Dusit ever think of him?

He had no clue.

Unlike him, Dusit wasn't active on social media. Dusit kept his life private, and other than a few actors whispering about seeing Dusit drunk in some bar, Gamon had zero information. Had he changed much in five years? But Rose had said Dusit was doing well, and that was all that mattered.

He pulled his hands out of his pockets and tried to shake the numbness out.

Had Dusit scrubbed away everything they'd been to each other? After what Gamon's mother had done to them, it wouldn't be surprising. Would Dusit ever forgive him for believing her over what they had shared? New as their relationship had been, he should have had more faith in Dusit. Even if Dusit forgave him, it didn't mean they'd be back together.

How could Gamon have been so young and insecure? He believed his mother when she said Dusit had ended things through her because he didn't want to be contacted by Gamon. There had been a big part of him that didn't believe he deserved such a love, so that fit his narrative.

His mother had even held him as he sobbed.

Anger slashed through him at the reminder that he'd let the man he loved slip through his fingers. If he had a chance, he'd never let go again.

An assistant entered and touched his arm. "It's almost time, Mr. Chaisit."

"Please call me Gamon." He hated the airs some actors put on.

"Yes, sir—Gamon." She inspected his suit and adjusted his collar.

He accepted the briefcase and muttered, "Typical day. Drove through the city and hit a lot of traffic. Now I'm running late for an appointment."

"An interview," she reminded him.

"Right, an interview, but why didn't I recognize the interviewer's name?" Why hadn't he thought of this when he'd first read the scene?

The assistant's eyes widened. "Um, you didn't pay attention to the interviewer's name, or perhaps you couldn't believe the world would be that small. Up to you."

At this moment, he believed in the impossible. His character was getting a second chance… was this his as well? How could Dusit ever forgive him?

"I need to up my imagination." Gamon tried to chuckle. At least he'd put a smile on the assistant's face.

She handed him the clipboard with a made-up résumé. “Thank you for doing this. I’m a big fan of the series and this… well, your fandom is ecstatic.”

No formal announcement had been made yet, but the inevitable rumors contained too many details to be wishful thinking.

Guilt and embarrassment flooded him. “I’m glad. I hope this is as successful as the first season.”

He hoped for so many things, but the top hundred had nothing to do with the series. Gamon took another small sip of the Sprite before the intern took the can away and left the room.

The assistant touched her earpiece. “We’ve got the go.”

Someone shouted, “Take one” on the other side of the door.

Gamon clutched his briefcase and stared at the clipboard. He wanted to run now that he had the go-ahead, but he forced his feet to move at the measured pace of an executive. He was unsure of the reception he would get.

He shifted his briefcase and the clipboard into the same hand. The doorknob felt cool against his palm. This is it.

Dusit is behind this door. Only a few meters away….

Swallowing hard, he kept his head down, readjusted his hand on the knob, and opened the door. He stepped into the room and put all his energy into focusing on the clipboard as he muttered his line. “Sorry to have kept you waiting. I—”

His gaze traveled from Dusit’s shiny brown laced-up shoes to the perfect fit of his suit, which accented his broad shoulders, and then their gazes locked. He stared at the only man he’d ever loved.

He dropped his briefcase and took a step forward. All his breath was stolen, and he couldn’t draw another.

Dusit!

The world vanished and left only the two of them. Gamon inhaled, filling himself with Dusit’s signature cologne, Jaguar Classic Black. The scents of cardamom, black tea, and geranium mixed with Dusit’s unique smell and tantalized Gamon.

His frozen heart beat again. Air seeped into his lungs. Gamon was alive once more.

Dusit looked incredible. He was less boyishly handsome and more stunningly masculine. His shoulders were wider. The rumors of him working construction and other hard manual jobs must have been true if the way his suit highlighted his muscles was anything to go by. Lines creased the corners of his soulful brown eyes to highlight them—eyes that saw everything about Gamon and still wanted more.

"I told you before, I'll always wait for you." Dusit's deep voice wrapped around Gamon's heart.

Emotions broke over him. Hurt and anger warred with sadness over the loss of time, but the strongest was pure, unconditional love.

One thing was certain; he was still completely in love with Dusit. Five years might have passed, but it could have been five minutes. Time hadn't changed Gamon's heart.

"I told you before, I'll always wait for you." Dusit repeated the line.

Gamon pulled himself out of his stupor and spit out his lines with the raw hurt that was right at the surface. "How was I supposed to believe that? You didn't call. You didn't email. You didn't even post on social media."

His voice trembled and his eyes misted at the hurt of abandonment. He didn't have to pretend. One of the reasons Gamon posted nearly his entire life online was on the off chance Dusit would want to contact him… but never once in all this time had he done so.

Maybe Dusit hadn't felt the same.

Dusit took a casual step forward, bringing him almost within touching distance. "I was told you were no longer interested in me, so I should spare you the burden and avoid causing you trouble."

The irony of *Don't Break My Heart the Series* season two echoing their own story made the words taste bitter. In the first season, their parents had separated them for their "own good," and as in real life, that hadn't been the case. Their parents ripped them apart based on their own needs, wants, and prejudices.

A long moment stretched between them. Amid the hurt and pain, Gamon simply absorbed being near the love of his life.

Finally Gamon found the ability to grind out his line. "You shouldn't believe everything you're told."

Genuine anger at his mother slashed through him, leaving a chasm across his heart. A single tear slid down his cheek, which made him feel weaker and even angrier. He swiped the offensive evidence of his hurt away.

Dusit reached out for him.

Gamon stepped back, holding the clipboard to his chest like a shield, and pressed his lips together to stifle the sob that tried to escape.

If Dusit touched him now, Gamon couldn't pretend to remain professional on set. Everything was too real.

Pain registered in Dusit's expression, and he dropped his hand, making Gamon sigh in relief even as disappointment flooded him. He longed to comfort—

"And cut." Prem Li clapped his hands. "That was perfection."

Someone unpeeled Gamon's fingers from the clipboard he had clutched.

Cut meant stop… end scene. But that word didn't curb his feelings for Dusit or the chaos that was drowning him.

He needed to stop staring at Dusit, but he was afraid of waking up from this dream.

"Since we're keeping this confidential, I've organized a small dinner in one of the conference rooms. There will be a few key—Gamon, do you hear me?"

Shit! He shook his head and turned his focus toward the director. Taking a shaky breath, Gamon asked, "Yes? Sorry, I'm just—"

"Yes, I know. We captured it on film." Gamon had followed Prem's career and reached out to praise his work. They had become friends online and Prem had directed some of the smaller roles Gamon had taken since he'd been back in Thailand. So it wasn't unexpected when Prem went on to tease, "I wish the camera was still rolling. Your befuddlement is adorable."

Gamon tried to glare at him, but with Dusit still in his line of sight, he failed, and before he could say something witty, Prem turned away.

Prem said to Dusit, "I'm glad Rose talked you into taking on this role again. I heard you weren't answering Kanawat's calls."

The assistant bounced back to Gamon. "The scene was everything. And—are you all right?"

Gamon wanted to scream, "No!" but he smiled and said, "Of course. I'm glad you think the scene came out well."

Prem headed out the door with Dusit, pausing to look over his shoulder, "Coming, Gamon?"

Gamon followed the two of them, but he kept his eyes fixed on Dusit, even admiring the back of his head. His hair looked soft, making Gamon want to touch the strands.

In the hallway, Dusit and Prem continued to chat. Gamon was sure they had things to discuss… but so did he.

Gamon selfishly wanted all Dusit's attention on him. Okay, if he were honest, he wanted to drag Dusit off to one of the single bathrooms in any of the workshop rooms. In a simple white room, similar to where they'd shared their first kiss….

Rose's boyfriend, Nok, rushed to Dusit. "Dusit Sitwat. Sawasdee krub. Rose said you would be here."

"And you are?" Dusit steepled his hands and put them to his lips.

Prem gestured and said, "This is Noknoi Ayutthaya. He and Rose—"

"Are together, right?" Dusit said without missing a beat.

Gamon was pleased to see that Dusit no longer had any of the old hesitation he might have had in the past.

"You were my first," Nok gushed.

What now? Gamon liked Nok a lot, but not right now.

"Excuse me?" Dusit's smile dropped as he squinted at Nok. "What?"

Gamon could only hope they hadn't heard his gasp.

That hope vanished when Prem, Nok, and Dusit all turned and stared at him.

Dusit graced Gamon with a slightly smug smirk and then turned back to Nok with a smile. "You weren't my first."

"Rose was right. You are funny." Nok snorted. "I meant *Don't Break My Heart* was the first Y-series I watched. Could I get a picture?"

"Of me?" Dusit put his hand over his heart and stepped back.

Prem laughed. "You'd better get used to that request again. Nok, give me your phone."

Nok threw a careless arm around Dusit.

It meant nothing. Gamon knew how Nok only had eyes for Rose… but still, he needed to keep his hands to himself.

"Gamon." Dusit gestured for him to join. "Get in the picture."

He stood next to Nok, but Dusit grabbed his wrist and pulled him to his other side. "Next to me."

Mmm, that was hot. International audiences may hate shows of possession, but the gesture turned Gamon on and made him feel secure and wanted.

Dusit turned his head, bringing his lips near Gamon's mouth.

It would take nothing to lean toward him for a moment, to brush his mouth against—

"Closer." Dusit wrapped his big hand around Gamon's waist and tugged him so he was flush against Dusit's body.

God, he smelled right and familiar. Gamon had almost bought a bottle of Jaguar Classic Black but didn't, because it wouldn't be the same.

Gamon wanted to rub his face all over Dusit and inhale his clean fresh scent. He couldn't pull himself together, so Gamon held his breath.

The warmth, the strength, and the feel of Dusit against him was everything he'd missed. He didn't want to move a millimeter.

Dusit squeezed his waist and blew a gush of spearmint air across his cheek. "Smile."

Right. Pictures.

Muscle memory kicked in, and Gamon ran through basic poses including a sweet smile, a peace sign framing his face, and a silly expression.

"My mother and sister are going to love these. Thank you." Nok stepped back and took his phone back from Prem.

"Let's give them our love." Dusit held up his hand cupped in the shape of half a heart.

Gamon took in a ragged breath and touched his fingers to Dusit's. His camera smile broke into a real one.

After snapping a bunch of pictures, Nok steepled his hands. "Thanks so much. I know you'll be busy with the series, but maybe Rose and I can have you over for dinner."

"That would be great after filming," Prem chimed in. "Our schedule is tight."

Nok glanced at the pictures. "Thanks. These are going to score major points with my sister."

"Remember, don't post them yet," Prem said with a wink, which meant leak them to start the craze.

"Will do." Chuckling, Nok gave the director a wave and hurried back down the hallway.

Glancing sideways at Dusit, Gamon tried to read him. Dusit still had his arm around him and held him tight. Maybe this time the crazy wouldn't be so bad.

Prem cleared his throat. "The investors are waiting for us."

"That's nice." Dusit shrugged. Never taking his arm back or moving away from Gamon, he guided him down the hall at a leisurely pace.

The satisfaction that gave to Gamon was stupid. The gesture was probably meaningless, but perhaps Dusit didn't want to let go of him yet.

When they got to the room, Prem held the door open.

Dusit gestured to him. "After you, Gamon."

Ridiculous that such a small thing should make his heart flutter, but he missed all the gentlemanly things Dusit did. This wasn't fan service; this was simply how Dusit had always been with him.

Gamon didn't need anyone to take care of him, but the gesture made him feel like someone saw him and that he was worth treating well.

"Thank you." Gamon stepped into the room, and in an instant he was swallowed into a group of investors. Some of them were with their daughters—or possibly younger girlfriends—but all seemed to be interested in the show.

After endless selfies where people seemed far too close, he faced the dilemma of where to sit. Usually in situations like this, his mother—no, he didn't need his mother to tell him where to sit.

Prem and Dusit were in a conversation with two investors who were praising what they had seen.

This interaction reminded Gamon that the BL industry was like any other business: Money was the driving factor. These investors weren't coughing up baht for charity work. They wanted to see a return on their money. But directors like Prem and many actors used the opportunity to gain visibility and public support for LGBTQ people.

Gamon recognized one investor who had been key to having Dusit removed from the reality show. The man now backtracked and kissed up to Dusit to get on his good side. The audiences' demands and interests would guide the investors' spending. Reversing their feelings and swallowing their pride was par for the course. It was business and not about their egos.

Hiding a smile, Gamon grabbed the closest chair and sat.

Young women scuttled to sit beside him on either side.

Time to be charming. He bit back a sigh, gathered the better parts of his personality, and asked the woman next to him, "What is your all-time favorite Y-series?"

"*Don't Break My Heart* of course." She grinned. "It was an amazing story. Both you and Dusit, I mean Mr. Sitwat, are incredible together."

Gamon kept his voice even, as if he didn't feel harpooned, and said, "Thank you."

"It's why I love Thai Y-series so much." She waved at an older gentleman. "I asked my father to invest in this series for my birthday."

Ahs echoed around the table.

“Quite a present.” Even though Gamon had money now, he really couldn’t understand *that* kind of money. “Do you watch BL dramas from other countries?”

She grinned. “Oh yes. I love K-BL but they are usually too short.”

“True, they are only eight to ten episodes and usually only twenty to thirty minutes each.” Gamon frowned as if he were bothered by that and not at Dusit being grimaced at by an investor.

A woman wearing a devilish smile asked, “How about the BLs out of Taiwan?”

The woman on Gamon’s other side answered, “They are spicy and a tad unhinged.”

Someone squealed, and the entire table became immersed in a conversation around the sex scenes in Taiwanese BLs. This was a relief because it allowed Gamon to focus on Dusit. But he was no longer sitting with the investors.

Where was he?

As if on cue, Dusit appeared to Gamon’s left and tapped the woman sitting next to him on the shoulder. “May I steal your seat?”

She opened her mouth, but another woman tugged on her arm to pull her out of the seat. “Of course she can move. You two probably have a lot to talk about.”

Lots of “ahs” went through the women as the investors grinned, probably seeing the reaction as confirmation that they were on the right track. One woman was making a video.

Gamon glanced at Dusit but couldn’t read his motive.

Was this simply part of their ship work? In the past, they had to do a certain number of posts and fan meetups while acting to exhibit their ship as per their contracts. Or could it be real?

There was so much Gamon wanted to say, but with this audience surrounding them, nothing he could say.

Dusit slid into the chair, and his knee brushed against Gamon’s.

Gamon jumped away, but Dusit eased toward him again until his leg rested against Gamon’s.

Hailing a waitress, Dusit ordered, “Two Sprites, please.”

Did he remember?

Dusit turned toward him and smiled. "I haven't had a Sprite in forever."

Gamon tried to swallow past the emotion. "Neither have I. Today was the first in almost five years." Hurt broke his words.

He plugged his brain back into the conversation.

Prem was discussing the evolution of social change in Thai Y-series and BL series in other countries and how it was affecting the LGBTQ issues in Asia. "Isn't that right, Gamon?"

"Yes, the social messages under Prem's direction resonate with our audience." Gamon knew Prem had handed him this opportunity with expectations, so he added, "Allowing the fans of *Don't Break My Heart* a season two where their favorite characters get a happily ever after, and the special episode, if granted by our success, will allow fans to see same-sex relationships can work not only in fantasy. The global BL industry, not only the Y-series in Thailand, is using its soft power to promote equality for everyone."

Most of the people's heads bobbed in agreement, and some women clapped softly.

Feeling Dusit's gaze on him, Gamon's heart fluttered, but he wasn't brave enough to look in his direction.

A woman asked, "Mr. Sitwat, are you looking forward to acting again?"

Dusit's leg remained against Gamon's, and as he shifted, his thigh rubbed along Gamon's.

Gamon bit his lip to stop from moaning, but he couldn't avoid longing to straddle Dusit's lap and ride him. He could almost feel Dusit's hands on his ass, helping him move at the right—stop!

He never had any control when it came to Dusit.

Ensuring the tablecloth was over his lap, Gamon schooled his face to appear interested in the conversation. What was wrong with him?

Dusit didn't look at him but grinned. "Um, sorry, a memory had me lost. Could you repeat the question?"

The woman giggled.

Was Dusit just pretending? This was all for show… right?

If Dusit had cared about him, why hadn't he gotten in touch with him? Even though his mom had restricted Dusit's access, he could have gotten someone to get a message to Gamon. Couldn't he?

Servers put plate after plate along the conference table.

Each plate of food looked delicious, but Gamon didn't plan on eating much. This was an investor dinner where he needed to sell himself and the series, not enjoy the food. Though his nerves had such a hold on him he couldn't imagine being able to choke much down.

This seemed lost on Dusit because he kept putting pieces of chicken on Gamon's rice and uttering a soft command. "Eat."

Every time, Gamon's heart pounded harder. He wasn't hungry, but each time Dusit spoke, he obeyed and filled his mouth.

Gamon tried to stay attentive to the guests and to Prem, but all his attention kept slipping to Dusit each time he moved or took a breath. He tried not to shiver as Dusit ran a finger around the rim of his water glass or casually leaned into Gamon as if he needed to get closer to whichever speaker was asking a question.

Wait! What was that latest question?

"I'm not sure." Dusit turned to Gamon and asked, "Do you know when we'll be moving in together?"

Gamon had made sure he didn't drink more than one glass of wine, but that question made him feel drunk and giddy.

"Soon," Prem jumped in. "Based on the filming today, we need to get started, but I haven't spoken to either of them about the actual schedule."

Living together. Living together. Him and Dusit in the same apartment. Living together? Living together.

Gamon hadn't let his mind go to all the things accepting this part meant….

This time his mother wouldn't be there to run interference, though not even she had been able to prevent them from sneaking into each other's rooms back then.

The gathering finally ended, and an assistant appeared. Gamon accepted the page she handed him. "Here's the current schedule, Mr. Chaisit. Please report at nine in the morning. The car will pick you up at eight tomorrow. And there is a car outside to take you home right now."

He didn't want to part from Dusit. They hadn't truly gotten to speak to each other.

Although if Gamon was being honest, postponing their conversation relieved him of his concern about what might be said. He needed time to find the right words and the perfect opportunity to apologize so he wouldn't lose Dusit… again.

Staring at Dusit, Gamon longed to refuse to leave. He wanted Dusit's number; he simply wanted Dusit.

Dusit stared back with a small smile, one that let Gamon know Dusit could read his mind. Dusit opened his mouth to say something, but an assistant appeared behind him.

"Mr. Sitwat, I'm afraid there's a meeting you need to attend right now."

The assistant behind Gamon began to guide him away from the table. His eyes were still fixed on Dusit. "They've got us surrounded. Good night."

Dusit waved to him. "Wishing you the sweetest of dreams."

Gamon's heart fluttered at the familiar parting. Their gazes remained fused together, and they both sighed.

There was so much to say, but nothing would come out of Gamon's mouth.

The assistant said, "This way, Mr. Sitwat."

It wasn't until Gamon was in the back seat of the town car that he glanced at the schedule. He had meetings all day tomorrow, the workshop started next week, and they were moving in together the day after tomorrow.

He had to talk to Dusit. Five years apart had been horrible, but tomorrow seemed like forever away… and they hadn't even exchanged numbers.

CHAPTER 7

"I STILL DON'T know why you insisted on helping me move. It's not like I have that many things." Dusit's life fit into a beat-up suitcase and a couple of boxes.

"Speak for yourself." Charong struggled to balance all the bags of food Chat had commanded her brother to carry into the condo building.

"Hush, watch the steps." Chat guided her brother up the complex's staircase.

Dusit swallowed down the emotions. This family took him in and helped him stay on a sober path. He'd miss sharing their noisy meals and daily chaos. "I appreciate the help."

"This isn't about helping you… well, it is, but this is also about rebranding your image. We are your entourage… your people… your crew." Charong failed to sound as cool as he was clearly trying to.

Lyric scoffed over the box she carried. "Entourage? I'm here for dinner. Chat gave you everything she cooked. If I didn't come to your new place, I'd have starved."

Dusit pressed his lips together so his smile didn't escape. The kid had made it clear she wasn't a silly fangirl who would be wowed by an actor. But he decided since he was an only child, she'd be the little sister he'd dote on. "Not to worry, I'll make sure to feed you."

Lyric glared at her biological siblings and then graced him with a contented smile. "Well, at least someone cares about me."

Both Charong and Chat frowned at him for the betrayal.

Charong waved Dusit off. "You spoil her, and it goes to her head."

Dusit threw his hands palms out to Charong and then winked at Lyric. "I've got your back, Lyric."

The doorman rushed to open the door and said, "Welcome home, Mr. Sitwat. The elevator is on the right side of the lobby."

"Mister! See that! Your rebranding is already working," Charong whispered with too much confidence.

"You sound like the production company." He was still irritated by the investors who had kept him from talking to Gamon after the investors' dinner.

The long meeting had not been enjoyable for anyone. But they insisted he work on rebranding himself with respectability.

Glancing around at the group, he thought maybe it wouldn't be so bad. "I never really had a brand."

Charong wagged his finger at Dusit. "You did, and according to what I read today, every entertainer has to develop a platform based on who they want to be seen as."

"You researched?" That touched Dusit's heart. His parents—and maybe for a time Gamon—were the only people who would have taken such time for him.

Charong nudged into him. "Of course. We are your crew. It's our responsibility to figure out the things you don't know."

Unsure of where he could focus, Dusit blinked away the blurriness and remained silent.

"Chat, what was Dusit's brand?" Charong asked.

Lyric elbowed the elevator button, and the doors slid open.

As she stepped inside, Chat sighed in the dreamy way fans used to exhibit in relation to him. "Cool, kind, handsome, and devoted to Gamon Chaisit."

Dusit didn't know about the first three, but the last continued to be accurate. He followed Lyric and Charong into the elevator.

"Fancy building," Charong teased as he studied the polished panels that held golden swirling designs.

"Yeah, better than the three-bedroom apartment they put us in last time." And this time Gamon's mother wouldn't be there.

How did Gamon feel about that? What happened there? He had many questions, but he'd tried to follow the advice of the production company, not trying to get those answers and focusing on the series.

Chat smiled. "The condo is better, because now you two are big stars and because the production house has expanded. The Thai Y-series industry is a global phenomenon going beyond the BL community. And they know *Don't Break My Heart 2* is going to be the best BL ever made."

"Overstatement," Lyric grumbled.

The elevator door binged open, and Dusit rolled his suitcase down the hall to his new condo… and new life.

He pushed open the door and let his self-assigned crew in.

Chat whistled. "Wow, really nice."

Too good for me, he sighed to himself but smiled at her. "I think Rose Thongsi and Nok Ayutthaya used to live here while they were shooting their series."

Nodding, Chat circled the room. "Yes, they did. I remember this room from their lives, and now they have moved into a condo near Lumpini Park, working and living together. Eeeeee!"

Looking around at his centrally located, beautiful condo, waiting for Gamon to come home, he couldn't help the excitement rushing through him. Even though it hadn't really started yet, he wanted this temporary situation to continue.

Dusit took in the white sofa and chairs, the cream-colored walls, and the whitewashed carved woods. The condo screamed upscale luxury. When he first came to Bangkok, this might have impressed him, but now he knew everything came with a price. The question was, how would he be expected to pay for all this?

Charong set the bags of food on the table.

Chat assigned tasks to everyone. "We'll set up dinner. Go unpack."

Dusit transferred his meager collection of clothing into a dresser drawer. When Dusit peeked into the closet, he discovered various luxury brands filling it exactly like last time, possibly ones that wanted the actors as brand ambassadors. He wasn't much on labels, but he did like coordinating his clothing to Gamon's. Silly how that small connection meant so much.

Chat called from the dining room. "Come eat. It's still warm."

He headed out of his bedroom.

Charong sat and smiled at him.

"What?" Dusit asked as he grabbed an empty chair.

"Even though you've moved here, it's close enough that cooked food doesn't get cold." Charong put some vegetables on Chat's rice and then on Lyric's.

Dusit almost reminded him that was because traffic was unusually light this time of day, but he didn't have the heart. Hopefully, they'd continue their friendship.

Charong must have read his insecurity because he said, "Hey, you can't get rid of us by moving here."

"Big star or not, you've got a responsibility to make sure these two don't mistreat me," Lyric said, which was probably the closest Lyric would come to saying she liked him.

"Pinkie swear." He held out his finger and waited.

She rolled her eyes and scoffed but was quick to shake pinkies.

He looked around the table. There was something incredible about having people not part of the BL Industry, other than his parents, in his life. "I have a feeling even if the food got cold, we'd still get together often."

Chat shook her head. "Well, not when you're filming… shooting? I hear the schedule for shooting a series is brutal, but we will work around your schedule. When do workshops start?"

"Workshops? Are you building the sets?" Charong asked, half joking, but he probably really didn't know.

Dusit filled in the blanks. "Workshops start next week, and those are classes where we work on key or difficult scenes and get comfortable with our partners and co-stars."

The door's keypad beeped, and the door opened.

Gamon!

Dusit held his breath. The concept of living with Gamon again had been an idea, a fantasy, but it was happening.

Dusit needed to keep his distance and perspective. He didn't want to be hurt again.

Gamon rolled in like a prince with his two pristine monogrammed Louis Vuitton suitcases and bowed his head.

Lyric's spoon clattered to the plate as she stared at the visitor.

"Oh, sorry. I didn't mean to startle anyone," Gamon said with a serene smile.

Dusit's hope of keeping his feelings in check was as possible as counting clouds in the rainy season.

How did Gamon make a simple white T-shirt, jeans ripped at the knees, and bare feet look like he could walk a runway in them? His hair was perfectly styled.

Dusit had enjoyed every time he broke through Gamon's calm, almost icy perfection and left him sweaty, satisfied, and clinging to him.

"Ow." Dusit rubbed his shin and frowned at Lyric.

She growled. "Why didn't you tell me? I would have worn something else."

"In a different shade of black?" Charong smirked in big-brother fashion and then followed Chat to his feet.

Charong and Chat paid Gamon a proper greeting. Charong cleared his throat, which seemed to help Lyric find her own feet and do the same. With the spoon she'd dropped now clamped between her steepled hands, she waied to him.

"This is…." Dusit hesitated for a second but then realized it was true. "This is my good friend Charong Rattana, and his sisters, Chat and Lyric. They helped me move in."

Gamon smiled at them behind steepled hands that he touched to his lips. His full lips—Dusit pulled his thoughts from going places they shouldn't and finished the introductions. "I know Chat already knows who Gamon is, but this is Gamon Chaisit." *My everything.* "My partner in the *Don't Break My Heart* series."

Gamon's gaze lingered for a moment on Dusit, but then he snapped into the role of gracious actor. "I didn't know you had friends over. I don't want to interrupt. I'll head to my room."

Dusit waved Gamon in, not wanting to spend a moment apart from him. "You should—"

"No, please join us." Lyric jumped out of the chair and almost tripped on her way to getting Gamon a bowl of rice, a dish, and utensils. "I love your music."

Gamon abandoned his two suitcases and joined the group with apparent reluctance.

Even with all Gamon's success, he appeared shy and uncertain in social situations, calling up Dusit's need to protect him.

In the brief time they had been together, Gamon shared how he constantly found it surprising that people wanted to spend time with him. But after Dusit met Gamon's mother, he got to know the root of that insecurity.

Chat smiled at Dusit with enormous eyes that widened a little, and then she moved her eyes but not her head, as if he was missing something he should be doing.

What was she expecting?

Then she studied each of his and Gamon's movements and kept looking between them.

Dusit racked his brain for something to say and pulled out, "I think it's going to rain."

The weather?

Gamon nodded too vigorously to avoid showing his desperation. "Yes… um…. The sky darkened on my way over."

The silence droned on.

Dusit needed to make this less awkward. "Chat is a superb cook."

"Smells delicious." Gamon picked up his rice bowl.

Lyric stared openly at Gamon as he ate some rice.

Charong cleared his throat several times, but his youngest sister ignored him and kept gawking at Gamon.

"Need some water?" Dusit asked Charong while keeping a straight face.

He always found people's first reactions to actors as if they were aliens amusing, and while Lyric didn't care about many BL actors, apparently singers were another thing. She did not disappoint.

Though tonight he was no better around Gamon.

Charong glared at Dusit and then put some chicken on Lyric's plate. "Eat. We don't want you to accuse us of starving you."

Sparing him a quick frown, she then turned to Gamon. "Did you really write "No Other Love" when you were only seventeen?"

"I was a bit older, but yes, I wrote the song. I was surprised that it became the OST for *Don't Break My Heart*," Gamon said, nodding slightly.

Good for him! Dusit smiled. Gamon was finally taking credit for his accomplishments.

"I knew it." Lyric waved her finger as if she'd solved a mysterious case. "Did you two know it would be such a success?"

"No, I hoped I—we—did the series justice." Gamon glanced at Dusit for half a second and then stared at his plate.

Singing with Gamon had been the start of… everything. Dusit had sung in school choirs and karaoke with other people, but the experience had not been life-changing. He had never imagined how fulfilling and spiritual merging his voice with someone else's could be until he sang with Gamon. The blending of their voices—

"You cold, Dusit?" Gamon asked. The concern in his voice tempted Dusit to believe he still cared.

"Um, no."

"Because you shivered. Let me lower the air-con." Gamon was on his feet and adjusting the temperature.

Dusit stared at him. The man was still the sweetest… kindest….

"Thank you, Mr.—I mean, Gamon," Chat said. "It is a little bit cool."

"Chat's chicken is the best." Dusit put another piece of chicken on Lyric's plate, hoping to stop her questions, and then put some on Gamon's plate, because he longed to take care of him in even the smallest ways.

Lyric acknowledged Dusit serving her with a head bob and then leaned toward Gamon. "So you have been in love? Did it not end well? Because the next song you released was 'Total Mess.' And, well, the lyrics were devastatingly sad and heartbreaking. You wrote that one too, right?"

"'Total Mess'?" Dusit had never heard that song. He hadn't listened to much music; it reminded him of Gamon. Plus alcohol wasn't conducive to paying attention to music.

Gamon stared at him with wide eyes. His nose wrinkled as if Dusit had pinched him. "You… um, you never heard of it?"

The hurt in Gamon's broken words stabbed Dusit's heart.

"No, I—"

Lyric took a deep breath and blasted out, "Never again. Never like this. So much love, but not enough trust. Broken and lost, I don't know why you've gone. I don't know what I did. I still need you. Yes, I still want—"

"Are those the words?" Dusit failed to keep the shock and hope out of his voice. Maybe Gamon hadn't wanted to break up with him. Perhaps—no, he needed to stay grounded in the facts. Gamon vanished, didn't connect with him, and they were apart for five years.

But when Gamon gave him a slight head tilt even though he wouldn't look at him, Dusit's heart soared.

Lyric continued the song. "I still love you. I still want-want you. You are always in my heart. Even though now we are apart."

Dusit's breath caught, and he forced himself to think these lyrics weren't meant for him.

Charong stepped in. "It's a beautiful song."

"Why didn't it get more play?" Lyric apparently didn't read the pain written on Gamon's face.

Gamon took a shaky breath. "My manager threatened anyone airing the song and canceled my appearances where I would have performed the song, so 'Total Mess' faded away."

"No! That's insane. I hope you got rid of your manager. Wait! Wasn't your mother managing you?" Lyric covered her mouth. "That's so sad."

Charong's head swiveled between every one of them as if seeking help.

Lyric didn't understand how uncomfortable she was making things.

Gamon appeared to be plotting an escape, and Dusit wanted to avoid that.

"Wait, call the newspaper." Charong forced a chuckle. "Something is sad to you other than my life, Lyric?"

"No one reads news on paper anymore." Lyric made an are-you-ancient face at Charong and then turned back to Gamon. She appeared to be determined to continue her investigation. "They say you need to write what you know, so I guess—"

"Here, have some egg, Lyric." Charong added a portion to Lyric's untouched plate.

She waved her brother off. "I mean—"

"Try some of the bean sprouts. They're your favorite." Chat scooped a big spoonful onto her plate.

Lyric covered her plate as if to fend off the food offensive. "What is happening?"

Charong smirked. "You said we never feed you, and now that we are, you shouldn't complain."

Chat whispered, "Read the room."

Lyric glanced at Gamon, and her mouth dropped open, hopefully with the knowledge of what was dancing beneath the surface.

The group fell silent until Chat said, "Dusit told us the workshop begins next week."

"Yes. Looking forward to working with… um, everyone again." Gamon pushed some rice into his mouth.

"Will you be doing live streaming together?" Chat asked with a smile, as if she didn't know the answer to such a basic question.

Grateful, Dusit chimed in, since Gamon was sipping his water. "Yes, as per our contract, we have to do at least two a week."

Smile growing larger, Chat said, "I can't wait. It'll be something to look forward to in between studying."

"What do you study?" Gamon asked.

Charong puffed up his chest and said, "Chat goes to Chulalongkorn University and studies pharmaceutical science."

Gamon's eyes widened. "Impressive."

"Not as impressive as your career. You're an actor, singer, model, reality star, influencer, and you've had success with each of those abroad too." Chat gleefully rattled off Gamon's résumé, but at the mention of working abroad, Gamon's smile dropped a bit.

Gamon gestured toward Charong. "What do you do?"

"I own a bar, and I've got a side gig of befriending actors who end up on my floor."

Dusit choked on his chicken.

Gamon rushed around the table to hand him water and pat his back.

Through his coughing, Dusit said, "That's how Charong and I met. He took pity on me. They all did."

"It wasn't pity. You… you are ours," Chat stated, as if it were simply a fact.

Charong and even Lyric gave a nod.

The rest of the evening passed pleasantly with light conversation as everyone cleaned the dining room and did the dishes.

"We should go." Chat said when she looked at her phone. "You've got a busy week coming up."

"Already?" Lyric folded her arms and pouted.

"Yes. Dusit has things to unpack." Charong's emphasis on "unpack" didn't need his whispered explanation of "You need to talk to Gamon."

"You don't say." Dusit rolled his eyes and then grinned. "Thank you all for coming and helping me settle in."

"Take care, Mr. Chaisit," Lyric said, then turned to Dusit and said, "Take care of him, would you?"

"Yes, of course." She did not know how much Dusit longed to do that. Maybe he should be careful, but everything in him dragged him to Gamon. He couldn't blow this second chance.

"Let us know when you're free so we can bring you dinner," Chat said, as if she needed to bribe him.

"Absolutely. I'll email Charong my schedule and put it in the group chat." Where did that come from? The need to share with them shouldn't have surprised Dusit, but he'd only ever done that with his parents.

After a long goodbye, Dusit's self-proclaimed people left him alone with Gamon. How many nights, drunk or sober, had he spent thinking about what to say if Gamon ever gave him the opportunity?

He might be afraid of being hurt again, but that fear paled beside the possibility of ruining this chance.

Gamon thrust his hands in his pockets and gawked at him.

The connection between them strengthened and wrapped around his heart tighter.

Dusit couldn't believe he was standing in front of the love of his life. This was it. He should say something. What could he say without ruining this simple moment?

All the questions and all the declarations started and ended with, "Gamon—"

"Dusit… no." He took a step back from Dusit as if the distance would limit what was between them.

"No?" No? What did he mean no? The only acceptable answers between them should be yes, now, and please.

"I know we have a lot to talk about, and I have a ton to explain…." Gamon bit his lower lip for a moment and then sighed.

Explain? Would the explanation push them further apart? Maybe they should get used to each other again before they reopened the wounds that had never quite healed.

Gamon took a deep breath with his eyes closed. He opened his eyes as he exhaled. "But I think we should listen to the management company."

"Yeah? I mean, yeah. You're right." Relief at avoiding the spot they were in flooded Dusit.

"We have a series to do," Gamon pointed out the obvious.

Dusit took a step forward to close the distance between them. "We do. I never thought I'd be excited about acting again, but doing a series with you…."

Dusit lost the rest of his words when Gamon smiled at him gently.

"I'm happy about that too," Gamon said.

Staring at the man he was still hopelessly in love with, Dusit was caught somewhere between happy and terrified. His emotions must have been painted on his face, because Gamon's smile faltered and morphed into a frown.

"I mean it," Gamon insisted. "We should focus on the series. I can't tolerate losing—I can't bear to have things end badly again."

"They won't end badly if we don't let them." Dusit couldn't help but make promises he had no business making. He wanted to explore forever between them. Would Gamon let that happen?

Gamon waved his hands as if he were swatting away the negativity. "You don't know that."

True…. Dusit reached out to Gamon. "But I want—"

"Me too." He reached a hand toward Dusit and then dropped it to his side. Stepping back, Gamon raked his fingers through his hair. "We should get to know each other again."

Dusit dropped his hand, and like the sunlight he was trying to capture, it slipped away. "Get to know each other again? What don't you already know about me? What do you want to know? I'll tell you anything."

Gamon's joyous laugh echoed through the condo. "Let's go slow. We should go slow, right?"

"You're not saying no?" Hope was a dangerous thing, but Dusit couldn't help it.

Gamon rolled his suitcases to his side of the apartment. He stopped and grinned over his shoulder at Dusit. "Have I ever said no to you?"

Dusit's mind spun with images of how accommodating Gamon could be.

The door clicked shut, alerting Dusit to Gamon's disappearance.

Strategically this was a good plan and lessened the risk of things blowing up. By taking their time, Dusit could hope they could avoid wasting this opportunity.

He could do slow. Slow was safe. He'd do a snail's pace if he had to—if it meant he'd get Gamon back in the end.

CHAPTER 8

"GREETINGS. I'M your acting coach, Achara Saetang." Her grand sweeping entrance came to a scuffing stop. She looked around and dropped her professional persona. "Gamon, my sweet one. You're the only one here?"

Jumping to his feet, Gamon gave her an air kiss near each of her model high-boned cheeks. He gestured for her to turn. "You look beautiful."

Her smile said she agreed with him as she turned in a circle to show off her suit. "Gucci. Believe it or not, they want me for their fall line."

Happiness flooded him. He was glad she was getting the recognition she deserved. "Of course they do. You'll be stunning. And the color palette coming up—"

Achara patted her updo and then waved her finger at him. "Don't distract me with fashion talk. How are you doing?"

"Me? Fantastic. Why do you ask?" He was a better singer than actor… and it showed.

She dramatically choked. "You saw him for the first time in years, and now you're living with him. I mean—how do you expect me not to ask?"

"It's fine." Wanting to reassure her and himself, he opted to downplay the upheaval living with the love of his life caused in his mental well-being.

"Don't let that boy ruin you. Last time it was not pretty."

He wished he could pretend he didn't understand what a disaster he had devolved into. He'd allowed his mother to cancel fan meets, appearances, and then he gladly fled overseas to avoid news of Dusit. "There were lots of reasons for what happened. I take full responsibility. I—"

"Sweetie, you were in the darkest of places." She grabbed his shoulders. "You scared me."

"I felt trapped. I allowed the person I wanted most to leave—to be taken away from me." Anger bubbled within him.

"I'm sorry I wasn't there for you. I regret we only saw each other a couple of times." She sat down on the sofa and gestured for him to do the same.

He followed, taking some deep breaths, and sat facing her. "You were abroad, and we kept in touch through emails. Then I was…. Look, I'm fine now."

"Are you? You've passed on so many parts I thought you'd given up acting."

"Not so many…." Okay, perhaps quite a few.

"The fans believe it was because you didn't want to be in a ship with anyone other than… with him." She held up her hand to stop his untruthful denial. "I know from your emails how much you've gone through."

He shrugged and tried to smile. "Yeah. Felt like I was starring in my very own drama. And I was the character who couldn't piece everything together."

"I'm glad you trusted me enough to share what happened to you. I can only imagine the pain you felt finding out what your mother did."

"Years of not knowing. How could I not have seen how manipulative she was and how she engineered everything?" If only—but maybe….

Achara studied him and tilted her head. "I'm so sorry… but wait!"

"What?" He tried to school his expression.

She gasped. "You can't be looking at this like a second chance with him, right? No! How could you think that?"

He glanced away from her, hoping she'd stop reading him. She had always been a "cut your losses and move on" type of person. But how could he not hope that he and Dusit could recapture the love that was stolen from them? "How can I not?"

"Sweetness, he's not the same boy you knew. He's a drunk, and he even got abusive—"

Gamon would never believe that. "No, someone baited him."

She rolled her eyes. "I'd believe that, but I also saw him in a bar fight a couple of years ago. It was not pretty. He's got a problem."

"It's called self-medicating with alcohol, and from everything I've seen, he's not doing that anymore."

She stared at him. Silent. Waiting.

"Look, in the past five years, I've done things I'm not proud of. I tried self-medicating with sex, then alcohol, then work. I get it." Nothing worked to ease the ache in his chest except—

Dusit waltzed through the door, looking too good in jeans and a vintage T-shirt. "Sorry, the director stopped me with some questions."

Achara stood and spun on her heels, a professional mask in place as she extended her hand.

Taking her hand, Dusit gently pressed his lips to her knuckles. "You're even more beautiful than I remember."

"I've had some work done." She circled him.

Dusit stood still for her inspection.

Her assessment complete, she said, "You look good, probably better than before."

"Er, thank you." Dusit shifted from foot to foot.

He was so adorable and apparently still not used to the frank appraisal of your appearance, talent, and voice people gave freely in the entertainment business, as if you'd asked for their opinion.

Achara leaned toward Dusit and smelled.

"What are you doing?" Dusit pulled his T-shirt to his nose and sniffed. "It's the new shower gel. Gamon and I are ambassadors for this brand. We have a promo shoot later this month. Don't you like it?"

She stood in front of him with her hand on her hip. "Are you still drinking? I'd like to know if it's something we need to work around. Or—"

"I'm not, and I stopped months ago. I have the occasional beer, but that's it." Dusit's gaze was on Gamon. "I don't want to screw this up. I'm all in."

"Whether you're talking about the series—" She turned to follow Dusit's stare. "—or something else, I hope you mean it. I'll take you at your word that you're ready to work, because I have no choice."

"I won't let you down," Dusit insisted.

Achara tapped her finger to her lips and then clapped her hands. "Let's begin."

They sat around a table. Dusit sat close to Gamon's side, making him grin like his crush had asked him out.

Achara handed them each a sheet of paper. "This is the list of the scenes I think will be more difficult and may need some extra attention. I assume you both read the script, so let me know if you want to add any."

"Why is the one that takes place in Patpong and Silom Soi 4 marked with my name next to it?" Why did she think Gamon needed help with this?

Achara glanced between him and Dusit, and then her focus narrowed to Gamon. "Your character tries to forget Dusit's character by going to dance clubs and then eventually ends the night with someone who offers services of sex."

"Still doesn't answer why you'd think I'd have trouble with this scene." Gamon was miffed.

Why did everyone assume he was a virgin made of spun glass? Did he not tell her he'd used sex to get over Dusit? Gamon was far from innocent. Did she not believe him?

From her tilted head and small smirk, it was clear she did not.

Fine. Gamon adopted a casual tone to emphasize this wasn't a big deal. "The scene with the sex workers reveals a lot about my character and how he tries everything he can to escape the pain of losing the one he loves."

Achara stared at him.

He gave her the "told you self-medication was a thing" expression. "When my character runs out of options trying to forget… he goes to a sex worker."

"Right, it's a pivotal point in the story." Achara appeared to be waiting for him to fill in more of the blanks.

Dusit cleared his throat. "My character shows up and stops him—is that realistic? How does he know?"

Achara pointed at him with a smirk. “He still has the GPS tracker installed on his phone from season one. Though his reaction shows growth.”

“Right, he’s understanding.” Gamon wonders if Dusit would be as compassionate.

Dusit snorts. “My character is a red flag if ever there was one. He has been following yours all night like a stalker and drags him out of there immediately.”

“In a quick second.” Achara smirked as she studied them. “Stalking, nonconsent, and rescuing aside, Dusit’s character has grown. That’s where the emphasis needs to be, but he still will not let his man have someone else.”

Gamon pointed out, “These scenes also allow us to get the message of equality and the importance of increasing protections for service workers out.”

Achara added, “The director said he’s adding numbers and web sites where people can go for more information about sex trafficking and protective agencies.”

“Okay, but I still don’t understand why this is on the difficult list and with my name next to it,” Gamon said. Why was he tagged as needing help with the scene?

Achara arched her perfect eyebrow at him. “Do you have experience in Patpong? I can’t imagine your mother would have allowed you to spend much time in Patpong.”

Before his mother hired a driver, she’d never let them get off the SkyTrain at the Patpong stop, even if it was closer to their destination. Looking back, he realized she hadn’t even let taxis go that way, but he would not share that. “I’m not a prude… and why aren’t you asking Dusit?”

Achara let out a long-suffering sigh, as if Gamon were talking nonsense. She snapped her head to assess Dusit. “Dusit, have you or have you not been to Patpong?”

He frowned and then shrugged. “I have.”

Dusit had shared his abysmal experience with Gamon. It was a typical coming-of-age story. His friends dragged him to a bar and paid the fine to the owner for a hostess to take him to a hotel. She tried to get him aroused with her hand, but he stopped her from using her mouth by saying he'd already come.

Achara leaned in. "Did you have sex—"

"Achara." Gamon glared at her. He wasn't jealous, but did she really have to dig this deep into Dusit's past?

Achara patted his hand. "I'm an intimacy coach. The question isn't to be nosy, but I want to make everyone comfortable. I need to assess each of your experience levels so we can start discussing how I can best support both of you through this scene."

Gamon sighed. Here he was, proving her point. "I apologize for overreacting."

"Trust me, I get it." Her look said that she understood on how many levels this affected him and how the entire situation befuddled him.

Dusit folded his hands on the table and stared at them. "I had one unfortunate experience when I was eighteen, on my birthday. Unlike most of my friends, it wasn't something I ever wanted to repeat."

Gamon wished he could hold Dusit close, like the day he originally shared the unpleasant memory.

"Many men have their first experience in Patpong." Achara tapped her finger on the pages of the script. "In the script, Gamon's character goes to a bar and finds a sex worker. It's not his first time, so he's not that awkward, but he's determined."

Gamon could feign familiarity.

She tapped her nails on the table. "I think you two need to make a wee itsy-bitsy field trip to Patpong and Silom Soi 4."

"So much for taking it slow," Dusit said for Gamon's ears only, and then he chuckled.

Dusit's chuckle turned into a deep laugh, digging into places Gamon didn't even know were tight and loosening them, making him open and ready.

"A field trip?" Gamon's voice was a bit too high.

"Real emotions are hard to tame, while you need to sculpt your character's." Tilting her head, she smiled and suggested, "I recommend the night market at Patpong, which is where your darling character begins his sad little misadventure."

“He’s got a right to be sad. Losing the love of your life does things to you.” Gamon didn’t mean to reveal how much he could relate.

Dusit threw an arm around him like he’d done so daily in the past. He caught Gamon’s gaze. “Agreed, it’s an epic nightmare.”

His words were light, but there was an undercurrent, or maybe Gamon was projecting his own issues onto Dusit’s words.

Gamon stared at him in the foolish hope Dusit would leave his arm around him forever.

“Glad you two agree.” Achara cleared her throat.

Dusit dropped the embrace but continued to hold Gamon’s gaze. “Shared experience.”

Hurt, pain, and loss surged in Gamon, but under it all was potential. However, acting on this hope was the one thing that had the power to tear everything apart. He needed to manage the effect of the possibility on him for both their sakes.

Sighing, Achara rolled her eyes. “Okay, back to the field trip.”

Gamon dragged his gaze from Dusit and asked a basic question. “It was easy for me to avoid recognition abroad, but how can we go to Patpong without being recognized?”

Achara grinned. “The pandemic was good for something. Wear a mask in Patpong, and do your hair differently like in the recent photo shoot. When you get to the clubs in Silom Soi 4, no one will recognize you. If they do, they won’t want to admit where they saw you. Unfortunately, many people aren’t ready to step out of that closet.”

“Will a mask be enough?” Gamon was doubtful the disguise was sufficient.

Achara leaned toward him. “Will you be able to handle it?”

Gone were the days of Gamon the Pristine. He’d done things. He’d been places… not Patpong or to a sex worker. “*L’habit ne fait pas le moine.*”

“Excuse me?” Achara asked in her should-I-be-insulted tone.

Hoping to make his point, Gamon translated, “The exact saying is ‘the robe doesn’t make the monk.’”

Achara tapped her nails on the table for a moment and then said. “Another way of saying don’t judge a book by its cover.”

Gamon glanced at Dusit.

Dusit grinned at him. "Or the man by how innocent he appears. Though innocence passes quickly with enough eagerness."

Touching his hot face, Gamon tried not to remember how enthusiastic he was for Dusit.

"Well, if you wear what you did in the photo shoot, no one will accuse you of being innocent." Achara put a hand to her heart. "I almost didn't recognize you with that wicked expression."

"You mentioned that before. What photo shoot?" Dusit asked with big eyes.

Gamon's covering his face with both hands didn't block out the chuckles from his ex-friend and his ex-boyfriend.

"Look at him on the cover of *Allure*." Achara must have pulled up the images of the photo shoot on her phone.

Dusit whistled. "Whew. That is… you look… I mean…."

"What Dusit is so eloquently saying is that you look lovely in a noncupcake sort of way."

Nodding, Dusit added, "You definitely look delicious, and you know how I love cupcakes."

Achara sighed, probably because she felt her tease wasn't getting enough appreciation, and Dusit used it. "Let's figure out where you'll go in Patpong."

A FEW HOURS later, Dusit's eyes widened as Gamon stepped into their condo's main area. He pointed. "Is this the exact outfit you wore in the photo shoot?"

Gamon glanced into the mirror and fussed with his messy hair. He touched the black leather collar that encircled his neck and smiled. "Yeah, but I wore a white racing-back tank top, not black, but it's evening, so…."

"Aw, well…." Dusit's look lingered on Gamon.

He felt the gaze physically, but the silence made him insecure.

"What?" Gamon arched an eyebrow at Dusit. Maybe he didn't look as good as he thought.

"I mean, you look—" Dusit's gaze connected with Gamon's eyes. Then he licked his lips, conveying everything Gamon had hoped for.

"Too much?"

"Makes me want to take an actual field trip—like the ones we used to take." Dusit's words invoked the memory of a steamy adventure they'd shared.

They were on location. The director called a lunch break, but instead of eating, the two of them slipped away to a secluded part of the woods. When staff questioned their whereabouts, Dusit told them they had gone on a bit of a field trip. The makeup artist smirked as she plucked leaves from their hair.

Gamon's cheeks heated, but he kept his head clear of the wishes that sprang forth. "Shall we head out?"

"Sure." Dusit handed Gamon a black mask and put on his own.

Their driver dropped them off a few streets before the night market, so they walked the remaining blocks.

As Gamon wove through the tables of the open-air night market with Dusit at his side, he was thrilled by the novelty of the activity. The potential of the night crackled like electricity all around him, especially whenever Dusit was close.

The night-market stalls sold everything from clothing and knockoff designer handbags to household goods. Tents covered some, while others dared the weather.

Another section made his stomach rumble. The smell of meat cooking reminded him he hadn't eaten since lunchtime.

"What is that?" Gamon pointed to a light that someone shot into the sky, and then it came spinning right back into the seller's hand.

Dusit grinned at him. "You've never seen these?"

The guy behind the table slingshotted the lit spinner high into the air. The toy arced and slowly spun back to the man.

"You want one?"

Gamon was an adult and shouldn't want a toy, but his mother had blocked him from these basic experiences. "We're not here for this."

Dusit's eyes widened, and he smirked. He leaned in and said, "No, we're here to meet with some sex workers who we need to chat with."

Snorting at the ridiculously unlikely reason they were there, Gamon conceded, "Point taken. Yes, I'd like one."

Dusit handed the man some baht and nabbed two devices off his table. He handed one to Gamon.

"Thank you. Did you want one too?" Gamon felt less childish.

"No, this is for when that one gets lost." Dusit pocketed the flying spinner.

"Oh." He slipped the toy into his crossbody bag. So much he didn't know.

A group of drunken foreigners came bumping down the aisle, headed on a collision course with him. Dusit wrapped his arms around him and swirled him out of the way of the tramping mob.

Gamon absorbed Dusit's closeness. He loved how Dusit's strong hands guided him to safety. "Thank you."

"Sure." Dusit smiled at him and released his hold on him. "Should we head over to Silom Soi 4?"

And it was time to fill in his other knowledge gaps. "Sure."

Dusit led him down a few short blocks, and then they turned onto one of Bangkok's gay-friendly streets. Restaurants, bars, and clubs outlined in neon lights lined both sides of the small street. The only difference seemed to be the high ratio of men.

Overhead lights were strung between the buildings in rainbow colors. There were even a few rainbow flags hanging off buildings and smaller ones tied to tables.

Out of habit, Gamon tried to avoid eye contact. The looks he was getting had nothing to do with fan recognition but were heated invitations.

Dusit put a claiming hand on Gamon's lower back. "You're being eyed like a piece of candy."

The sign of possession encouraged Gamon. "I've been told I'm very sweet."

"Without a doubt, because I know you are. But come on, let's get you off the street and into a club." Dusit grabbed his wrist and tugged him into a nearby dance establishment.

"You've never accompanied me to a dance club," Gamon said. Despite not being vain, he knew these clubs valued a handsome face, slim body, and well-toned backside, things he worked on daily.

"What?" Was Dusit double-checking what Gamon had said or daring him to say it again?

Gamon needed to keep his heart on lockdown, but being with Dusit made that impossible. He couldn't stop smiling. "Nothing."

All heads turned, and gazes fixed on them. They were new—not to mention Dusit was gorgeous and fierce in that alpha-male way still favored.

Dusit frowned and pointed over to the quietest corner of the club. "Let's get that table."

Gamon would no longer hide. He had the freedom he'd always wanted. He was with Dusit, and he was going to enjoy the experience.

He grabbed Dusit's hand and pulled him toward the dance floor. "No, I want you all to myself."

Dusit groaned. "But—"

"Sitting makes us a stationary target. Besides, I will not sit on the sidelines anymore. Dance with me." Gamon let the music seep into him and started to move.

Dusit's mouth dropped open, and he froze on the edge of the dance floor, making no attempt to react to the music.

Gamon drank him in. "Not used to me refusing you? Or you didn't realize I'm better at reading other people's intentions in places like this?"

Dusit studied him and then gave him a slow smile. "You've changed in interesting ways."

"I'd ask you how, but I can only hear you if you're dancing." Gamon rocked to the beat.

How many times had Gamon wondered how different his evenings in Paris would have been if Dusit had been there?

Perhaps he could find out.

Closing his eyes, Gamon let the music soak into him. He moved to the beat of the popular song, one that told of the magic of discovering one's soulmate, and he sang along, wishing the lyrics could erase the past. As he mouthed the words of the elation that comes when one finds true love, Gamon craved that feeling as his own future.

"Where did you learn to dance like this?"

Gamon opened his eyes to find Dusit dancing close to him. "I went to dance clubs in Paris."

Dusit frowned as he waved off another man trying to encroach on their space. "I bet you got even more attention than you are getting here."

Oozing a bit more of "come hither and take me up against a wall," Gamon smiled. He'd always had the skill of capturing attention. "Sometimes."

Dusit's expression dropped. "Were there many?"

"Clubs?" Gamon pretended not to know the real question.

"You know what I'm asking." Dusit studied him.

Was his sex appeal lost on Dusit? "We're having this conversation here and now?"

Nodding, Dusit's gaze pinned him, and he ground out the word, "Yes."

"Right now?" Gamon teased because he loved riling Dusit, and he needed to postpone answering.

"Gamon," Dusit growled. "Were you with lots of other men?"

Jealousy usually annoyed Gamon, but Dusit's possessiveness turned him on. Wrong as it may be, Dusit's fierce you-are-mine stare was reassurance that Dusit still wanted Gamon for himself.

"Were there?" Dusit folded his arms over his chest and stopped moving.

Gamon exhaled hard and undid Dusit's arms. He danced in the space between them. "A few. Sometimes I couldn't stand the thought of being alone," he said, leaving out how he longed for Dusit more when he left with someone else. "You?"

Glancing away, Dusit said, “I don’t know.”

“What?” How was that possible? Gamon feigned a pout. “That’s not fair. I told you.”

Dusit sighed. “When I’d get blackout drunk, it was hard to remember how I ended up in some of the places I did. I think I had sex in a bar bathroom once or twice, and maybe once in an alley. I don’t quite remember any of it.”

A dark emotion Gamon tried to avoid flooded him and overwhelmed his good sense. He couldn’t name the need to reclaim and mark what was his as jealousy. That word was too tame for what he felt.

Stop. They needed to keep this light. The production house was right. Don’t get entangled. He needed to take this slowly. The slash of emotion revealed that he wasn’t prepared for Dusit.

But Gamon had to know more details. He couldn’t stop himself from asking, “With who? Men, women…?”

“Probably both.” Dusit frowned and said, “I’ve done all the testing, and the results came back with no issues.”

Gamon might not remember their names, but he couldn’t block out the various men he’d been with. “You don’t remember?”

“Nope… and I’m good with that.” Dusit reached and cupped Gamon’s face. “I don’t want to remember the last few years.”

Gamon understood that feeling and didn’t know what to add, so he went back to the original topic. “I’ve also done all the tests and haven’t been with anyone since I received the results. No issues.”

Dusit stared at him.

What was he thinking?

Leaning in so Dusit could hear him over the music, he said, “Next time you have sex, I hope it’s more memorable and that you want to remember every single detail.”

Without missing a beat, Dusit grabbed Gamon by the waist and tugged him against his body. He held him close and said in his ear, “If it’s with you, it will be etched into my mind for all time.”

Gamon envisioned how he would compose Dusit’s next sexual experience, one that would be immortalized in a song. Excessive, yes, but desire flooded him.

He needed to compartmentalize these wayward cravings and tried to step back. There was a reality they should deal with, so he suggested, “We should talk.”

“Nope. Let’s wait. Stay close. I need to enjoy you for a little longer.” It appeared Dusit wouldn’t allow him the space. He hooked his thumbs into Gamon’s pants and locked him in place.

Moving from side to side, Dusit pressed his hardness against Gamon’s. Dusit gyrated with the music, sending filthy thoughts spiraling through Gamon.

This man still could make him pant with a look, a touch, but dancing with him? Well, that was another thing altogether. Rubbing against him—

“Maybe we should cool down,” Gamon suggested, resisting the urge to fan himself. “On to the next stop?”

Dusit chuckled. “Because going to find a sex worker is the way to take things down a notch?”

Shrugging, Gamon grinned. “What do you want me to say?”

He wanted some time—they needed some space.

Dusit’s eyes sparkled with mischief in a way that had always thrilled Gamon. “Off to the next stop in taking it slow.”

CHAPTER 9

OVER THE last few years, Patpong had undergone a cleanup, and the bars Dusit had known disappeared. Though his not so splendid memories remained.

He and Gamon hadn't taken but a few steps outside the dance club before a younger kid approached them. "Go-go girls?"

Ah, he was a tout. Someone who drummed up business for a club. Gamon raked his fingers through his hair. "Um…."

The guy looked them up and down. He leaned in, and in a quieter voice he asked, "Go-go boys? Nice pretty boys…?"

Dusit asked, "Did all the bars move?"

"Some, yes. The pandemic made others go out of business." The tout gestured to the right and the left. "You want go-go boys? I can show you where you can take a boy for a private party?"

Gamon's eyes widened as he stared at the guy. He then turned to Dusit and asked, "Boys?"

Dusit made a fist and clenched then released it. He did several times, though he couldn't shake off that terrible reality of trafficking. He clarified for both his sake and Gamon's, "You mean men?"

The tout shrugged as if it made no difference to him. "You want men?"

No! He wanted Gamon.

Gamon said, "Yes, we want—"

"A private party?"

"A party?" Gamon schooled his expression as if he were trying to play cool, but his voice squeaked, telling the truth of how he felt about this whole situation.

Dusit needed to make this as painless as possible for him, so without a better suggestion, he said, "Sure. Let's go."

The tout, who in the streetlight looked to be only a teenager, led them down several streets. With one last turn, they were finally outside a noisy club glowing with red and purple lights.

Gamon glanced over at Dusit.

Dusit peered inside. The place's bar appeared safe, so he grabbed Gamon's hand and stepped inside what looked like a get-a-beer type of bar.

"Have fun." The tout waved to them and then collected a token from the bouncer.

"What's that?"

Not a hundred percent sure, but Dusit took a guess. "I believe that's for bringing us to this bar. He'll turn in the chip for baht at the end of the night."

Gamon took one step inside the club, and three men with short white sarongs wrapped around their waists, numbers pinned to them, descended upon him. Hands were gliding over Gamon's arms and back.

"Um, Dusit?"

Their unwanted touches needed to stop.

Dusit played interference and slipped an arm around Gamon. He tugged him close. A voice in his head that sounded surprisingly like Lyric snarked, "Ownership much?"

The octopus men hadn't taken the hint, so Dusit said, "Later, guys. I want to take my man to a seat."

"My man?" Gamon gasped, though his eyes sparkled.

Too soon to argue about the facts, so Dusit shrugged and led Gamon away from the men, who were now pouting and glaring.

A man dressed in a white suit waved them over. "Sit here. You'll get a good view of the show."

Glancing up at the stage, Dusit understood what "out of the pot and into the fire" meant. They were seated in the front row.

"Oh! Look at that." Gamon gestured with his chin to the stage.

Two men were having intercourse, which would have been fine, but this was more like an acrobatic feat. The smaller man with bleached blond hair was on the bottom, and he gasped. He clutched two poles in front of him with his hands while his toes gripped the back poles. He supported his own weight while the other, more muscular man held the same pose over him and, with a look of determination, fucked him. By the blond's moans, the big guy seemed to be doing it well. Or was that all for the show?

"How do they do that?" Their strength and stamina amazed Dusit.

"Their toes must be strong." Gamon continued staring.

After a few more minutes of their vigorous humping, the guy doing the thrusting simply tapped the other guy on the shoulder and they gracefully disengaged from each other and the poles.

Gamon pointed out the obvious. "Did I miss something? They didn't—"

"Orgasm? No. I guess they may have multiple shows a night, and it's about the performance, not their climax." Did he sound like he knew what he was talking about?

Gamon's mouth dropped open.

The performers who had been onstage were now standing next to them, wearing sarongs. The smaller one's sarong jutted out in an obscene way as he smiled at them. "Hello."

Dusit nudged Gamon out of his silence. "Hello."

"I'm Niran, and this is Somchair. We haven't seen you at the club before and thought we'd say hi."

Somchair frowned as he glared harder. "Welcome."

That did not feel welcoming, not even a bit.

Dusit pressed his lips together so he didn't annoy Somchair further.

Niran tilted his head and studied Gamon and then Dusit. "You look familiar."

Gamon adjusted his facemask and shifted closer to Dusit.

Happiness zipped through him, and Dusit tried to ignore how incredible having Gamon closer made him feel. He reminded Niran, "How can we? We've never stopped in before."

Shrugging as if he'd heard that before, Niran asked, "Shall we have a drink, or do you want to leave?" It seemed like he was checking how they felt about the weather rather than asking if they wanted to have sex with him.

Gamon looked around as another couple took the stage. "It's hard to talk in here, so let's get out of here."

"I'm part of the deal." Somchair stepped forward.

Gamon glanced at Dusit, but what did he know? Dusit simply went with the flow.

Niran raised his hand and gestured to the boss for attention.

Each establishment had a boss, or *mae-lao*, who managed the place. They appeased local law enforcement, catered to the customers, and took care of the workers. All while counting the baht that rolled in.

The mae-lao, dressed in a gold duster jacket, wide-legged pants, and high heels, rushed over. "You don't have to take Somchair if you don't want to. Somchair, stop the nonsense."

Somchair's glare said they did or he'd break something… possibly them.

Gamon used his rescue-me-please hand-squeeze on Dusit's forearm.

What did one do in this situation?

Preferring not to have his bones broken, Dusit said, "We'd like to spend time with both of them."

"Ah, yes. They are very… *entertaining*… to talk to." Snapping her fingers at Somchair and Niran, she demanded, "Get dressed." Then the mae-lao laughed behind her hand. "I must collect a bar fine for you to take out two of our greatest performers."

Even though they were probably charged double the baht as newbies, Dusit didn't hesitate to hand over the money.

Before sailing away, the mae-lao turned to them with a smirk. "And you work the rest out with them."

"The rest?" Gamon asked.

The mae-lao tugged on her gold suit. "Yum-yum, fucking, ropes…."

Gamon's eyes went wide. "Oh."

Niran appeared before them and waved. "Follow me. I know a decent hotel that's not too expensive."

"We only want to talk." Gamon's voice was an octave higher than it usually was, alerting Dusit to the fact that he was incredibly nervous.

Somchair rolled his eyes. This guy was truly not interested in customer satisfaction, or even general politeness. In fact, he was actively rude.

Niran smirked in a way that said he'd heard that line a hundred times before. "Sure. I know some *places where we can talk*. The room will be quiet."

As they followed Niran and the scowling Somchair, Dusit put a hand on Gamon's lower back.

Gamon glanced at him. "What's yum-yum?"

How could this devastatingly hot man—his man who embodied sex—be so innocent?

Dusit made a circle with his index finger and thumb in front of his mouth and moved his hand back and forth twice.

Gamon's eyes widened. "Oh? A blowjob."

The man was too cute.

Grinning, Dusit asked, "You okay?"

Frowning, Gamon said, "Do you think I'm not okay?"

He hated making Gamon unhappy. Why did he say that? It was clear Gamon had something to prove to Achara, to Dusit, and probably even himself.

Thinking fast, Dusit asked, "If you're okay, I'll let you do the talking."

Gamon shook his head with an appeased smile. "Good save."

Impossible to fool Gamon, Dusit couldn't deny the truth. "I do my best."

When they got to the hotel, Somchair woke the receptionist. After a brief discussion, he handed Somchair a key card.

Niran waved at the group and led the way down the hall and up two flights of stairs. "Here it is."

Somchair, with silent waves of anger rolling off him, opened the door. He held the door open for Niran and then stepped into the room himself.

Dusit was sure if he hadn't caught the door, it would have locked with them in the hallway. Somchair was not a people pleaser, so his choice of career didn't make sense.

Niran smirked at Somchair and then shook his head. "Sorry about him. Have a seat and get comfortable. Take off your mask or your pants… or both."

There were two double beds and a TV on a dresser with a broken handle, but no chairs in sight.

Gamon took off his mask and sat on the farthest bed.

Maybe they should have had Niran and Somchair sign something so they wouldn't blab about their time together.

Too late.

Dusit pocketed his own mask and settled next to Gamon. He tried to jumpstart his brain, which had gotten stuck on the thought that he was on a bed with Gamon. The last time they were—

Gamon shifted a tad closer to Dusit and smiled bigger at Niran. "Do you usually work together?"

"Whenever we can." Somchair dared someone to disagree.

Niran sighed, placing a hand on Somchair's arm. "I got banged up a bit, so he's protective. It happens…."

The casual way Niran shared such a devastating fact about his job broke Dusit's brain.

"More than once." Somchair looked away and swiped a hand over his face.

"I'm fine." Niran gave Gamon and Dusit a bright smile. He touched Somchair's back. "I'm fine."

"They admitted you to hospital," Somchair bit the words out. He gently touched Niran's face.

The makeup that covered the bruise around Niran's eye onstage had long since worn off. Dusit's stomach tightened.

The business they were in put them in the dangerous situation of going to a private place with a stranger, dangerous especially for someone Niran's size. He was fit but only one hundred and fifty centimeters tall and without much muscle mass.

Niran patted Somchair's arm. "I'm fine, Som-Som, but most of the time, the client enjoys both of us."

No one added anything.

Finally Gamon filled the silence. "So what usually happens?"

"Sex," Somchair answered. His clipped tone suggested he thought the question unnecessary.

Not to be detoured, Gamon asked, "Yes, but how does that—"

Somchair opened his mouth.

Niran elbowed Somchair before he got a word out and smiled at Gamon. "We usually ask what the client wants to do. Then the price is negotiated, we shower, and then…."

"And then…?" Gamon didn't seem to know how to ask for further details.

Niran reached out and put a hand on Gamon's thigh. "What do you want?"

"Nothing." Gamon jumped closer to Dusit, knocking Niran's hand off him. "No, I mean…."

Dusit put an arm around Gamon, hoping to reassure him.

Somchair grimaced at Dusit. "What do you want?"

Customer service didn't seem to be Somchair's strong suit, but Niran's black eye explained why.

Niran rolled his eyes. "Sorry. Somchair's in a mood. He's usually better after a show."

Somchair tucked Niran under his arm as if to protect him from all the bad in the world. Right now the *bad* appeared to be Dusit and Gamon.

"Well, I guess you must be frustrated," Dusit pointed out the obvious. Somchair had fucked Niran within an inch of his life and still hadn't come.

"What do you mean?" Somchair's eyes narrowed as if Dusit were trying to trick him.

"You didn't…." Gamon gestured to below Somchair's waist.

Dusit helped Gamon. "Finish."

"It's a performance. Work. We don't 'cause then we couldn't spend an enjoyable time with you." Niran pasted a sweet smile on his face and reached out a hand toward them.

Gamon gave his hand a shake like the foreigners did and then let go.

A giggle bubbled out of Niran. "So what do you want?"

Dusit's mouth opened. "Nothing. I mean—"

"You want nothing?" Somchair sneered as if to cover his unease. "You overpaid for our bar fine, but you want nothing? People always desire something."

Dusit did long for something, but it was nothing either of them could grant him. He shifted closer to Gamon.

Niran skimmed a hand down Somchair's arm as if trying to soothe the beast.

The big muscular man melted and gave Niran a small smile.

Gamon wrung his hands. "We hope to understand what you do and—"

Somchair jumped in with, "Since they want nothing and you want to understand what we do, perhaps we can show you."

They disappeared into the bathroom.

Gamon opened his mouth several times, but Somchair and Niran returned from the world's quickest shower with towels wrapped around their waists.

A sharp inhale said Niran was onboard with this plan. He turned to Dusit and Gamon. "Do you like to watch?"

"Um…." Gamon's answer summed up Dusit's feelings on the matter.

"We love to perform, but before we do, let us tell you the costs." Niran ran down the list of activities they could do to them or to each other.

Somchair added, "No hurting him at all. If you want to do anything painful, it's done to me."

That said it all. Dusit completely understood that sentiment. Somchair was not simply protective of Niran—he wanted Niran for his own.

Gamon gasped and put a hand out in front of him. "We don't want to hurt anyone."

Niran batted his eyelashes and then said, "Think of us as your servants. You can do things to us you can't do to someone you have feelings for…."

Dusit's brain hurt. The idea of paying to use someone. "There's nothing we—"

Niran gave a wink. "Maybe we can give you some inspiration? Somchair and I could continue to—"

"Yes, why don't you do whatever you'd like to each other. We are not looking to take part, only watch, and we will take the option of the full night." Gamon's voice didn't even waver as he handed over a pile of cash.

Niran's mouth dropped open for a moment before he grinned at getting paid for probably doing exactly what he wanted. "You got it," he said and dropped the cash on the dresser.

With lightning speed, Somchair dropped his towel, grabbed Niran, and tugged off Niran's towel. He let the towel fall and nibbled Niran's shoulders.

"Kiss me," Niran boldly demanded.

Somchair affectionately nuzzled his cheeks and then worked his lips over to Niran's mouth.

Somchair's tongue grazing over Niran's lips differed completely from the show they put on in the club.

He claimed ownership of Niran's mouth. There was no rough possession, only confidence that Niran's lips were his to kiss.

As they kissed, Gamon touched his own mouth as if wanting the same.

Somchair didn't end the kiss but eased onto the empty bed, pulling Niran on top of him. They were both beautiful in different ways. Niran was slim, almost petite, and his blond hair was cut in a schoolboyish style. Somchair was mostly muscle, and his hair was longer, with a part that allowed it to fall on either side of his face.

They remained locked in a kiss. Both were hard.

Whispering loud enough for Dusit to hear, Niran asked, "Want yum-yum?"

Was Niran asking to give, or did he want—

Niran spun with the grace of a dancer so he faced Somchair's erection. His body hovered over Somchair's.

Other than a couple of jerk circles, and vague memories of a drunken encounter or two, Dusit hadn't been too close to cocks that weren't his own… except for Gamon's.

Dusit had seen movies of people doing 69. Porn was one thing, but smelling the pheromones from other men was something else. The musky scent mixed with Gamon's cologne made Dusit feel drunk.

Niran looked over at them and grinned, then broke into a moan.

Somchair licked Niran's shaft without warning.

Gamon gasped as if he had felt a wet tongue on his own cock.

Niran's eyes squeezed shut as Somchair sucked him into his mouth.

Holding his hips still, Somchair controlled the action. Dusit could appreciate the rush of making your lover savor the moment to build the sensation to something more.

Not to be outdone, Niran opened his eyes and licked the long length of Somchair's cock. Then he laved his tongue over the wet tip in gentle flicks.

How Dusit wanted to do that with Gamon. To taste his sweetness again would be a miracle—no, Dusit shouldn't do anything with Gamon. They were taking it slow.

He wrapped an arm around Gamon's shoulders. Holding him needed to be enough, so he tried to keep a grip on himself by analyzing the scene.

Niran and Somchair exchanged long, slow, sexy licks. Next time he sucked Gamon, he wanted the lights on and—

Gamon shifted restlessly on the bed.

Should Dusit do that to him right now?

No, of course not. They had recently reunited, and things still felt fragile between them. It was way too soon. They hadn't even talked about what had happened.

But maybe he could—no.

Gamon turned toward him. The heated need in his eyes overwhelmed any of Dusit's cautious thoughts—wait, pause, stop?

Maybe they could get off a little. "You want to—"

Whimpering, Gamon nodded his head but otherwise didn't move.

His eyes begged Dusit to make it better, and that was intoxicating.

What could this hurt? He was giving in to what they both wanted.

Dusit should resist. "We probably shouldn't do this…."

The outright want in Gamon's eyes did Dusit in. How could he refuse this man anything?

"But we are going to." Dusit moved back on the bed to lean against the headboard. Then he pulled Gamon to him and positioned him to sit between Dusit's legs with his back to Dusit's chest. Dusit wrapped his arms around Gamon's middle.

Gamon stayed put and let his head drop onto Dusit's shoulder. He purred.

God, Dusit had missed the simple pleasure of hugging Gamon from behind.

Gasps and soft moans that didn't sound practiced drifted over from the other bed.

What should he do?

Gamon shifted restlessly in his arms and sat forward a bit.

The best of this bad idea would be to get Gamon off and then go into the bathroom to take care of himself.

Dusit's hand rested on Gamon's stomach, and what had once been the cutest little belly was now flat and hard. "You've lost weight but gained muscle."

Gamon leaned back onto Dusit's shoulder. He nuzzled Dusit's neck and then whispered, "I'm finally working out."

Niran and Somchair were showing off their sucking skills. Somchair's hands guided Niran's hips.

If Dusit were alone, the scene playing out in front of him might have been interesting, but Gamon had his total focus.

But Gamon lay in his arms.

He could have easily—no.

Trying to keep his wits about him, Dusit asked, "Do you work out at a gym or—"

"Dusit." Gamon's exasperation sounded in his tone and was echoed in his wide-eyed, what-the-fuck look.

"What?" Dusit mouthed.

"We should pay attention." Gamon sat straighter.

"I am… to you."

"Not to me, to them. Look how beautiful they look."

They had moved out of their sucking-cock pose and onto all fours. Somchair readied Niran with his fingers.

Niran grinned over at them and mouthed a "Thank you" that ended in a groan.

Dusit whispered for Gamon's ears only, "I used to love putting my fingers in you to open you."

"Dusit" came out of Gamon like a twisted moan.

There it was. That breathlessness he had missed so much. Dusit wanted to build on it… a little. "You would get so impatient."

Gamon moaned and rubbed against him. "You'd go too slow."

"I didn't want to hurt you." Dusit traced his fingers over Gamon's zipper.

Gamon exhaled his name. "Dusit, please."

"Am I going too slow again?"

"You loved making me beg for you." Gamon's words mixed with gasps as he thrust against Dusit's teasing fingers, searching for a bit more friction.

Dusit admitted, "I couldn't resist. You beg so sweetly."

"I've begged no one… but you." Gamon shifted restlessly against him. "I miss begging for you."

"Want to beg me again?"

Gamon froze. "I want to do a lot. But we shouldn't."

Dusit's mouth grazed Gamon's neck in all the places that drove Gamon crazy. "No, we shouldn't. We are taking things slow and focusing on the series."

"We can stop." Dusit unwrapped his arms from around Gamon. "You're right."

"No. Please." Groaning, Gamon turned in Dusit's arms so they were facing each other. Gamon sat between Dusit's legs and slipped his hand under Dusit's shirt.

"We can stop." Dusit bit back a moan. "Is that what you want?"

"Only thing I want is you. Can I have you?" Gamon looked through his long eyelashes, melting any good intentions Dusit tried to have. His fingers teased Dusit's nipples. "We can take it slow."

Dusit would not point out Gamon's hand under Dusit's shirt and how this wasn't the definition of going slow.

Gamon grabbed Dusit's hand and put it on his thigh, near to where Gamon's erection was pushing against his pants. It would be so easy to unzip him and stroke him to a quick orgasm.

Dusit rubbed Gamon's thigh. He caressed Gamon's erection through his pants.

"Please." Gamon scratched down Dusit's chest and stomach to the top of his pants. "Please?"

"You're sure?"

"I can't wait. I need you…." Gamon's words broke.

All Dusit's remaining doubts shattered, allowing his own desire to satisfy every need Gamon ever had to take control.

Shifting and leaning in, Gamon kissed Dusit on the mouth. No gentle press of lips, this was desperation. His lips clung and sought more.

Dusit opened his lips immediately and let Gamon's tongue sweep in. Gamon kissed like he was starving for Dusit's mouth.

Sparks of long-missed pleasure danced through Dusit. He teased Gamon's tongue with his own, their heads twisting and turning as their need surged.

Gasps and an "Mm, you two are sexy" interrupted the moment.

Gamon broke the kiss and froze. His eyes showed confusion and want.

Shit! Not alone.

They needed some privacy, so Dusit suggested, "Lie down."

Dusit lay alongside him and pulled a blanket from the end of the bed over them.

"Hurry," Gamon demanded, making a shiver go through Dusit.

He'd always loved Gamon's urgency.

Niran's voice reached Dusit. "Look at them."

"So hot." First nice thing Somchair had said.

But this was a moment Dusit didn't want to share. He unzipped Gamon's pants.

Gamon's breath turned into gasps as he shifted around to help Dusit with his vintage button-fly jeans.

"Too many buttons," Gamon growled.

Dusit had never imagined adhering to the fashion trend of wearing vintage would cause him so much regret.

Their breaths mingled. There was not much light coming through the thin blanket that covered them, but Dusit could make out Gamon's anxious expression.

"Help me." Gamon begged, wiggling his hips impatiently as if he could wish his pants off.

"You want…?" Dusit didn't know why, but he needed confirmation that Gamon desired him.

"Yes." Gamon teased a finger along Dusit's erection under his jeans.

Dusit made quick work of pushing down his pants. His movements almost shoved the hot blanket off him, so he repositioned it.

Gamon licked his hand, then wrapped his fist around Dusit's shaft. "Mm, yes."

Trying not to die, Dusit did the same. He started tugging on Gamon. Gamon liked it tight and hard.

God, he'd missed Gamon's noises. His gasps and moans went right to Dusit's erection.

Gamon stroked him hard and fast.

"Slow down." He didn't want this experience to be over before it started.

Thrusting up through Dusit's fist, Gamon whined, "I can't."

Dusit stopped jerking him off. "Yes, you can."

Gamon exhaled hard, and his cock throbbed in Dusit's hand.

Recalling that Gamon enjoyed dirty talk, Dusit said, "Look at you. In a hotel, so desperate to come you don't even care that there are two guys fucking in the next bed."

"Yes. Dirty." Gamon tugged on Dusit's cock at the perfect speed.

"Do you want to come?"

Gamon whimpered.

"What if they hear you? Then they will know you are a horny, filthy mess." Dusit knew there was no way Niran and Somchair wouldn't hear his and Gamon's completion.

"Quiet. I'll be quiet," Gamon promised as he trembled.

"I don't know if you can." Dusit twisted his fist as he jerked him.

Gamon whined as his body moved against Dusit's motion, causing the blanket to drop.

Dusit didn't think it through. He demanded, "Beg me."

Gamon sighed and pulled the blanket back in place. "Please, Dusit."

"Please what?"

"Let me… come." Gamon had gotten more confident. "Jerk me off. I don't care who knows. I'm too hot to think straight. You make me so crazy I don't care about anything. I need to come with you."

Dusit could feel Gamon's body poised on the edge.

"Dusit, please." Gamon shoved the stifling blanket off them.

Their only privacy now was Dusit's body blocking him, and the fact that Gamon didn't care lit a fuse in Dusit.

Stroking at the exact speed and strength he knew Gamon preferred, he whispered, "Come, but everyone's going to know."

Gamon's hand faltered on Dusit's dick as his entire body froze, then spasmed.

Fuck, the sounds Gamon made were almost enough to make Dusit explode. He stroked Gamon through his orgasm.

When Gamon was done, he smiled dreamily at Dusit.

Dusit needed him. He wrapped his hand around Gamon's fist to stroke himself off.

"Mm, yes." Gamon took over stroking duties. "Come for me, Dusit."

Too many times had he longed to hear that. His tenuous hold snapped, and he came. Pleasure radiated from his core and rolled out in pulses.

Gamon stretched and pulled the blanket back over them once more.

Dusit glanced over at Niran and Somchair, who were gently kissing and whispering to each other. Did he really get off with other people three feet away?

How was Gamon with all this?

Gamon was already in dreamland. His nose wrinkled in his sleep, and he shuffled closer to Dusit. Dusit ran his fingers through Gamon's hair, pushing the damp strands off this precious man's forehead.

All the love and wishes he'd had roared to the surface. He wrapped Gamon in his arms. This time he would not let go.

Sleep. He wasn't tired. He wanted to absorb every moment of holding Gamon. Dusit needed to close his eyes for a minute….

WHAT A DREAM.

The blanket was down around Dusit's waist, and—wait, Gamon wasn't there. He was across the room, dressed, and whispering to Niran.

It wasn't a dream. They were in a hotel.

Gamon glanced over and gave Dusit a smile.

It was his dearest fantasy come true.

Dusit couldn't stop grinning. It hadn't been his imagination or a jerk-off hallucination.

All was right in the world.

He adjusted and rebuttoned his pants, felt eyes on him. Glanced around.

Somchair glared at him from the other bed. Or maybe that was his resting face.

Dusit used his chin to gesture toward Gamon and Niran. "What are they talking about?"

"Whatever they want." Somchair sat upright and then leaned toward him. "You should tell him."

"Tell him what?" Dusit didn't think he was so obvious that an angry stranger would notice.

Somchair clarified, "Tell him how you feel."

Hadn't he done that last night? Lyric's "words matter" echoed through his head.

CHAPTER 10

A FRESH BURST of affection and love clenched Gamon's heart as he tried not to stare at Dusit lying there in bed. Not looking was impossible since Dusit kept smiling at him.

Ah, Dusit.

Dusit was everything Gamon had been missing, and being with him made Gamon feel he could do anything.

Not wanting to be rude, he refocused on Niran.

Niran smirked and whispered, "You love him."

No longer wanting to deny reality even to a stranger, Gamon nodded his admission. "Sorry, I got distracted. You were saying Somchair wants to become a chef, and you want to run a restaurant?"

Shifting from foot to foot, Niran peeked up at Gamon. "Yeah. We can't do this forever. He loves cooking. His mother and grandmother taught him, though right now he gets little opportunity. Somchair and I are saving up to get some place where people can come and be themselves. And maybe some of our friends from the club can change their careers too."

"That sounds incredible." Gamon hoped that happened for him and Somchair. Niran didn't want pity, and Gamon would give him none. He was doing this work because he had few options. He had only a little education and needed to send money back to his mother.

"And I thought once we are out of this… situation," Niran went on, "we can hire others that want to do something different as well." The entertaining, free, sexy imp was now a prospective business owner.

"If you need investors, I might be interested, along with a couple of other—"

Niran took a step back with a frown on his face. "No. My intention when I told you that was not try to get money from you."

Hating that he'd insulted Niran, Gamon tried to make it better. "I know you didn't. But I like to invest in new businesses for first-time business owners."

"Why?" Niran seemed honestly surprised.

"Same reason you want to hire people—so they can change careers if they want." Gamon made little on these investments, but he got enough of a return that his accountant didn't scold him, and he loved helping people succeed.

"Oh." Niran smiled and waved him off. "Don't worry about it. We've almost got enough saved."

"Then email me when you open so I can support you that way." Gamon was usually not so insistent. But recently he'd decided if he wanted something he'd find a way to have it.

He forced himself not to look at Dusit.

"Your email?" Niran's mouth dropped open, and he put a hand on his heart. "An enormous star like you is going to give me your email?"

Gamon's pulse raced, and he tried to steady his breath. These two men knew who he and Dusit were the entire time? Panic crept in.

Niran must have seen Gamon's distress. He immediately said, "Don't worry, we'd never out you or tell anyone you visited with us.... You wouldn't believe some people we've spent time with. Right, Somchair?"

Somchair grunted.

"We've seen a lot of actors from Thailand and other countries, singers, and even a few politicians. Outing any of our clients would go against our ethics."

"And be bad for business," Somchair added.

Niran laughed. "That too."

"Then let me give you my email." Gamon found a notepad and pencil near the phone. He scribbled his email address and handed the square of paper to Niran.

Niran glanced at the paper and then peeked up at him. "Thank you. It's rare that people trust us with their personal information."

Dusit crawled out of bed, came over to Gamon, and threw an arm around his shoulders. "He's not most people."

"I see that. And you're nothing like what I thought." Niran looked Dusit up and down.

"Ah, you thought I'd be the drunk who beats people up?" Dusit sighed.

Gamon bristled slightly at the reminder of Dusit's ill reputation, but he had to admit that it explained Somchair's behavior last night.

"No insult, man, but we can't be too careful." Somchair shrugged unapologetically and took a step closer to Niran.

Niran gave Gamon a big smile. "Well, I'm glad you lived up to who I thought you both were."

Relief swamped Gamon. He always worried about the impression he made on people, especially his fans. "Good. I'm glad."

A phone alarm went off.

"It's mine." Somchair turned it off. He opened his bag and pulled two bottles, both labeled with the name of the new type of PrEP medicine. He held a pill out to Niran. "Your meds."

They both swallowed a pill without water.

"Water?" Dusit tried to hand Niran a bottle of water supplied by the hotel, but Somchair snatched it out of his hand.

His glare lessened. "Thanks." Somchair uncapped the water bottle and handed it to Niran to sip. Then he took a swig himself.

Gamon was glad they seemed vigilant about protecting themselves from contracting HIV.

"Are the meds expensive here? I know abroad they can be."

"No. Because of our job, we can get them for free through a program." Somchair looked much less scary today.

Gamon didn't quite know what to say. "We really want to thank you both for spending time with us and allowing us to understand… what happens."

Niran scrunched his face. "Wait, was this, like, prepping for the second season?"

Dusit smiled at Gamon as he silently agreed, making Gamon's heart melt.

"I can't wait." Niran clapped his hands. "Somchair, a second season! How did I miss this news?"

"I'm not sure, but it's time to go." Somchair sounded like he was daring someone to object.

Dusit checked around the room and of course found Gamon's phone on the floor near the bed where they…. Gamon took it from him with a wink.

"Thank you again," Gamon said as they walked downstairs with Niran and Somchair.

They all paused at the entrance.

"May I have a hug?" Niran asked.

Gamon usually declined, but he couldn't refuse such a sweet man. "Um, sure."

Niran gave him a quick hug and then grabbed Somchair's wrist. "Bye. We have plans."

Niran and Somchair hurried down the street.

The memory of last night and the begging he'd done surged to the forefront of Gamon's mind. He'd orgasmed with other people in the room… and why did he find that so hot?

Dusit probably hadn't processed last night any more than Gamon had, and they still needed to talk, but… being next to Dusit fulfilled him.

Gamon glanced at Dusit, who had expectations written all over him.

Dusit smiled at him as he took his hand and squeezed it with reassurance. "Everything will be okay." As usual, Dusit gave Gamon exactly what he needed.

The feeling was familiar and so right Gamon wanted to drown in happiness.

Dusit used an app to arrange a car. It arrived before they could do much more than smile at each other.

A laugh bubbled out of Gamon as he got into the car. He was so happy standing next to Dusit it was ridiculous.

Dusit put his hand palm up between them.

Gamon couldn't resist the invitation and put his hand in Dusit's. Warmth and joy seemed to triple, making Gamon frown.

Dusit leaned in with a serene smile. “What’s wrong?”

“This happiness scares me.”

Squeezing his hand, Dusit asked, “Why?”

“It can’t last.” Gamon’s brain faltered on that reality.

Dusit took his hand back and pressed a kiss to Gamon’s knuckles. “Why not?”

The closeness, the giddiness, and the joy were too much. Gamon couldn’t deny they were on the cusp of getting back together, and that overwhelmed him. “Perfection can’t last. I don’t get—”

“To be happy? You deserve to be happy. You should have someone much better than me, but—“

“You are what I need to be happy.” Gamon couldn’t stop the honesty from spilling out of his mouth.

Throwing an arm around him, Dusit chuckled. “Well then, prepare to be thrilled, because you’re going to have me.”

Gamon thought he should stop tempting fate, but stupid elation made him grab the moment. “You’re right.”

At that moment the taxi hit traffic, and they inched along for a bit and then ground to a halt. A row of digital billboards lined the side of the road.

“You look great.” Dusit pointed out a billboard featuring Gamon with the latest luxury must-have watch and a faraway look in his eyes.

“Thanks. I was still jet-lagged.” He had returned a few days prior to the photo shoot.

The next ad spot with the caption “The Moment We Have All Been Waiting For” flashed across the screen, followed by a clip of them during the reunion scene. “You made dropping the briefcase natural.”

“It was. I wasn’t acting. I couldn’t.” That was true. “Seeing you overwhelmed me.”

“Glad to hear that.” Dusit slid a bit closer to him.

Three billboards down was a stationary picture promoting *Don't Break My Heart 2*.

Last night was a priceless fantasy, but in a low voice Gamon reminded Dusit… and himself, "We can't afford to let things get out of hand."

They had been careless, gotten carried away.

Two more billboards featuring the two of them mocked him and wouldn't allow him to escape.

The green light ahead turned red.

How could Gamon have let himself get so swept away?

Dusit was rebranding himself, and his career was restarting. Everything was on the line for him.

"The second season is still in the cancelable phase." Gamon probably said that more for himself than Dusit.

What they'd done could end everything if one of the investors found out and deemed it inappropriate. How could Gamon be so happy when they had risked throwing everything away?

"It's not going to be canceled," Dusit stated as if it were a fact.

The red light turned to green as fear and worry zigzagged through Gamon like their taxi wove through the traffic.

Gamon slipped his hand away from Dusit and pretended to scroll through his phone.

"Don't shut me out. Not this time." Dusit's voice broke. "Please don't do that to me again."

How much Gamon's disappearance must have hurt him. Fury at what his mother had done to them slashed at him.

Gamon shook his head but didn't have the words yet to apologize; at the same time he was also incredibly hurt.

How could Dusit have believed her? Hadn't he known how in love Gamon was with him?

Crazy how immature and inexperienced Gamon had been. No more. There had to be a way of making this work. Maybe hiding their relationship might be enough to protect them. "We must be careful. No one can know."

Dusit stared at him for a moment.

Gamon was tickled that he had the power to surprise Dusit. He enjoyed doing the unexpected.

The way Dusit's expression heated meant he approved. He took Gamon's hand and held it beneath the vision of the driver.

They were almost at their condo.

Dusit traced a thumb across his palm, and the sensual touch made Gamon's breath catch. How could such a simple gesture be so erotic?

Fear had always overridden his baser instincts, so Gamon had never been overtly sexual. However with Dusit, from the moment they met until now, his body always reacted. His body knew what Dusit could do and had signed up for those activities, regardless of the consequences.

Even now he struggled not to be inappropriate in the Grab car. Gamon was burning up as he tried to keep his breath even. "How much farther?"

"Patience." Dusit's whispered words carried a tone that promised many dirty and wonderful things. "We are almost at our condo's gate."

Anticipation grew.

"We are home." As soon as the car stopped, Dusit grabbed his hand. He tugged Gamon out of the car and into the building.

They hurried into the elevator.

Whoosh!

Gamon against the elevator wall with Dusit pinning his hands above his head.

Dusit leaning into him and approaching Gamon's lips with his own.

Then their mouths connected, and sparks that had been flickering in the car ignited.

Gamon pulled his mouth off Dusit's and reminded him, "Cameras."

"Don't care." But then their gazes caught, and with a small nod, Dusit stepped to the other side as the elevator went up. "See, I am the model of responsibility."

Straightening his shirt, Gamon grinned over at him. "You know where there're no cameras?"

"My bedroom." The elevator door dinged open to their floor, and Dusit yanked Gamon into the hallway. "Come on."

Gamon laughed as Dusit rushed them down the hallway.

The hurrying stopped when they noticed two people in front of their door.

"Have you no sense of decency?" One investor, whose name escaped Gamon, continued to scold them and ended with, "How could you do this?"

Everything in Gamon froze.

Their hands unlocked. Gamon's empty hand fell to his side.

Prem gave them a small smile that tried to say everything was all right, but the concern in his eyes told a different story. He turned to the investor. "Keep calm."

The nameless investor stepped forward and held up his phone, emblazoned with his social media feedback. "Have you seen this?"

It was an old picture of Dusit passed out on the floor of a bar.

"Or this?" The investor flashed another picture; then a video came up on his phone. He demanded, "Play it for them."

The director sighed and frowned but hit play. The screen flickered with Dusit as he ordered another drink from the floor with slurred speech. When someone tried to help him up, he refused. The caption was "Don't let Dusit Sitwat drag Gamon Chaisit down this low."

Why were they acting like they didn't know these clips were floating around? Gamon stated the obvious. "That's an old clip."

"Do you think that matters? Look at the fan reaction," the investor growled.

Dusit spoke up. "But I—"

"You will leave this apartment immediately while we try to manage this situation while we still can. The two of you will not have any contact." The investor folded his arms and waited.

Gamon stood there. How was this happening?

He glanced at the director, who grimly nodded. "It was a caveat in the contract Dusit signed. This doesn't have to affect shooting. We are still workshopping for a few more days. Let's see where we land."

"Where we land?" Gamon repeated as his dream that had finally been in his hands evaporated… again.

"I know where you're going to land." The investor stomped down the hall. "I'll be in the car."

Prem shrugged as the irate man got in the elevator and out of earshot. "There are only two kinds of news to the investors. One that makes money and one that doesn't. We don't know how the investors will receive this round of dragging up the past."

"I'll grab my things." Dusit's expression was blank, and he didn't put up a fight. He entered the apartment and came out a minute later with his old beat-up suitcase. He patted Gamon's shoulder. "Maybe you're right. Perfection can't last."

The director talked, but Gamon couldn't focus on the words.

He simply kept nodding until the man left with Dusit.

Gamon's heart ached.

All Gamon could do was watch the love of his life disappear into the elevator.

He let himself into the apartment and sat.

All alone… again.

GAMON COLLAPSED on the sofa. He felt chilly after his shower, so he pulled on a blanket. He'd gotten settled when there was a knock on the door.

Could it be that Dusit was back but forgot his keycard?

He rushed to the door and threw it open. "Dusit?"

"Afraid not, sweet one. I'm here." Achara brushed past him.

"What's this?" He pointed to the several bags she carried that clinked as she moved.

Achara shrugged as she unpacked. "I know you probably haven't eaten."

"What's with the bottles of wine?" Leave it to Achara to come to his rescue.

"You need some pain management so you can relax a teensy bit." She set too many bottles of wine on the table.

"*Some?* Looks like a lot."

"I didn't know what went best with roasted pork." She held up a bag of food to prove her innocence of encouraging a liquid dinner. "So let me guess. The investors have a huge issue with Dusit and his less than pristine past. They are clutching their pearls as if this is new information to them. Now Director Prem is being forced to halt the project."

"Why would an old picture—"

"Not everyone knows it's an old photo, and that video clip doesn't make him look like a leading man. And someone turned this picture of Dusit throwing a punch into a meme."

He simply didn't understand that. "How could people be so cruel?"

"I'm glad you don't know the answer to that, sugar. But there's also this one of him on a different barroom floor. These pictures, video clips, and the memes are all on social platforms."

Gamon frowned. The basic fact kept swirling in his brain. "These pictures are old."

"Do you think that matters to the investors?" Achara pointed out what Gamon already knew. "This series is a product. The Y-series industry is a business. Those people aren't interested in you or Dusit unless you are making them money, and if either of you has done something that jeopardizes their investment…."

Gamon stomped into the kitchen to get plates, glasses, and silverware. "I know but—"

"Bottom line, it's a business." She poured the wine and put the food on the table. "Some fans are supportive of you and Dusit working together again, and it's not a surprise others are not happy. They are worried about your safety, and pictures like these—"

"I'm a grown man who can take care of himself. Why do the fans insist on seeing me as fragile? They insist on purifying me and casting me in the role of a virgin in need of protection."

She pulled out a chair for him and took a seat herself. "In that role, they can identify with you and understand you. There is a power in protecting someone else."

He exhaled hard as he plopped into the chair. "Why can't they understand I can run my life without help?"

"It's changing slowly. I remember several actors losing their careers completely for having a girlfriend or boyfriend. A simple picture of them standing too close to someone was at times enough to have a career implode."

"Why is that? I'm simply an actor. I play a role to the best of my abilities and then want to live my life." Gamon understood the visibility his characters gave to fans was important, but so was his sanity.

She clinked glasses with him and took a sip. "You know, the expected fan service is transforming. I think that's a good thing, because it will help fans understand the character and the actor are not the same."

Gamon was feeling put upon and swirled his wine in his glass. "It's not changing fast enough. I will say I appreciate that France doesn't expect purity."

"Not much of the West does. They are used to reality. But whether it's a K-pop idol, a stage actor, or a TV or movie actor, people still expect the person to pour everything they have into the role and their fans to the point that there should be nothing left."

"It's a terrible way to be forced to live." He took a big sip. His real frustration was less about industry politics and more with having Dusit taken away.

Achara tapped her purple nails on the table. "You know, when I started acting years ago, I could only play certain types of roles. I could have refused and done something else with my life, but I wanted to change this industry from the inside."

Gamon tried not to feel guilty about whining to someone who'd had it probably much harder than he had. She and other trans actresses were changing the presentation of what it looked like to be transgender in Thailand. "There is much better trans representation now. There are very few roles that are over the top now."

"In the past we appeared nonthreatening with a purpose. There is always a price to pay for acceptance."

He admitted there was a dramatic change. "You succeeded."

"It's evolving, and now many of the Y-series studios are adding education to their story lines." She drained her glass and poured herself more wine.

"I think that's great. But—"

She held her hand up to him palm out for a moment. "I know it's taking a long time, but you're up against generations. I don't find it surprising how many K-dramas and J-dramas incorporate a plot or storyline centered on toxic fans and the chaos they can create."

Another notification chimed on his phone. Gamon took a second sip of wine to steel himself and then peeked.

Gamon stared at his phone. There was a picture of him and Dusit at a club from last night. Luckily, the club wasn't identified. He read further. "They are accusing Dusit of being out until four in the morning and causing problems. That's not true."

With an arched eyebrow, she asked, "How do you know?"

"He was with me… doing research." Gamon looked around the room.

"All night?" She smirked. "Was it deep research?"

Gamon huffed. "Oh, stop. We were on our field trip you assigned to us and didn't get back until today."

She fanned herself. "I didn't tell you to stay out all night."

"Nothing happened." Much. Gamon hated being not completely honest, but he couldn't handle hearing another speech.

"Okay, but don't expect me to believe nothing happened." Achara was not successful at hiding her disapproval. "I want you to be happy."

"I was until this." More notifications chimed. He glanced at his messages and read, "Dusit Sitwat continues to be a problem. Poor sweet Gamon is trapped by his contract to remain with him. Social media keeps getting worse."

Achara sipped her wine. "Situations like these always do before they get better."

Gamon took a gulp from his glass. "You know what the worst part is of being pulled apart by an investor?"

"What?"

He needed to voice his failure. "I froze and didn't stand up for him. I didn't stop him from leaving and didn't even say anything. Once again, I let it happen all around me like I always do." Gamon hated the part of himself that couldn't react quickly enough.

Achara said nothing. What could she say?

Tipping his head back, Gamon finished all the wine in his glass and then poured himself another.

"So last night… was it a good night?" Achara asked as she studied him.

"The best." Gamon ran into his room and came out with the toy Dusit had bought him. "Look what he got me, because I never had one."

She inspected the spinning toy and handed it back. "Well, it's not a car or a luxury bag, but I admit it has heart."

"I know." Gamon stared at the toy and sighed. "He even bought a second one for when I lose this one."

*Tsk*ing, Achara studied him. "You are still over the moon for him, aren't you?"

"What?" He tried to play innocent.

Achara pointed a perfectly manicured nail at him. "You still love him, don't you?"

"With all my heart." No point in lying.

She tilted her head and frowned. "Does he know?"

Gamon groaned. "I didn't tell him…" with words.

There was still too much between them, but last night that hadn't seemed to matter. All he wanted was to be so consumed by Dusit that he couldn't tell where he ended and where Dusit began.

Achara sighed. "Are you going to let him know?"

"Why are you asking?" Gamon needed to know the reason behind her question in order to determine the context to put his response to.

"A couple of reasons. First, my cold black heart would like to be wrong to help prove the existence of love. And second, I want to be ready to catch you if Dusit disappoints you."

A shiver of fear wound through him. He wanted to deny it outright, but he still had trouble believing he could have what he wanted. "I hope I can tell him I'm sorry about doubting him and not being there for him."

"You really need to have that discussion with him so he understands," Achara said.

"I know, but I missed him so much. I think he missed me too. It's been an unspoken pact for us to enjoy each other for a bit before we dig up the past." Gamon tipped his glass to her.

"Here's to you getting a lot more than the tip… I mean, bit." She clanged their glasses together.

Gamon tried to glare at her, but chuckled instead. His phone buzzed with a text message. "It looks like Prem convinced the investors not to make any announcement or response to the pictures and video, keeping Dusit's suspension quiet."

Relief swamped Gamon, but this text made the suspension real. "Suspension? Is that what they are calling it?"

Achara rolled her eyes at him.

Gamon twirled his glass and watched the red liquid spin. He could relate to the wine. "Yes, but we know what it is. They want time to see where the fans fall. Do they support Dusit and his comeback with this series or not?"

Achara spooned rice into a bowl and put pork with some vegetables on his plate. She served herself. "Eat."

He huffed out a breath. "It's upsetting."

Gamon would bet the investors had tied Prem's hands, because this was simply business to them. If Prem wanted to direct for them on future projects, he'd need to follow their wishes now.

Not for the first time, Gamon's wish to oversee a production house floated to the front of his mind. He could use his savings and—one thing at a time. "I should post something. Why didn't I think of that before?"

"The investors wouldn't like that. They expect you to distance yourself from Dusit and his mess like other actors would and not comment on the situation."

Gamon frowned. "They'd probably also want me to pull off pictures of us together on social media. Not happening."

Achara sipped her wine and then said, "Of course, because a social media scrub signals to the fans that the actor believes the rumors are true. That you haven't done so is positive. You know the fans are scoping out your accounts for any kind of sign."

Shaking his head, Gamon muttered, "There's got to be more I can do."

"As a member of the crew, I can't recommend doing a live stream." Achara's eyes sparkled.

Gamon snapped his fingers. "Yes, that's it. I'll do a live stream."

She held up her hand. "Wait. Be careful. Don't let the fans direct what you say. Decide what you'll say, then work it in."

Gamon was already reaching for the pad of paper and pen on the end table. Not keeping that he'd been insulted out of his voice, he said, "I'm not that much of a rookie."

He wrote some notes and showed them to Achara. "As an actress, what do you think of this for the subject?"

"Brilliant, if you also discuss the workshop, the filming process, and give them a few stories of your time in Paris. Mention how great it is to work with Dusit again." Achara added these to the list of topics. "Go get camera-pretty."

This must help.

He changed his shirt, fixed his hair, added the right touches of makeup to his skin and lips, and used a touch of mascara on his eyelashes. The fans read a lot about his emotional state through his appearance, so he needed to be on guard.

Achara smiled at him. "You look better."

Gamon sighed. "Concealer and mascara do wonders. I wish I felt better."

"You should feel better. This is you doing something positive to support Dusit and bring the fans on your side."

Nodding, he took some deep breaths as he tagged each of his social media accounts and began the live.

"Greetings! *Sawasdee krub.*" There was a lot of English in the comments, so he added, "Hello to my international fans. Thank you all for coming."

Out of the corner of his eye, he caught Achara motioning for him to call out her comment.

"In response to BLForever, I can confirm that we are currently in the workshop phase of *Don't Break My Heart 2*. I know how long the fans have been waiting, because I've been waiting too, and from reading the script I'm sure you'll enjoy it."

A question about the amount of time filming takes floated by, so he answered it. "The workshop phase can take days to months. I'm not sure how long it'll be, but living with my acting partner will help speed things along. Yesterday we even went on a field trip."

He ignored the tons of questions on Dusit and laughed as he found something to answer. "No ThaiBLNow26, I will not tell you what we did for our research. That's a secret." He held up a playful finger to his lips.

Gamon purposefully worked in their secret mission on the off chance the location of last night's picture came out. The fans and the investors would chalk it up to him being thorough in his role.

He smiled into the camera. "Having a partner like Dusit makes everything easier. He makes me feel safe." There it was—the truth he had to get out. The one thing he hoped his fans would take away from this live.

The comments section went bananas, flowing with hearts and angry faces. He needed to turn the tide.

Gamon turned on his megawatt smile as if he were doing a product placement ad for toothpaste. "I'm grateful Dusit agreed to come back to acting to work with me. Yes, I know he went through some personal matters in the past, but he has resolved them. It makes me angry when people aren't forgiven for their mistakes or allowed to move past them even after they worked hard to correct them. We are one hundred percent into our roles, and we want to play them to the best of our abilities."

Smiley faces and hearts floated up the comment section more than angry faces, but he had to seal the deal. He held up his phone to his computer.

"Here are some pictures I can show you of the workshop rooms and the first scene we shot." As someone asked about the rumor, he smiled. "Yes, YaoifiedLove28 it's true the very first scene we shot was the first time Dusit and I saw each other in several years."

All the dreadful lonely years spent without Dusit. He would not lose him now.

Gamon sprinkled in the information he wanted out in the world.

"Sorry I didn't catch your ID, but yes, my heart was beating fast when I first saw him. I was so nervous but very excited. To capture all that emotion on film was a brilliant move by the director. He caught the characters' first reunion as our own real reunion. The director told me not to act, simply to feel all my emotions deeply and let them come out."

"Yes, Rose4U, the characters are still in love." And so am I. But is Dusit?

Achara waved at him to wrap it up.

He did. "I need to end here because I've got to go study my lines. See you soon."

Clicking off of the live stream, he breathed a sigh of relief, but then worry skated through him. "Do you think that helped?"

"You did well. Additionally, you also derailed some misinformation on the dates the video and pictures were taken."

Gamon felt like he'd run an obstacle course and was grateful he hadn't fallen. "I hope it works."

Achara shrugged. "Well, at least you'll find out how Dusit reacts to a stressful situation."

That was true… but he couldn't help but feel it was too soon to run *any* tests.

CHAPTER 11

DUSIT HADN'T wanted a drink in months. He didn't even like the taste anymore. What he craved was the numbness the bitter liquid gave him. It would have been easy to find a new bar and drink until he didn't feel… anything.

An image of Gamon drifted to the forefront of his mind. Dusit wanted to feel everything he could have with Gamon.

Alcohol would steal that from him… them. He couldn't do that to Gamon or himself. Not giving the bastards who wanted him to fail a win was a side bonus.

Instead of heading down a destructive path, he went to Charong's.

He hesitated outside. Maybe he shouldn't show up unannounced. His parents had taught him to keep his problems to himself and never impose on others.

But he didn't know where to turn, so he lightly tapped on the open sliding glass door.

"Did you call him?" Chat yelled out from the kitchen.

Charong glanced from his phone to Dusit standing there and grinned.

At that same moment, Dusit's phone buzzed with a call from Charong.

Disconnecting the unneeded call, Charong waved him in. "I don't think we have to."

More banging of pots, and Chat hollered, "Of course we do. Dusit needs to know we support him a hundred percent."

Dusit's heart clenched. He really had people.

Lyric dashed out of her room and beelined over to him. "Those were old pictures… right?"

"Of course. The last bar floor I was on was your brother's, months ago." Dusit hadn't gotten drunk since. There was no deep compulsion to forget, so he didn't need to drink.

Even now he didn't reach for an escape. If anything he wanted to remain clear-headed so he could deal with this mess.

Chat stomped into the room. "Charong, I don't know why you don't call—oh, you're here."

Charong gave her his I-got-you chuckle.

Ignoring her brother, Chat squeezed his arm. "Thank you for coming. I'm glad you knew enough to come home."

Home. It was so nice to—

Lyric stepped into his space. "Yes, we're all glad you're here. Yada, yada, yada. But why haven't you made a statement? Why haven't you walked this back? How come you haven't…" the social media to-do list Lyric ticked off went on and on.

Overwhelmed, Dusit plopped down at the dining room table. "Um, the production house told me to stay off social media and listen to—"

"They are covering themselves, not you." Shaking her head, Lyric pointed out the obvious.

"Have you talked to your agent?" Chat asked as she set dishes on the table.

"No, good point." He really wasn't thinking clearly.

"You didn't do that? You need to call the people representing you right now," Lyric stated with absolute certainty. "Why haven't they called you?"

Dusit fished his phone out of his pocket and held it up. "Phone's on Do Not Disturb for everyone except you guys and Gamon."

"Not helpful." Lyric grabbed his phone and changed the settings.

Dusit closed his eyes for a moment and sighed. He hadn't changed the settings back from the night before.

"Going to be okay, man. You're breathing, and sometimes that's all you need to do." Charong patted his shoulder.

Things were happening around him, but all he could do was inhale and exhale. How could everything go so terribly wrong in such a short amount of time? He and Gamon had been happy. They'd been about to—but the investor.... The guy reeked of the power to destroy Gamon's career. Gamon had worked too hard to get where he was for Dusit to screw things up for him.

Lyric handed him back his phone. The phone was buzzing with incoming text messages.

He stared at the phone.

Lyric pointed. "Open them."

Dusit forced himself to hold his phone up. Face ID didn't recognize him. "When your phone judges you look bad...."

"Try it again," Lyric demanded.

He did. Nothing.

Damn, he must look awful. He put in his password. Would Rose call him or text? He'd never given up on him before but... "He texted and called. Rose called."

Relief calmed him as he saw several missed calls from Rose. Nobody had abandoned Dusit.

Charong handed him a glass of water. "Of course. He's part of your people. You've got your people, and we've got you."

"Or he's calling to cut me loose." Even as he said that aloud, it didn't ring true.

"Nonsense." Chat rushed through the kitchen door carrying a tray with dishes of all Dusit's favorite foods. "Make the call and get ready to eat."

Her caring command was familiar and gave him comfort.

"Thanks," he said to everyone in the house. They really had his back.

"Of course. Make the call before Lyric does it for you." Charong used his head to gesture toward his youngest sibling.

Lyric paced behind him. "Any day now. Or are you going to wait until the next scandal before you return his calls?"

Chat said, "Bite your tongue."

Dusit scrolled to Rose's number and called. "Hey."

"Why didn't you return my calls or texts?" Rose's annoyance bled through.

"My phone was on Do Not Disturb." Last night with Gamon in his arms, the last thing he'd wanted was to make it easy for anyone to break into their bubble.

Rose exhaled hard. "Oh. Okay. Fine."

"Did you think I was blackout drunk somewhere?" Dusit would have been insulted, except he couldn't deny that it had been his only answer for the last few years. But no longer.

"I was worried, yes. Where are you?" Rose didn't deny the truth, which made Dusit feel better. He didn't want to be handled like he would break.

"With my people." Dusit said it loud enough to make Chat smile at him. Lyric stopped pacing and folded her arms, glaring at him and gesturing for him to get on with the call. Charong sat down, not even pretending he wasn't trying to hear the entire conversation.

"Good. I'm glad. Now I can represent you properly." Rose sounded like a general about to set strategy.

This was what Dusit needed. It moved him. "Thank you. What should I do?"

"Where can we meet? Not in public." Rose's clipped words told Dusit this wasn't something he could sleep on.

"Hold on." Dusit muted the call and asked, "Can Rose drop by?"

Charong said, "Of course."

Chat gasped and put her hand to her chest. She sank into a chair at the table. "Rose… as in *the* Kulap Rose Thongsi?"

"I'll send you the address. See you soon." Dusit ended the call and turned to a very pale Chat. "Yes, that Rose."

"I'm going to die. I'm for sure going to die." Chat vibrated out of her seat and fluttered her hands in front of her face.

"Oh, get a grip. He's just a guy." Lyric rolled her eyes, expressing how very unimpressed even the most famous of ex-BL actors made her.

"Will he bring Nok Ayutthaya? I mean, if they are together? They are together, right? It's not fan service?"

Not sure if he should confirm anything, Chat's face made him tell her the truth. "Yes, they are a couple in real life."

Chat clapped her hands and did a happy dance. "I knew it. They came out, but sometimes even that's for the fans. I'm so happy for them."

The enthusiasm no longer surprised Dusit. "But I doubt Nok will join him."

"This is work. Why would his boyfriend be joining him?" Lyric sighed and tugged on her sister. "Let's go change your clothing."

Chat looked down at her food-stained apron and hurried out of the room.

Charong cleared his throat and offered, "If you want, we can stay out of your way and give you privacy."

"Nah, it's your house… and you are my people." Dusit tried to grin at him.

His grin failed because Charong punched him playfully. "It's going to be all right."

"Yeah, but—"

"Look, even if it's not, you're going to do what you can. I don't know your agent well, but when he came to the bar, he seemed to have your interests above all else." Charong studied him, maybe attempting to see if his words had an impact.

Dusit tried to be confident in what he was saying. A part of him believed it, but another part of him was stuck in a place of loss, and that look of helplessness on Gamon's face had been…. "You're right. This is bad timing."

"Is there a right time for this type of scandal? But don't they say there's no adverse publicity—"

"The investor who told me to leave the condo was furious." Dusit raked his fingers through his hair. "These pictures of my past put his investment in jeopardy."

Chat returned with a pretty dress on and pointed to the food. "Please, eat."

He didn't want to disappoint her, so he put a bit of black-pepper pork, rice, basil chicken, and steamed okra on his plate. After taking a couple of bites, he said, "It's superb."

Everyone remained silent for the rest of the meal, and that intensified the drama playing out in Dusit's head.

"So, Lyric, how is school going?" he asked and ate some more, hoping to keep everything down.

Typically, Lyric huffed and ignored the question.

Soon after they'd cleared the table, there was a knock at the door.

Charong greeted Rose with Chat standing behind him, blushing. Lyric stood there with a hand on her hip, assessing Rose.

After introductions, Lyric rolled her eyes and walked to the kitchen. Charong suggested Rose and Dusit go into the living room.

As soon as they sat down, Chat brought in coffee and treats. "I appreciate your work, Mr. Thongsi."

"Thank you, and please call me Rose." Rose gave her his star smile.

"Okay." She didn't swoon, but she smiled big and then scurried from the room.

He and Rose shared a knowing look.

Having fans felt surreal most of the time. He'd been relieved when Chat got comfortable around him, but it had taken a couple of days. Or perhaps it was the poor shape he'd been in when he came to them.

While "his people," even Lyric, milled about the dining room pretending like they weren't hanging on every word, he got to the point. "Rose, I'm sorry for this mess."

It was his fault. His past was on view for everyone to see… again. Why did he have to lose it in such a specular fashion? A fraction of the pain and loneliness surfaced to remind him of what he had been trying to escape.

Rose put his hands on his own knees and leaned toward Dusit. "Everyone involved knew this might happen. But they hoped it wouldn't. And we know hoping doesn't make it so."

Action. He needed to take action to make this right. "What should I do? Tell me what to do."

"Nothing. Do not answer the attacks with counterattacks or justifications. You'll only make the situation worse. It's good you aren't on social media all that often, so staying off it doesn't say anything to the fans."

To stalk Gamon, Dusit thought. But Rose's suggestion didn't sound right. It was crazy-making to do nothing. "There must be something I—"

"The key is admitting your past and owning your mistakes. The fans will respect you for it. Let them see you as human." Rose took a sip of coffee.

"What? Are you asking me to admit that I felt devastated because the man I loved abandoned me?" Hurt came to the surface, and anger followed closely behind.

He still didn't know why Gamon had never contacted him. Why had Gamon let go so easily of what they were to each other? Wasn't he important to Gamon? Hadn't Gamon wanted what they had?

Rose sat upright and waved his hands in front of him. "You don't have to be specific. It's best if you remain vague. This will shift the energy devoted to attacking you to finding out who and what broke your heart."

"I can do that.... On a live?" He hated doing those, especially without Gamon, but he'd do whatever it took not to lose this chance to be with Gamon again.

"To start you can make a simple statement post on your social media. Apologize, acknowledge you know it was wrong to drink so much that those pictures and videos were possible, and say how much you regret it. Promise nothing like that will ever happen again."

Doubt surfaced. "How can you be so sure?"

"That it won't happen again, right?" Rose clarified and narrowed his gaze at Dusit.

Dusit gave him a rueful chuckle. "Doesn't it appear like I enjoy floors and fights? What makes you think it won't happen again?"

"Because you're not stupid. You learn from your mistakes, and you've got something—someone—you want to be better for." Rose patted him on the shoulder.

That was true.

"And where are you right now? You're not passed out on a bar floor. After what was probably an intense meeting, you went to be with your friends, not to a bar."

Intense? Ha, abusive would be more accurate, but whatever. He'd barely heard the investor's rants because he was so worried about Gamon.

Dusit glanced over at his people hovering near the entrance to the living room. Once again they tried to look busy but came across as ready to defend him if need be.

Someone's phone beeped with a notification.

Chat pulled her phone out of her pocket and gasped. "Gamon is doing a live."

Lyric rushed over to her sister. "Really? I wonder if he's got a new song he's introducing."

Rose's mouth dropped open, and he stared at Lyric for a moment.

Charong chuckled. "Not everything is about music."

Scrunching her face, Lyric said, "No, but the important stuff is."

"Shh, it's starting." Chat waved her sister quiet.

"Did you know he was going to do this?" Dusit asked.

"I haven't had a chance to speak to him." Rose pulled out an iPad from his bag. "We should watch."

Dusit's heart jumped at seeing Gamon. He looked handsome but sad. Pushing aside his need to run back to the apartment to give Gamon a hug, he studied the comments section.

The comments section was a sea of mad faces and thumbs-down emojis.

Rose clenched his fist and talked to his iPad. "Turn it around, Gamon. You've got this."

Within the next ten seconds, hearts and hands clapping floated past.

Gamon was charming but seemed worn out. His cheeks were a bit pink, so maybe he'd had some wine.

When the live concluded, Rose jumped up and pumped his fist. "Yes! He did it."

"He did?" What did that mean?

"Yes, he did his part to let his fans, as well as your combined fandom, know that he is one hundred percent on your side." Rose grinned.

Affection shot through Dusit. Gamon hadn't done the wise thing, which was to distance himself from Dusit and the scandal. He'd come to Dusit's defense. Wait. "But this won't hurt his career, will it?"

"No one can know. We can only guess, and mine is that Gamon did what he needed to do, so now it's your turn to do your part."

Dusit rubbed his hands together. "I'll do whatever you say I should. I trust you."

"Good, let's get started continuing to turn this around. We need to acknowledge how wrong it was to drink so much." Rose studied Dusit.

Did Rose think he'd disagree? "I was a grand mess."

"You were. Emphasize these events were in the past. You turned yourself around. What turned you around?"

"Friends and a steady job." Dusit stated the facts without hesitation.

"Good, that's relatable. Okay, let's write some drafts."

After the fourth go-round, Dusit read the current draft to Rose.

To my fans,

No one should ever drink to the extent portrayed by those pictures of me in the past. I make no excuses, but I was not myself. I was heartbroken and had a rough few years, but with the help of my friends, I've turned my life around. I'm sorry for any distress or embarrassment these pictures and videos from the past resurfacing may have caused. I pinky promise I will never do anything like this again. Please forgive me, and I hope you will support me in Don't Break My Heart 2.

Much love, Dusit Sitwat.

"Great, but I'll pass it through Kanawat before we post."

"This must be your first time spinning a scandal." Dusit tried to smile. "I'm sorry, man."

"Hey, don't be. This happens. I should know, right?"

Dusit exhaled hard. Rose had had a couple of scandals himself back in the day. "I guess."

Rose grinned. "I have to make sure this ends well, and not only because you're a friend. It's my job, as well as a personal responsibility."

Dusit cocked his head.

"Nok's mother and sister are big fans of *Don't Break My Heart*, and well, if a season two doesn't happen, I won't be able to go there for dinner. Nok's little sister will gather fans and do bodily harm to me."

Laughing felt good. "I'm sure Nok won't let anything bad happen to you."

"I don't know. He's counting on a season two as well." Rose chuckled.

Dusit smiled. "Do you think this will work?"

"All we can do is wait and see," Rose sighed. "It is troubling that any misstep can equate to you being canceled and losing your career. The fans love you… until they don't."

"Well, you're still loved by your fans." Dusit knew Rose had a strong fan club, and together with Nok, it had to have at least doubled.

Rose sighed and grimaced. "Some. When Nok and I came out with our relationship, there were rumors that we weren't together, that we were only saying we were in a relationship."

Chat's cough said she was uncomfortable.

Continuing, Rose sighed. "We got a ton of hate mail, and fans dramatically left our ship to become antifans."

This always confused Dusit. "I guess I haven't really interacted with the BL industry for a long time, but it's hard to understand. If the fans want your fictional characters to get together, why wouldn't they want you together in real life?"

Rose threw up his hands. "It ruins the fantasy."

"Fantasy?"

"Possibility of an actor falling for a fan."

The missing pieces fell into place for the first time for Dusit. "So that's why Gamon's mother wouldn't let him come out."

"It was especially bad around the time when your show aired. But now with marriage equality passing, as well as the international audiences' voice in support of the actor's happiness and not their orientation, it's a little easier. They hold up a mirror and have no issue chastising any type of homophobia."

"Well, our society is not as progressive as the West. Though we are moving in that direction."

Rose chuckled. "I don't think the West cares. They are impatient for LGBTQIA+ rights to be accepted everywhere yesterday."

Dusit sighed and imagined being able to hold hands with Gamon anyplace in Thailand. "That would be nice."

Nodding, Rose added, "Yes, it would. Someday."

"I also noticed in the contract there was no fan service expected. My first contract was very specific on what type, when, and where." Dusit had been uncomfortable having anytime he was out in public scripted.

"Yeah, we don't put that in our contracts anymore. The actors may be asked to do ship work during their fan meets, like acting out scenes onstage, but they don't cuddle each other… unless they want to." Rose winked.

How would that affect how he and Gamon acted in public, assuming they didn't kick him off the series? "I guess you figure that out with your acting partner."

Dusit glanced at the doorway where his people were and smiled at them. Everyone should be so lucky as to have a safety net like what this family provided him.

Dusit needed to find out how Gamon was doing. Even though he did great on the live, maybe he could use some support, and Dusit wanted to be that for Gamon, to help make the world seem bigger, more explorable.

He'd liked how they had connected with Somchair and Niran. Learning about their dreams and aspirations made them more than a field trip assignment, real people rather than stereotyped sex workers. Maybe even friends.

CHAPTER 12

"WHAT'S THAT?" Gamon glanced around his condo to locate the strange ringing.

Achara laughed. "That's the condo's landline."

Landline? They had a landline.

Maybe it was Dusit calling. How did he even have the number?

Gamon tripped over his feet but found the phone. "Hello, Dusit?"

"Sorry. This is Charong, Dusit's friend."

Why was Dusit's friend calling and not Dusit? Many horrible scenarios of Dusit being in an accident or drinking or worse raced through Gamon's mind. "Is he okay?"

"Yes. I'm glad I caught you. Dusit is meeting with his agent right now and will spend the night here. If you'd like to—"

"Yes! Please send me your address." Gamon was grateful and desperate.

"Of course. It'll be late when you arrive, so if you want to spend the night, you're more than welcome."

Gamon didn't bother with the politeness of trying to turn him down. "Thank you. I'll be there as soon as I can."

Achara must have overheard because she was in the bedroom packing an overnight bag. He grabbed his toiletry kit and hurried out of the condo five minutes later.

A sleepover with Dusit had seemed like a great idea, but now that he was in the taxi, anxiety hit.

What if Dusit didn't want to see him?

What if someone found out? He and Dusit were going directly against the investors' and director's orders.

Was Charong calling because Dusit was out of control? Perhaps he needed assistance....

No, that didn't sound right.

Achara was right. This was certainly a test to see if Dusit really had given up drinking. Gamon believed that was the case, but not even he could be one hundred percent sure. If Dusit had a relapse, Gamon would be there to get him back on the right path.

Regardless of the situation, at least Gamon could see Dusit.

The taxi pulled over in front of a small white house. Gamon paid the driver and got out. Since the gate was unlocked, Gamon hurried along the plant-lined path and stood at the side door.

Catching a glimpse of Dusit through the glass put Gamon at ease. Dusit looked good and was even smiling.

Gamon tapped lightly on the sliding glass door.

Charong rushed over and welcomed Gamon in. "Glad you could come."

Dusit lit up when their gazes locked.

Maybe this was a good idea after all.

Gamon grabbed both his hands and asked, "Are you okay?"

"Yes, and I'm even better now." Dusit grabbed him into a hug.

"Really?" Gamon wished he could make the entire situation disappear.

"Really. I'm glad you're here. How are you handling everything?"

"Achara stopped by and watched the comments as I did the live." Gamon was grateful for her support.

"Thank you, that was incredible." Dusit glanced at their audience.

Gamon had forgotten they weren't alone and dropped Dusit's hands.

Dusit grabbed his hands and gave them a squeeze. "I'm happy you're here."

Smiling back, Gamon said, "How could I say no to a sleepover?"

"Sleepover? That would be great!" Dusit glanced at Rose.

Would Rose say no?

"There should be no issue, as long as you keep it quiet," Rose warned them.

"Got it." Dusit couldn't stop grinning at Gamon.

Rose smiled at Gamon and gestured with his thumb toward Dusit, "I'm counting on your discretion, because we know your man—I mean, acting partner—has little."

"Ha." Dusit faked annoyance, but his smile diminished its effect.

"Ms. Chat, thank you for the coffee. It was delicious. Nice meeting you, Lyric, and thank you, Charong." Rose waved.

Dusit and Gamon walked him out.

Rose patted Dusit on the shoulder. "This will blow over."

"I hope you're right." Gamon crossed his fingers.

"I usually am. Plus, that's Kanawat's take on the whole thing."

A bit of calm seeped into Gamon. Kanawat understood this industry better than almost anyone in the business.

"You two take care of each other." Rose waved and then got in his car and drove off.

Dusit took Gamon's duffel bag, which was still slung over his shoulder, and grabbed his hand to press a kiss to his knuckles. "You're right, you know. Perfection can't last, but there's nothing to say we can't have more perfect moments."

That made Gamon smile from the heart as he allowed Dusit to lead him back into the house. In truth, he'd go wherever this man led.

Gamon said a proper hello to everyone.

Charong intercepted Lyric, who was on her way straight for him with a stack of sheet music in her hands. "Lyric, he's been through a lot. Why don't we let them get some rest?"

Before Lyric could object, Dusit said, "Thanks. We are exhausted," and tugged Gamon down the hallway and into a room.

The room had a bed to fit two and a desk with a chair pushed under it. Cheery bright yellow walls picked up the abstract pictures on the walls.

Gamon looked around. "This is a lovely room."

Although a pantry with Dusit would have been like a palace.

Dusit waved a hand around at the room. "Yeah, Chat and Charong set this room up as a guest room and an office. Since I no longer work at the bar, Chat insisted I sleep in here instead of the bar's backroom. The bathroom is right through there if you want to take a shower."

Gamon quickly showered, and then Dusit did the same.

When Dusit returned, Gamon didn't know what to do. He couldn't stop pacing.

Sitting on the bed, Dusit said, "Why so nervous? It's not like we haven't shared a bed before."

Sexy images of last night flashed through Gamon's brain. Dusit over him, rubbing against him, touching and feeling and—

"Right. It's been an exhausting day. We should go to bed." Gamon slid into the bed and under the comforter.

They needed to clear things between them on so many levels, but Gamon struggled to find a way to start that conversation. Dusit had been through so much, and Gamon didn't want to add to the insanity by dragging up the past.

Besides, it was hard to concentrate when Dusit looked yummy in his T-shirt and boxers. He'd gotten much broader and seemed even more manly than before. His hands were nice and strong, and his fingers were long.

He tried to stop thinking about Dusit putting those hands all over him, but failed. Sighing, he rearranged the bedding to avoid announcing his arousal.

But then Dusit climbed into the bed right next to him.

Why did he smell so good? Having him near shouldn't feel this incredible. The anticipation was as delicious as it was hellacious.

Gamon didn't expect to have the same overwhelming reaction to him as he did five years ago. Age and maturity had set in. He was no longer a virgin sleeping next to a guy for the first time. Gamon was in control of himself.

Now, if he could convince his body of this; it had shifted now to *very* aroused.

Maybe he should have jerked off in the shower, but all his focus had been on hurrying to get back to Dusit. He probably should have taken care himself, but would of, should of, could of….

Here he was, lying next to Dusit in Charong's newly made pretty yellow guest room, trying not to put the moves on him… or outright beg him.

This wasn't the time or the place to go down that road.

Mm…. Going down—stop!

They needed to deal with one crisis at a time. Besides, they needed to talk so that he could ask for Dusit's forgiveness for not having more faith in them as a couple and for not figuring out what his mother had done to separate them. He should wait until the timing was better.

Gamon shifted over to his edge of the bed. The bed should have been big enough, but they needed to share a comforter.

Each time Dusit turned or moved, the sheets rubbed Gamon's erection through his pajamas. How many nights had he fantasized about simply lying next to Dusit? But now that fantasy was sensual torture.

He was so out of control, he yearned to thrust so the sheet dragged across his erection with the weight of the comforter assisting, but he feared moaning with pleasure.

Dusit turned toward Gamon and propped himself on his elbows. "You can't sleep either?"

"No." Gamon's fists tightened on the comforter.

Pulling the comforter taunt, Dusit tucked the comforter around Gamon's shoulders. His head turned to the end of the bed. "Oh. You are—"

Could the bed swallow him whole? Swallow…. Images of Dusit swallowing him tripped through his brain. He couldn't lie, so he groaned, "Sorry."

Smirking, Dusit whispered, "I remember whenever we slept together, you could never sleep without coming."

Gamon tried to make it a joke. "Hey, I'm not *that* bad. Look, I'll go to the bathroom and—"

Dusit grabbed him and halted his departure. "Why don't you let me help?"

Was Dusit suggesting he would take care of Gamon? "You? Help? Me?"

Dusit chuckled. "Yeah, like last night. I already jerked off in the shower, but I'd love to be of service to you."

Images of water cascading over Dusit as he stroked himself off in the shower, mixed with the affectionate romp they'd had the night before, heated Gamon to boiling.

He wrinkled his nose. "That's what I should have done. I didn't think I would—"

"That you'd still want me this bad?" Dusit arched an eyebrow at him. He was giving him the option of playing his suggestion off as a joke but studied him carefully.

Gamon's dick throbbed with need. He stopped pretending. "No… I mean, yes. Of course I'm still very attracted to you. I thought perhaps I'd be mature enough not to respond like I was thirteen."

Slowly, Dusit unwrapped Gamon's fingers from their grasp on the comforter. With gentle care, he pulled the comforter to Gamon's knees.

Gamon's erection jutted out invitingly, standing at attention. "I should go to the bathroom."

Dusit gave a soft moan, and caressed Gamon's cheek and down his torso to end at his waistband. "Or you can stay, and I can make you feel incredible."

Whimpering wasn't an answer, so Gamon forced the words out. "We can't do this here."

"You want to bet on that?" Dusit traced his index finger along Gamon's pajama-covered shaft, and when he got to the top, he made slow circles around the tip. "I definitely think we can."

Gamon had never been with anyone more focused on giving pleasure than Dusit. It felt like everything he did to Gamon was a gift he also gave himself. Without meaning to, Gamon thrust against Dusit's knuckles.

"Let me take care of you." Dusit's fingers were back to teasing Gamon's waistband.

As much as he needed this, he'd be mortified if he left his DNA on the blanket. "I should go take a quick shower."

Yes. That's exactly what he should do. It was not what he wanted to do, but what a mature person would do. There were still things to settle between them, and—

"Are you sure you want to go all the way over to the bathroom without me?" Dusit's hand moved away from Gamon's waistband and slid under Gamon's pajama top. He glided his fingers up to Gamon's nipples. He pinched one.

Gamon's body arched toward Dusit's hand, desperate for more of the enticing pain.

Dusit gave him a pajama-dropping smile and squeezed his other nipple.

The pain made Gamon sigh in pleasure. The bite of sensation brought his intense need into focus… and that need was Dusit.

But they shouldn't do this. They were supposed to talk.

Gamon's body wasn't listening to his firm instructions and was seeking more physical attention. He shifted closer to Dusit. Maybe a little more before he went into the bathroom and privately took care of himself.

Dusit's fingers swirled over his nipples and teased down to the waist of his pajama bottoms again.

Gamon was panting. He wanted everything Dusit would give him, but how could he do this? "I'll make a mess of the sheets."

Dusit smirked and licked his lips with his talented tongue. "No, you won't."

He could tell he was going to orgasm hard and leave a big puddle. "But—"

"Did you forget I suck and swallow?" Dusit's grin turned almost predatory.

For the love of all the Y-series scripts in the world, Gamon bit his lower lip to stop a moan. Now that was an offer Gamon did not have the will to refuse. He wanted to be consumed.

"I remember how you used to love when I took care of you with my mouth," Dusit nearly purred. "It's been so long. Don't you want me to do that again?" Dusit locked gazes with him and licked his lips, showing him what he had to offer.

Gamon couldn't find air, but he nodded once.

Wasting no time, Dusit reached beneath the elastic waistband of Gamon's pajamas. He touched Gamon's bare shaft. Without the cloth between them, Dusit traced a finger up and down Gamon's erection.

The pleasure of that simple touch burned Gamon, and he almost choked.

"Let me make you feel better." Dusit pulled the offending fabric out of the way and pushed it to Gamon's knees.

Gamon's cock stood out proudly. He gasped, "Please."

With lightning speed, Dusit slid down Gamon's body to bring his mouth level with Gamon's cock. He gave him a wicked grin and threw the comforter over his head, and then he grabbed Gamon's hips.

Immediately, Dusit covered Gamon's tip with his hot, wet mouth. He slowly pushed down along the shaft to the base and then dragged his lips back up. He started bobbing his head as he sucked.

The comforter rode up and down with Dusit's head movements.

There was none of the usual teasing Dusit used to do. Dusit was direct, as if he rushed to give Gamon what he craved. He seemed as desperate for this as Gamon.

They got into a rhythm.

Gamon tried not to thrust, but Dusit's hands on his hips invited him to do so.

Dusit slid his mouth up and down as he sucked.

It had been forever since Gamon's last blowjob. Dusit had been the first to use his perfect mouth on Gamon… and the last.

He needed to see and pulled the comforter away from Dusit's head. Dusit's eyes were closed as he sucked. He was gorgeous as he strove to please Gamon.

"I can't last long." Gamon struggled to get the words out.

Dusit smiled around Gamon's cock and sucked harder while bobbing his head faster.

Gamon gasped. "Your mouth… incredible… you are incredible."

Their gazes locked.

Pulling off Gamon's cock, Dusit whispered, "Come for me."

The demand was something Gamon could never deny, and when his cock was enclosed in Dusit's mouth again, the sensation was too much.

Gamon covered his own mouth as he came in long, shivering waves of pleasure again and again. He seemed to come forever.

He'd been right; he came a lot. But Dusit swallowed everything he had to give.

Gamon trembled as Dusit finished him off.

Dusit licked him clean and righted his clothing. "Better now?" he asked as he scrambled up to the pillows.

"Perfect, but what about—" Gamon pointed to Dusit.

Dusit waved him off. "I'm fine. I came a few minutes ago in the shower."

"Yeah, but—"

"Time for sleep. We've had an emotional day. There's always tomorrow."

He was right. Gamon had been on a roller coaster of emotions, from Dusit being pulled from the show, to scrambling into action, and now to being taken care of in the most essential way, with no expectations.

Dusit didn't ask. He tugged Gamon into his arms, taking him away from the overwhelming feelings.

Safe. Secure. And unbelievably happy.

Gamon fell asleep.

LIGHT STREAMED through the windows, but the alarm they set hadn't gone off yet.

Gamon looked over at the beautiful man sleeping next to him. The new angles and muscles he'd gained took Dusit from cute to hot.

Was Gamon dreaming? Would he wake from the fantasy to be disappointed by reality? How could—

Dusit moved restlessly.

This wasn't a dream. Shifting closer, Gamon basked in Dusit's body heat. So warm. Mm, so hard.

Then Dusit rubbed his hard-on against Gamon's thigh. Gamon's naked thigh.

Glancing to the floor, Gamon saw his pajamas lying in a pile. Dusit must have gotten hot in the night because his T-shirt lay there too, and he was only wearing his boxers. Fortunately they were no impediment to the freedom of Dusit's erection.

Thrusting, Dusit rutted said erection against Gamon.

Gamon pushed back. Skin on skin—there was nothing quite like it.

Dusit had always been ready to go first thing in the morning, and the years they'd lost hadn't changed that.

Dusit moaned and rubbed some more. His tip must be leaking because the wetness was easing his slide.

Gamon wasn't sure if he should let Dusit continue to the natural conclusion, but no, he was selfish and wanted to take part.

Moaning softly, Gamon said, "Morning."

"Come here, you." Dusit wrapped an arm around him and dragged him closer.

Gamon loved the way Dusit moved him around, positioning him exactly where Dusit wanted him. Closer, always closer.

Dusit caressed Gamon's stomach on the way to—

"Mm, yes," Gamon gasped as Dusit teased him with his hand. He could have easily come in a few quick strokes, but it wouldn't be enough.

Gamon wanted to prove to Dusit he no longer just lay there but could take the initiative.

He longed for the connection of having Dusit inside him, but they hadn't talked yet, and this was neither the place nor the time. Still, Gamon was desperate for something.

An image popped into Gamon's head, something he had seen in porn. He couldn't imagine asking anyone to try this… except Dusit. "I saw something I always wanted to try."

Dusit stopped kissing Gamon's neck and paused stroking his cock. "Sure. What?"

"It's fucking, but on the outside." He spit out the words like he used the word fuck all the time.

"Okay. How?" Dusit was always game, so he didn't need convincing to remove his boxers.

Gamon rolled onto his back and grabbed a tube of hand cream off the nightstand. He squirted some out and then coated his thighs. "Use my thighs. Push through them like you would if—"

"As if we were fucking?" Dusit asked. "How?"

Gamon took his lotion-coated hand and gave Dusit's cock a stroke. "I'm sure you can figure it out."

Dusit groaned, and his head fell back. "I think you're right."

Excitement tripped through Gamon.

With a bit of shifting, Dusit put his knees on either side of Gamon's slippery thighs and lay down on top of Gamon. "I'm not too heavy?"

"No. Feels good," Gamon moaned softly. He loved Dusit's weight on him, and his stomach was touching Gamon's erection.

Dusit thrust gently between Gamon's thighs. "Like this?"

"Yeah. More." Gamon needed Dusit's stomach rubbing his shaft.

Dusit started humping Gamon's thighs and kissing his way from Gamon's lips to his neck. He always gave Gamon what he needed.

In this position, he had no difficulty imagining Dusit was in him… minus the not-quite-comfortable fullness that he missed.

Gamon turned his head and allowed Dusit better access to his neck. He caught their reflection in the mirror and stared, watching Dusit's rounded ass moving up and down with the thrusts.

This angle was hot. It looked like they were fucking.

Not being able to resist, Gamon grabbed Dusit's sweet asscheeks and squeezed. He started guiding Dusit's hips so he could go deeper between Gamon's thighs. Still watching in the mirror, Gamon saw the exact moment when his own cock started getting the right amount of attention from Dusit's stomach.

He gasped, squeezing his thighs tighter, hoping to intensify the friction Dusit was getting.

Panting, Gamon shifted, giving and getting pleasure.

Dusit groaned softly and then froze. "Coming."

"Mm, yes." That was hot. Gamon yanked him in close by his asscheeks.

"So good." Dusit thrust a couple more times before rolling off Gamon. "Mm, let me finish you."

Having no will for argument, Gamon lay back and let Dusit stroke him off.

"Getting close." He kissed Dusit on the mouth and moaned as his orgasm hit.

Dusit finished him with perfect strokes, then slowed to a tender caress when he was done. "That was—"

Gamon wanted to shock Dusit. "All the fucking with no preparation."

"Yes. Yes, it was," Dusit snorted. "But so much for not getting the sheets dirty."

"Oh no. Get up. Get up." Gamon stood on shaky legs. He picked up his pajama shirt and wiped himself off, then removed the sheets from the bed.

Dusit accepted the ball of tangled sheets. "What do you want me to do with these?"

"Go wash them."

"Wash them?"

Gamon didn't understand how Dusit could *not* understand they needed to wash the sheets.

"That's not suspicious at all." Dusit smirked as if this was amusing him.

"Why would it be suspicious? Overnight guests should wash their own sheets." When Dusit still stood there grinning at him, Gammon broke the spell with, "I'm serious. Take these to the washer, or tell me where it is and I'll do it." Gamon didn't mean to be demanding.

"I'll do it. You go take a shower." Dusit grabbed a robe from the back of the door and gave Gamon the once-over.

Yum… no! "If anyone asks about you washing them, tell them you want the next guest to have clean sheets."

Dusit kept staring at Gamon's body. Though Gamon was no longer self-conscious, the attention was turning him on. "Go. And maybe if you're quick enough you can join me in the shower."

"How about you make sure you wait for me." Dusit patted him on the butt.

"Hurry up." Gamon was getting hard again.

Dusit slapped his ass. "Anything for you."

CHAPTER 13

DUSIT STOPPED himself from whistling as he almost danced out to breakfast. Charong would never let him live it down. His work life might be in jeopardy, but everything that mattered was falling into line, and he'd had some great sex with the man he loved.

Gamon sat in the living room with Lyric in what appeared to be a deep discussion about music.

"Hey, thank you for last night." Dusit sat at the table.

Charong smirked and quietly said, "I'm not the one you should thank for last night… or this morning."

No! Dusit couldn't look at him.

"Were we that loud?" Dusit whispered. "Did your sisters—"

"Nah, Chat and Lyric are on the other side of the house, and it was only when I went past your door to go to bed or the kitchen." Charong grinned. "He seemed to like whatever you were doing."

Dusit was embarrassed but a little proud. "What can I say?"

Charong snorted and then asked, "So I guess I did okay to invite him?"

"Yes. I—hold on, I got a text." He pulled out his phone. "It's from the director."

Would he tell Dusit he was off the series? How would that affect Gamon? And then…. Would it derail where he and Gamon were headed?

"Well, what does it say?" Charong gestured to Dusit's phone.

Dusit hesitated. A lot was riding on this text. He stared at Charong.

"Read it," Charong demanded, as if it were *his* life hanging in the balance.

"I'm expected back today. We can finish our workshops." Dusit rushed over to show Gamon.

Gamon's mouth dropped open. He grabbed Dusit into a warm but too-quick-to-end hug. "I knew it."

"I'm glad you did, because I had my doubts." Dusit wanted to acknowledge how Gamon turned the fandom around. "I didn't have time to tell you last night, but your live stream yesterday was what flipped the narrative. Thank you."

"I saw your tweet this morning. You handled it well." Gamon smiled as if Dusit could do anything in the world.

And at that moment, maybe he could. "Without Rose, I would have mucked it up." Dusit showed Gamon the time on his phone.

Gamon smiled at him and then touched Lyric on the shoulder. "What you have written so far is beautiful. Take a look at the lines I pointed out. But we will have to continue this review another time. I need to go to the set."

"Really? You liked it?" Lyric blushed and looked away. "That means so much to me."

"We should go." Dusit helped Gamon move.

After a quick thank you and goodbyes to his… his *family*, he grabbed Gamon's bag and his own. When decisions were made, action needed to happen immediately. Shooting a BL was hurrying up to wait, and then go, go, go.

Outside the house, Gamon stopped for a moment and simply smiled at him.

Dusit's heart clenched, and he was glad he could hurry and wait and go, go, go with Gamon.

AS SOON as he and Dusit got on set, Prem rushed over to them.

"Dusit, I'm sorry." The bags under Director Li's eyes suggested he hadn't slept in days.

Dusit understood the investors had the most say, so it wasn't the director's fault. "You had no control over the situation."

Frowning, Prem shook his head, raked his fingers through his hair, and sighed. "I shouldn't have allowed myself to get caught up with worrying about the investors so much. But the audience expects higher quality, so the series' success is more dependent on money."

Shaking his head, Dusit reassured Prem. “The industry is a business, and businesses run on money, which means investors and sponsors. I really get it.”

“Besides, all is well that ends well,” Gamon chimed in, helping Dusit out of the uncomfortable position.

“We’re workshopping some of your scenes today, but some others would like to speak with you.” Prem gestured toward a room often used for workshops.

As they walked down the hall, several actors frowned and then looked the other way. An actress not even working on the series rolled her eyes at them. A couple of the crew mumbled under their breath while glaring at Dusit.

Gamon leaned into him. “Ignore them.” Then in a louder voice said, “We are lucky to be doing *Don’t Break My Heart 2* as the first one launched so many careers.”

“Wonder who is going to throw shade now?” Dusit stepped into the room to find a small group of actors and actresses sitting around.

Were they angry that he put the series at risk? What did—

All assembled stood and began applauding.

Someone shouted, “Keep fighting!”

Dusit felt humbled.

Gamon threw an arm around his shoulders and gave him a squeeze. Then he took a step back and joined the other actors, who continued to clap.

Once the room went quiet, Dusit said, “I’m sorry my past actions reflected badly on our series. Those pictures are from a place I am no longer in and have no plans on ever returning to.”

Gamon grabbed his hand and pressed his lips to Dusit’s knuckles. “Of course not.”

“Let’s get back to work,” Prem ordered from the doorframe.

“DUSIT, CAN you escape?” Achara asked as she peered around him.

Dusit pulled at the ropes Gamon had wrapped around his wrists to secure him to the chair.

Achara paced around them. “Impressive rope work, Gamon.”

Gamon shrugged as if it were nothing.

"Where did you learn how to do this?" Dusit wasn't sure he wanted to know the answer.

Smiling, Gamon seemed to have read his thoughts. "Tutorial videos," he said. "Amazing the things you can learn on those skill-share platforms."

Dusit was still getting used to this version of Gamon who wasn't shy and easily embarrassed.

"I'm happy my character is rescuing you," Gamon said.

"Why?"

"I'm tired of the trope of the innocent bottom needing to be rescued."

Achara clapped twice. "Well, it's overdone. I was glad the author gave us the rights to change that outdated trope."

Gamon circled around Dusit's chair.

"Let me set the scene," she went on. "Gamon's character's father has kidnapped Dusit to separate and scare you."

Dusit struggled against the ropes to get into the mood of the frustrated captive.

"Remember, neither of you know if his father means you any harm. Gamon's character is finally breaking away from the hold his parents have on him. He's risking a lot to do this, and it doesn't come naturally."

"But it's important and about time he doesn't let his parents rule over him," Gamon said and grimaced; then he continued more calmly, "Although my character is getting to a place where he is an adult and is no longer going to allow himself to be controlled by his family. He is considering his wants and needs first, and while that's not easy, he's going to do it." Gamon's statement felt more like a promise.

Achara smiled and patted Gamon on the shoulder. "You're saying this with a lot of determination."

Gamon sighed. "And experience."

"Bring it all to your character," Achara advised. "Dusit, you've never been kidnapped, but imagine something or someone separating you from what you want most in life."

Hurt and anger tripped through him, as that experience was still fresh. "I don't have to put too much effort into imagining that."

Achara clicked her nails on the table. "On that note, let's run through the scene."

As they workshopped the bondage scene, Gamon's breathing grew quicker than usual. He kept wiping his hands on his pants as he stared at Dusit with hungry eyes.

"Is this really the logical place for my character to get… horny? I mean, shouldn't my character be untying Dusit as quickly as possible and escaping?"

Achara grinned. "Prem is working with the screenwriters to make the scene flow more logically. Let's take the scene from the top and assume it will make sense with what they figure out."

Gamon bobbed his head once in gesture for Dusit to start when he was ready.

"What's going on with you?" Given the script, Dusit could almost believe that Gamon was simply exercising superior acting skills. However, dilated pupils and the waves of neediness rolling off Gamon revealed the truth.

Shrugging, Gamon got back into character and gave Dusit a sheepish grin that made him look delicious. "Don't know. I like… I think I like you being tied up…."

Dusit stuck to the script. "So you like being in control of me? You enjoy being in charge?"

"No, it's just—I don't know." Gamon exhaled hard, with more frustration than necessary to project an inner conflict.

"I think you do." The thought tickled Dusit. He had another way to drive Gamon wild. Tugging at the ropes, he tried to appear helpless. He went off book. "You like me dependent on you and at your mercy."

Gamon moaned. "Under my protection…."

There was no moan or lines about protection in the script as far as Dusit remembered. "Do you like me under your control?" he asked, insistent.

Gamon finally hissed out, "Yeah."

Something more was happening beyond the erotic nature of bondage.

"I, um, love knowing you can't get away." Gamon's hands trembled, and then he wrapped his arms around his chest to hide that fact.

"You don't need ropes for that. Red flag or not, you won't get rid of me this time." Dusit felt these two lines deeply. His character wouldn't be letting Gamon's character go any more than *he* intended to let Gamon disappear again.

Gamon's breath caught in his throat. "Dusit, I'm so sorry. I—"

Achara cleared her throat. "As your friend, I know you two have a lot to work out on a personal level. But as your intimacy and acting coach, I need you both to get back into character and deal with your character's fear of abandonment. We must ensure we get this right since this scene will be shot early in the schedule."

Dusit wished he could hold Gamon right now, but he settled for telling him the truth. "I'm sorry too, and we can make anything work if—"

"Lines, and in your characters, please," Achara insisted.

Nodding, Dusit said, "Okay."

They ran through the scene several times.

Achara finally clapped. "Nicely done. Take a break."

Gamon's pocket buzzed, as it had several times during the scene. He retrieved his cell phone and stared at it.

"Everything okay?" Dusit asked, knowing he wouldn't get a proper answer.

"It's just… nothing important." Gamon frowned down at his phone. "But I need to take care of something."

Achara waltzed over to Dusit with her pretty smirk and an arched eyebrow. She handed him a length of rope. "For later."

"Um…." What could he say? Dusit gave her a curt nod and shoved the rope into his messenger bag.

Gamon trudged back into the room, looking like something was off.

Dusit put a hand on Gamon's shoulder. "Everything okay?"

"Yeah. Fine." Gamon gave him a small smile.

Achara clapped her hands. "Okay, you two. Do you want to practice the sponge bath scene here"—she dropped her voice to a low and sensuous tone—"or at home?"

In unison they both said, "At home."

"If you need me, call." Achara waved and glided out of the room.

"I'll call our driver." Gamon was already scrolling his phone for the number.

GAMON CLEARED his throat. "We really need to talk."

Dusit was leery of doing so. He was afraid that the connection they were reforging would be in danger of snapping. "We do, but maybe after we memorize tomorrow's scenes."

Gamon bit his lip for a moment, as if to stop himself from leaping into the conversation. Then he said, "I guess that makes sense."

Relief flooded Dusit. He wasn't the only one who was hesitant. Grabbing the script, he said, "Let's see the next scene. Why is there always a sponge bath?"

"You know what they say—if a sponge bath isn't involved, it can't be considered a BL." Gamon grinned.

"No one says that." Dusit laughed. "Though that seems to be the case."

"At least I don't have to poke your bruises like in season one." Gamon chuckled. "I know these minor scenes are to show a bond between the characters, but I like how we are moving away from the typical ones. Taking care of the other is one way to get that across, and at least Prem is breaking some of the cliched scenes. Like the scenes where you were tying my character's sneakers, blowing on hot food, or carrying his books."

Dusit lay back on the bed and tried to think of ways to appear feverish. "But not the sponge bath."

Gamon scanned the script one more time and then asked, "Ready?"

"Always." Dusit couldn't help but flirt with him when the reward was an adorable blush.

“Here. Let me take off your shirt,” Gamon’s voice became his character’s, which was higher than his normal speaking voice.

“No.” Dusit struggled to resist. His character didn’t want Gamon’s character to see the bruises he’d gotten from being kidnapped.

Gamon unbuttoned Dusit’s shirt. “Yes. Shh, don’t fight.”

Dusit slipped it off so they could stay in character.

“Let me—what did they do to you?” Gamon’s voice broke as if someone really had banged him up.

He wet the cloth, wrung it out, and wiped the cool rag on Dusit’s supposedly fevered body.

Gamon was thorough with the cloth and gently touched every part of Dusit’s torso and arms. The long swipes of the cloth became caresses, making Dusit long for more.

With every tender touch along his arm, Gamon seemed to communicate his love and affection.

Not even Dusit could miss that… unless it was only Gamon’s character.

No, this was how Gamon always touched him when they were together. No one had ever touched him like he was a precious treasure except Gamon.

Perhaps there was a reason for sponge baths after all.

Long after the cut would have been called to end the scene, Gamon kept stroking Dusit’s body with the cloth until Dusit had to press his lips together not to beg for more.

He squeezed his eyes shut so the need and desire in Gamon’s gaze did not overwhelm him. The man seemed to be trying to memorize every one of Dusit’s muscles.

“You rest, and I’ll go get some medicine for you.” Gamon finally spoke the line that was supposed to end the scene and stood.

“No. Stay.” Dusit opened his eyes and whined like his character would have. He locked his arms around Gamon, rewriting the ending of the scene.

Gamon toppled back onto Dusit face first.

Dusit grabbed him and held him close. He shouldn't enjoy Gamon's resting on him, but this face-to-face position brought back so many memories of being tangled in bedsheets with Gamon.

Gamon's eyes had widened, but now his lids shuttered the heated gaze, though not before Dusit saw the want in his eyes.

Shifting his hips, Dusit moved his body against Gamon's.

With a broken moan, Gamon straddled him.

"What do you want?" Dusit's voice had gone husky, which, if he recalled, aroused Gamon even more.

Gamon thrust his already erect dick against Dusit. He grabbed Dusit's hands to interlock their fingers. Groaning, Gamon pinned him to the mattress. The look of fire he aimed at Dusit was a gut punch and reminded him of the ropes and Gamon's interest in them.

After this afternoon, it was obvious Gamon enjoyed bondage. Dusit had never done that outside of today's workshop, but he was up to try anything as long as it was with Gamon. "You want to tie me up?"

For a split second, Gamon trembled, and then he stared at their hands. Or maybe he was focusing on *his* hands holding Dusit down. "What? No. I don't—"

"I think you do. I'd let you." Dusit studied Gamon.

His breath hitched, but then he rolled off Dusit like he'd catch fire if he stayed where he was. "No."

Dusit chuckled.

Gamon paced. "Besides, I have nothing to tie you up with."

Dusit scooted off the mattress and pulled the rope from their workshop out of his bag. "Luckily, I do."

Gamon's eyes went wide. "Why do you have that?"

It was probably too much to say outright that he wanted Gamon to do whatever he wanted to him, so Dusit hinted, "Achara thought we might want to run through that scene… or something."

"Most likely *or something*." Gamon's expression went from sweet to "I'm going to ruin you for anyone else."

Dusit smiled. Didn't Gamon know no one else could ever or would ever compare to him?

As he grabbed the rope, Gamon's eyes flashed with heat. His expression mixed determination and excitement. "Lie down."

Dusit swallowed hard. He had asked for this, so he laid his ass down on the bed and waited. What was he getting into?

Gamon inspected Dusit's hands and traced his fingers over his wrists. "The rope left some redness."

"It's very slight." Once again Gamon's tenderness melted Dusit.

Leaning down, Gamon kissed the marks.

Now this was going in the right direction.

Gamon snatched Dusit's hand and wrapped a loop around his wrist. He nabbed Dusit's other hand and slid the rope over that wrist too.

In a quick breath-stealing move, Gamon tightened the rope and wrapped it around both wrists, securing Dusit's hands together.

Out of instinct, Dusit attempted to pull his hands apart, but the makeshift rope handcuffs clasped them together.

Gamon tightened his hold on the rest of the rope that dangled.

Dusit peered up at Gamon.

Gamon checked the tightness exactly the way Achara had shown him to. "I caught you," he said with a grin.

He had captured Dusit forever ago, but Dusit would play along. "So what now? What are you going to do with me?"

"Anything I want." Gamon's grin widened, and he whispered, "All you have to do is say stop if you want me to."

Dusit acquiesced with a nod, as if there was anything he wouldn't let Gamon do to him.

The fluid grace with which Gamon slithered down the bed and tugged down Dusit's pants stunned him.

He wasn't hard yet, but that would change soon.

With liquid movements, Gamon undressed… slowly. He teased his shirt off one shoulder, then the other, and then dropped it. Gamon danced out of his pants with some hip action that made Dusit think of fucking.

Now he was hard and wanting.

Finally, Gamon's entire body became visible, revealing a fit and quite beautiful physique.

Dusit attempted to sit up and couldn't—an arousing reminder that his hands remained tied, hampering his movements.

This was Gamon's show, so his only option was to wait.

Gamon straddled him again. He grabbed the excess rope attached to Dusit's hand and used it to pull Dusit's hands above his head. "Leave them there if you can."

Dusit wanted to lighten the mood. "If I can—"

With lighting speed, Gamon shifted his position and pushed Dusit's unbuttoned shirt open but left it on. Then he slid his ass over Dusit's lap, right over his cock.

Dusit thrust up. He tried to say Gamon's name, but it came out as a moan.

With a look of determination, Gamon undid Dusit's pants. He pulled them down enough to allow Dusit's dick to jut out.

Staring down at him, Gamon stated again, "I've captured you."

"What are you going to do with me?" Dusit had some ideas if Gamon needed any.

Gamon ducked his head and licked Dusit's shaft.

"Yes," Dusit groaned and said a prayer that this moment would never end. So good, and—

Without further ado, Gamon sucked Dusit into his mouth. He bobbed his head, making his mouth go a little farther each time.

Dusit tried to touch Gamon but only met with the frustration of his wrists being tied together. Not wanting to disobey Gamon's request that he keep his hands above his head, he simply watched. "You… are sucking my cock."

Gamon slid his mouth off Dusit and smirked. "You noticed," he said and then went right back to pleasuring him.

Of all the things they had done together, blowjobs were at the top of Dusit's list of favorites. He loved to give head and watch Gamon spiral out of control… and he loved watching Gamon get high on the power he had over Dusit when he was the one giving.

The suction increased, and Dusit saw stars.

He needed to grab Gamon's head, but his wrists were still bound, and he had promised to keep them where Gamon had put them. But surely this fell under the category of "if you can."

Dusit couldn't help himself. "I can't. I really can't."

Gamon stopped midsuck and stared up at him.

"I can't. Can I put my hands on your head?" Dusit begged and didn't know what he'd do if Gamon said no.

Desire and triumph flashed through Gamon's gaze. He smirked around Dusit's cock and continued to stare at him. All the power was with Gamon, and his eyes sparkled with that knowledge.

Dusit was dying here. "Please."

Not bothering to take him out of his mouth, Gamon nodded and continued sucking.

After moving his tied hands to the back of Gamon's head, Dusit didn't push or guide. He rested them there.

Gamon had gotten better technically since their first bout of hurried passion, but he always gave everything his mouth could give.

Dusit's hands trembled as he tried to be gentle. Even though he was the captive, the need to possess this man rode him hard.

Gamon reached back and pressed Dusit's hands down on the back of his head.

Dusit's cock hit the back of Gamon's throat, making him gag.

He glanced down at Gamon. Did he still like to be forced to take more cock?

Gamon dragged his lips to the top of Dusit's cock, pulled it from his mouth, and licked it. "Please." Lick. "I." Lick. "Need." Lick. "You." Lick. "Too…."

Dusit's need to come increased tenfold. This was what they both wanted. Taking control of the situation, Dusit pushed Gamon's head down again.

Gamon's moan told Dusit he still enjoyed things being a bit rough. He wanted Dusit to not only take what Gamon offered, but what Dusit could yank from him.

Tears streamed from the corners of Gamon's eyes, but he didn't stop. He choked over and over but continued to suck.

Finally it was too much for Dusit, and he came, feeling every burst of pleasure as his orgasm flooded Gamon's mouth and his come leaked out and dribbled down his chin.

That sight alone was enough to make his cock throb a bit more. Once fully satisfied, he slumped back and petted Gamon's head.

Dusit made the offer with his tied hands. "Do you want me to—"

In one quick move, Gamon was on his knees above him. He took Dusit's tied hands and wrapped his own hands over them, then proceeded to use both sets to jerk off.

Dusit must have leaked a lot of fluid because Gamon's cock was wet to the touch.

"Mine. Mine. Mine…." He stroked faster and groaned.

Gasping, Gamon came all over Dusit's hands, the ropes and all. He trembled and fell to the side of the bed as the cum dripped off Dusit's tied hands.

"You, okay?" Dusit tried to clear his head.

"Yeah." Gamon stifled a yawn.

Dusit wanted the fluid that rolled down his hands. He couldn't resist and lapped up the taste he'd longed for. This is what contentment felt like. "Gamon."

Gamon sat upright and shifted to get next to him.

He tenderly brought Dusit's hands to his mouth and pressed a kiss on his knuckles. The look of pure love he gave Dusit made his heart melt.

"Let me untie you." Gamon worked on untying the cum-drenched rope from Dusit's wrists.

As soon as Dusit's hands were free, he tugged Gamon to the top of the bed. He wiped Dusit's hands with a discarded T-shirt and pulled up the covers.

Dusit hated to ruin the mood between them, but maybe they should talk about what happened and why.

Gamon's loud snore made Dusit chuckle.

Maybe later.

CHAPTER 14

GAMON PATTED around his nightstand to find his phone and stopped the alarm from jabbing spikes into his ears.

A flood of sexy memories involving a rope and some nonprudish activities came to mind. He was pleased with himself. "Dusit?"

No answer. Gamon looked to find no Dusit. Maybe he was still—the apartment was silent.

Dusit was gone but had left a note on his pillow. It read, *I've got to meet with the investors and then I'm going to Charong's. I'll be back late, but I will be back. Yours Always, Dusit.*

"Yours always… aw, he's so much more romantic now. So sweet." Gamon clutched the note to his chest and rolled from side to side.

He caught a view of his reflection and immediately stopped. Apparently Gamon had played in too many Y-series, and the BL characters had altered his brain chemistry. Shaking his head at his foolishness didn't stop him from putting the note in the drawer of his nightstand with care.

His phone buzzed with yet another text. He didn't have to look at it to know who it was. Why couldn't his mother leave well enough alone? She kept hounding him.

He ignored his phone and took a quick shower.

Opening his closet, he smiled. He truly loved fashion, and the perk of a full closet for being a brand ambassador for his favorite brands rocked. He selected a comfortable soft linen shirt in burnt orange and slightly wide-legged pants in dark brown. The clothing was from last season, but the outfit was too comfortable not to wear. He exchanged his messenger bag for one with in a dark brown leather and set the matching sandals near the door.

After grabbing a bottle of water and his laptop, Gamon sat on the balcony. The weather was mild, but from the look of the clouds, it would rain later.

High-rises and fancy hotels surrounded the condo complex. Gamon looked over the railing and studied the people who scurried below. Some seemed to be tourists who ambled along, pointing and taking pictures of everything, and others were workers trying to get to work on time.

He swallowed a sip of water, then sighed.

Time to deal.

He opened his email. There was not one but nine emails from his mother, all marked Urgent. He opened them one by one.

Son,

Please call me.

Mother

Gamon,

Please be reasonable. Stop your association with Dusit Sitwat. He is no good.

Your Mother

The next read:

Why are you being so stubborn? I didn't raise you like this.

Her frustration and anger started to show in the emails that followed:

How could you do this to me? I'm getting older, and you abandoned me. You won't answer my calls, texts, or even my emails.

I have no one.

Gamon's guilt surfaced. Was cutting all ties with her too much? Maybe going no contact wasn't the answer.

But the next email eliminated his guilt and reinforced why no-contact was the only answer right now. Her words only added sorrow to his pain. He read it out loud twice to make sure he heard as well as saw her words.

I've seen the disgusting pictures of you captured from the lives you did. I rejected every offer of a second season of that nonsense series because I didn't want you to be known as the gay singer. No son of mine is going to be that. I'd rather see you dead. If you continue down this path, you're dead to me, just not buried.

He closed his email, leaving several other messages from her unread, because he didn't need to expose himself to more. Once the words were spoken, there was no going back.

The emails proved she had no remorse for what she'd done to him. She had no regret that because of her deceptions he had lost the love of his life. Now, after years of loneliness and loss, she wanted to ruin things for him again.

He stood, paced the balcony, and tried to think of what to do. Facing the fact that she was toxic and didn't have his best interests at heart, he decided to go full no-contact with her. Avoidance was probably the healthiest course of action.

No contact felt harsh, and she didn't even know it was happening. Maybe he should meet her and explain what she was doing and why not seeing her for a while was vital for his mental health.

He needed to think logically. Calling Dusit wasn't an option since they still hadn't discussed what happened, so he called the one person who would give him clear advice. "Achara, what should I do? My mother is texting and emailing. I'm concerned she's going to show up on set."

"First, I'll let the production house know you can't have visitors. I'll advise them that this includes everyone."

He sighed in relief. "Yes, good thinking."

"Now let me ask you, do you depend on her to put food on your table?"

"No." If anything, he'd been the one to make money. It had been years since she had managed other clients.

"A roof over your head?" She probably had her hand on her hip, ticking this list off on her fingers.

"No." He made sure he squirreled away the money he'd earned in France and made sound investments.

"Okay. One last question. Are you still a child?"

"Absolutely not."

"So stop acting like one and be comfortable with the boundaries you have set. Hold the line or she will continue to trounce all over you. From what I can see, you've allowed her to be negative to the point of being abusive. I know it's hard, but you don't need that kind of treatment from anyone."

"I know, but—"

"She's your mother. I know. However, no one has the right to gaslight you, and—"

"I'm used to it." Gamon hated that was the truth. He let it happen.

"You were raised to accept whatever she gave you. Doesn't make her behavior right, and it doesn't mean you need to continue to seek the abuse. Learn a different normal."

Achara was right, but Gamon had no clue how to learn it. "How?"

"You've already stopped being available for her abuse. Do you see it's easier to see it now when she does it?"

"Yes. Like, before, her nasty emails would have made me think that there was something wrong with me. Now I can see her feedback—"

"As abuse." Achara wouldn't let him sugarcoat his mother's actions.

It hurt to admit and humiliated him for having tolerated it for so long. "Her abuse is more about her than me, but it still hurts."

"Of course it does. I'm sorry, but keep doing what you are doing."

Gamon didn't want to confess to Achara, but he did. "I decided I'd see her."

Achara gasped. “You what? Why?”

“I want to stand up to her and tell her how wrong she was… how much she hurt me and why I’m going no-contact with her.”

“Hold the line with her. If she steps over a millimeter, push her back. Consistency is the key. Remember, you matter,” Achara reminded him.

“Thank you. I’ll see you.” He inhaled and exhaled.

Gamon could do this. Through text, he set up a lunch meeting with her for later that day and went back to his closet to pick out some fashionable armor.

ARRIVING AT the restaurant early gave him time to pick his seat.

However, the extra time also gave him more of an opportunity to worry. Not for the first time, Gamon wiped his hands on his napkin.

Was he doing the right thing? Should he even see her? How would she react to what he was going to tell her?

Taking a deep breath, he reminded himself he wasn’t a little kid anymore. She couldn’t boss him around… unless he let her.

There she was. She sailed through the door with a pinched expression that screamed everyone was beneath her.

He could tell by her sigh of disappointment the moment she spotted him.

Gliding toward him, she frowned and pointed at his clothing. “What are you wearing?”

Restraining himself, he stood and gave her a kiss on the cheek. “It’s nice to see you too.”

He held out her chair and sat after she did. He’d taken the initiative to order a bottle of wine and pour her a glass, and she immediately took a sip, but he knew better than to expect a thank-you from her.

Absently, she nodded her lukewarm agreement to his greeting. “But what are you wearing?”

Gamon glanced down at his street-chic clothing. Maybe he should have stuck with the comfortable albeit last year’s style he’d considered, but he hadn’t. He wore these clothes on purpose, hoping the style would give him courage. He'd rolled up his blue jeans to show off chunky lace-up boots. He wore a leopard button-up shirt left open to show off the racerback black tank top underneath. On the shirt's corner pocket was a tiny rainbow button.

"The brand is called Be You. A new designer out of Chiang Mai who is always vocal about supporting LGBT rights in Thailand does this clothing line. Her clothing has a unique, vintage city vibe that I love."

This might be the first time he'd said so much to his mother at one time. She constantly interrupted whenever he spoke about himself. Her need to include herself by comparing her to him had derailed most conversations they'd ever had. So he never could get what he wanted to say out of his mouth. He'd given up years ago.

After a while, he didn't bother trying to share with her but only gave short answers to her questions and listened to her.

"Are you representing this line?" Her tone made it clear she was horrified.

He had reached out to the designer to compliment her, and she was preparing a contract for him. "I hope to, yes."

She glanced around at the other tables. "But then everyone would know you support… that kind of thing?"

In the past that would have hurt. Now he accepted himself and took pride in who he was. "I am that thing, Mother."

"No, you're simply confused." Then she leaned in. "Must you show everyone all of yourself?"

There it was: her homophobia. She'd shown who she was in less than two minutes. He traced a finger over his Pride Flag button. "Meaning I should be quiet in the closet? The rainbow offends you?"

"Yes," she hissed. "How are you ever going to break away from this type of thing if you dress like this and do that Y-series? Do you want *that* to be your entire personality?"

"What I do or don't do doesn't change who I am." Gamon sat straighter. That felt great to say. He added, "It's not the Y-series but what the visibility means to so many people."

She rolled her eyes yet again, reinforcing how little she respected him or the things he cared about or did.

Why was he even bothering? She'd never relent.

The server came and asked, "May I take your order?"

She huffed and made her are-you-stupid face. "Of course, I'm here to have lunch. You are a server. What else should you do? I'll have the chicken rice."

Gamon sighed. How many people spit into her food?

He grimaced and mouthed "Sorry" to the waiter and then said, "May I have the garden salad with dressing on the side?"

"Yes, sir." The server smiled.

"Why can't you eat like a man?" She sneered at him like he disgusted her. The expression was far too familiar. Was she ever proud of him?

"If I ordered something heavier, you'd criticize me for that. There really is nothing I do you approve of." Saying it out loud helped him understand he would never be good enough in her eyes.

She sniffed and drank her wine. "So you finally wanted to see me. Why? I'm not surprised you probably need my help."

Obviously it couldn't be so they could spend time together as a family. "No, I wanted to tell you how much some of your emails hurt me."

She rolled her eyes and grimaced. "*Tsk*, are you looking for me to apologize?"

"You told me I was dead to you." The words still cut through him.

"My words may have been careless, but I can't apologize for my feelings. I have a right to feel that way. It was late, and I was upset." She took a big swallow of wine.

Enough to disown him? "And drinking?" he asked.

She raised her glass to him. "Only some wine."

"You've always said with wine comes honesty." Wine loosened her sharp tongue.

Shaking her head, she exhaled hard. "All right, I didn't mean everything I said. Come back to me and let me manage you before you run your career into the ground."

He opened and shut his mouth without saying a word. Why was it so hard to stand up to her? *I'm an adult.*

Finally he choked out, "Absolutely not."

She stared off into space, ignoring him. "The first thing I'll do is get you out of this gay little drama. You shouldn't be associated with the BL industry. I hear Dusit is your co-star again."

"Yes." A bit of light in the dark world of her negativity.

She chuckled. "I was sure he was out of the picture for good. Though if those pictures of him keep surfacing—"

Wait a second? She wouldn't, would she? Why did he doubt it? "Did you—"

Smirking, she arched an eyebrow. "I can't take credit for that. Shame, because it seems to have the potential to work."

Anger swirled. If she had thought of sabotaging Dusit, she would have.

"Leave him alone," he snapped.

"As soon as you can stop associating with that piece of gutter trash." She took another sip of wine and stared at him, trying to make him feel small and worthless.

"Don't talk about him like that." His voice was low. He couldn't protect himself, but this time he would protect Dusit.

"Once the trash is back on whatever barroom floor you found him on, I'll get you—"

"Did you not hear what I said?" Her lack of consideration for anything he wanted stunned him. She simply didn't care what he needed or thought.

She *tsk*ed. "I know what's best for you, and—"

"No, you don't. Stop saying you do." His voice trembled, but he continued, "You will never be in charge of my career again."

She finished her wine and dabbed the napkin to her lips. "We'll see."

"What's that supposed to mean?"

Tilting her head, she sneered. "I mean, you are putting a lot of faith in a man who abandoned you without a word."

Apparently she didn't know he'd overheard her bragging at the production house. "That's not true. I know what you did."

Her eyes widened as she tried to feign innocence. "What do you mean? He just left without a word."

Anger whipped through Gamon. "You made him leave."

She refilled her glass. "He was eager to go."

Gamon shook his head, not letting a tiny seed of doubt grow. "You lied to him and me. We loved each other, and you broke our hearts."

"Ha, loved each other! He probably wanted someone easy to use, and you, my innocent dear, fit the bill."

Swallowing hard, he ignored her hurtful lies and said the words he needed to say. "You made us believe each of us broke up with the other."

She played with her wineglass, then looked him dead in the eye. "It was for your own good."

No denial. No remorse. No real explanation.

"It wasn't."

Shrugging, she whispered, "You were going to be labeled as gay."

"So? I am gay. There is nothing wrong with being gay, or bi or straight for that matter." He said those words in a normal voice.

She looked around to see if anyone was close enough to hear his declaration. "Lower your voice. I couldn't have that. No way could I have a gay son."

But she did. How could she think otherwise?

She continued, "You'd have lost everything. That would have been the end of your entire career."

Anger whipped through him again. "That's not true."

She rolled her eyes. "Okay, maybe you would have continued to work in the Thai BL industry, but that would be it. I removed all obstacles so you would have limitless possibilities."

"Even if my career ended with one Y-series, I'd have had Dusit by my side. I wouldn't have lost years with the man I love. We would have been together." Gamon took a sip of water because he was afraid of what he might say if he continued to talk.

She was silent for ten seconds and then shook her head. "Besides, I can't have a gay son."

Can't have? "What?"

"It's simply a filthy habit you can get over. And everyone knows men cannot stay faithful, and certainly not when there's two men in a relationship." She was gaslighting him with her projected reality.

He half choked and half laughed. That statement would have been funny if she wasn't serious. "That's homophobic and one of the stupidest things I've ever heard."

"Stupid? It is true. I can prove it to you."

"How?" What was she even saying?

"Never mind." She folded her napkin and placed it on the table. "I made your career. I took care of you. I gave up my life to be by your side. I did it all for you."

Did she really believe that? She had been the one who craved his fame, not him. "Did you?"

"How can you ask me that?" She pouted.

He couldn't let her get away with this nonsense. "You got a lot of perks managing me. Not the least of which was the ability to control me."

She stood. "You are nothing but ungrateful. You'll find out how right I am, and you'll come crawling back."

He shook his head, and with determination he whispered, "Never."

"You disgust me." She slapped him across the face.

Gamon laid his hand over his cheek. The sting of that slap was a physical representation of all the hurt her words had caused. "We will not be seeing each other anytime soon."

"What?" she gasped, as if he'd slapped her in return.

"I don't want this in my life. I wish you well." He wanted to say he didn't want her in his life, but that would have been a lie. Why couldn't she be in his life without all the abuse and negativity?

She stared at him for a moment as if she were waiting for him to backpedal. Not this time. Never again.

"What do you mean you're not going to see me?" She sounded confused.

"I want no contact with you." As he stated his need, he took back the power she had always kept from him.

She turned on her heels and stomped away.

He stared after her, shaking a bit—but with anger, not regret. He'd stood up to her and hadn't caved. It was a win, although he felt like he'd lost something he never had.

A woman at the next table came over and handed him a wet napkin full of ice. "Excuse me, but are you okay?"

He glanced at the makeshift ice pack she offered him and failed to stop a sob from escaping. Even a stranger was kinder to him than his own mother.

"Put this on your cheek so it doesn't swell." She took his hand with the ice-filled napkin and pressed it against his face.

He didn't know what to say, so he kept it simple. "Thank you."

"I had an abusive parent too. You did not deserve that, but I'm glad you stood up to her. I know how hard that can be." She went back to her table.

That concept swirled around in his head as he waited for the check. He did not deserve her abuse.

Gamon needed to stop giving her opportunities to hurt him. She would always lash out at him, because she had gotten away with it in the past. She never respected him, and now he was ready to accept the correct word: abuse.

He may have been used to the abuse, and was possibly even seeking it out because it was familiar to him and the only attention she ever gave him. As sad as it was, not being hurt didn't feel normal to him.

Even if he couldn't protect himself from her, he needed to protect Dusit from her. He wouldn't let her hurt Dusit ever again.

Gamon waved the server over. "I'd like to pay the bill."

"But sir, your food isn't ready." The server glanced at a manager and then at the doors leading to the kitchen. "I could have your meals packed up—"

"That won't be necessary." Gamon took the credit card machine, and even though there was a service charge, Gamon added a thirty percent tip. "Thank you."

"No, thank you, sir." The server left, staring at the machine.

Nodding his thanks to the woman at the next table, he stopped at the front to pay her table's bill and left the restaurant. He took a Grab car back to the apartment. There was so much traffic, the drive took forever.

Finally the car pulled into the circular driveway of his condo complex.

He trudged to the apartment. He was exhausted to his soul.

Gamon hoped Dusit was home or would be home soon. Thinking of him calmed his racing thoughts.

His mother was wrong about Dusit and him… and about everything else.

He stepped out of his boots and into his house slippers.

Dusit had sent him a text.

Investor meeting wasn't terrible. I'm heading to Charong's. Chat will insist I stay for dinner, so text me if you want to stop over. Or text me. (: Miss you. I'll see you soon, D.

Gamon wanted to see Dusit, but seeing other people seemed like an overwhelming idea. Maybe he'd take a shower and watch some TV.

He stepped into the bedroom and *whoosh*! A force threw him onto the bed as he entered the room.

"Dusit?"

"I can be anyone you want," an unfamiliar voice whispered.

Not Dusit!

Pinned to the bed, Gamon shouted, "Stop! Get off me!"

The guy tried to open Gamon's shirt with his mouth. "You say stop, but you want it. They said you might play hard to get, but that's how you like it. I'll give it to you any way you want it."

Shock was evaporating as Gamon tried to get out of the guy's hold on his wrist.

"Who are they? Get off me." Getting one of his hands free, Gamon pulled his fist back to punch—

"Get off him!" Dusit was none too gentle when he ripped the guy off Gamon.

The guy stumbled but didn't fall. He smirked. "Sorry you had to find out like this, but he's mine."

"What? Who are you?" Gamon had to stop this jackass's lies. He struggled to sit upright. "Dusit, I don't—"

"You okay?" Dusit asked as he skimmed his hands over Gamon as if looking for injuries.

"Yes," and then Gamon pointed at the guy. "Who are you?"

"I'm your lover. Stop trying to hide me from him." The guy must be an actor, because he kept his tone measured and logical.

Would Dusit believe him?

CHAPTER 15

DUSIT LAUGHED.

The guy simply stared. He appeared perplexed, which made Dusit laugh harder.

"What is so funny?" the guy demanded, sounding very put out.

"Someone sent you to make me believe Gamon was cheating on me." Although since they still hadn't talked, could it even be cheating? No! He would not second-guess. "My character I'm playing right now might have doubts, but I have none about Gamon."

Hand on his hip, the guy asked, "How can you be so certain?"

A million reasons, but the biggest one was what he shared. "We are meant to be together."

Gamon gave the cutest of gasps and then stared at him with dreamy eyes. "Destiny."

The guy scoffed and stalked out of the room.

When the apartment door slammed, Dusit's smile dropped. "Are you really okay?"

"Yeah." Gamon readjusted his clothing.

"Let me make sure he's gone." Dusit did a search of any hiding places, then changed his password and added the fingerprint verification. Once he was sure the door was locked, he hurried back to the bedroom and sat next to Gamon, who gave him a small smile.

"I shouldn't have used your birthdate as my password," Dusit went on ruefully. "I changed it to the date we first met and added the fingerprint verification."

Gamon's small smile turned into a big one. "You used my birthdate? I'll add my fingerprint verification when I change mine—I used *your* birthday."

Dusit ignored his heart doing backflips at that admission and the look on Gamon's face. "Birthdates usually seem like a good password. Even if fans knew the dates, they wouldn't know where we live. A person would have to know both."

Gamon slapped a hand over his mouth.

"What?" Had Gamon put together who would be on the short list of people who would know both birthdates and their address?

"How could she?" Gamon said.

Dusit swallowed the answer he knew would devastate Gamon. Taking Gamon's hand, he asked, "Can you tell me exactly what happened?"

Gamon wrapped his arms over his chest. "I don't know. I've never met him before in my life. You've got to believe me—"

"I do." Dusit took both of his hands and held them.

"Thank you. I came home. You weren't here, so I was heading in to take a shower. He threw me to the bed and started kissing me as he tried to undress me…." Gamon's voice broke, and then he closed his eyes.

The moment hit Dusit. Gamon said he was okay, but he wasn't. He had truly been afraid. "May I hold you?"

"Yes." Gamon leaned into Dusit's embrace, proving yet again this was where he belonged.

"It must have been scary and confusing." Dusit rubbed his back.

Gamon took a shaky inhale.

"Breathe." Dusit sniff-kissed his cheek. "It's okay."

"I thought you might not believe me that—"

"It was a setup," Dusit finished.

"And I think we both know it was my mother." Gamon picked at a hangnail. "I saw her earlier today. She said she'd prove to me men can't be faithful to each other."

"That's ridiculous." What a bizarre idea.

"I know." Gamon raked his fingers through his hair. "She probably got the address from the studio, and she knows my birthdate and yours. It was a logical assumption on her part that we might use them as passwords, so it was worth a try to try prove to me she was right."

By having her son molested. What kind of monster—

"I'm going no-contact with her." Gamon touched his own face. "She's toxic, and I'm done being her doormat. I can't let her keep ruining my life."

"Let me make you some tea." Dusit led Gamon out of the bedroom and into the living room. Once Gamon was seated, Dusit put the look-but-don't-use blanket over Gamon and tucked him in. Then he went to the kitchen, made tea, and tried to get his confusion and anger under control.

Dusit placed the tea on the side table closest to Gamon.

Gamon turned to him. "We need to talk."

Worry skated through Dusit. Those words rarely preceded anything good, but…. "We do."

"About what happened back then?"

"Yes." It was time. No more avoiding the past. Would this pop the magic spell that allowed them to be together?

"I want you to know I didn't know what happened until a couple of months ago." Gamon's words spilled out, and his eyes got watery.

Huh? "What do you mean?"

"I didn't know what my mother did until I overheard her threatening one of the newest production houses that she would cut my contact with them the way she did with… *you*." Gamon's voice dropped to a broken whisper as he gestured to Dusit.

Gamon hadn't broken up with him.

A grateful happiness covered him.

The love of his life didn't dump him without a word. A small piece of him had always believed that, but low self-esteem and poor decisions had been louder.

Grabbing Dusit's hand, Gamon sniffed. His words were shaky. "She told me you wanted nothing to do with me."

"She what?" That was the opposite of the truth. How that must have gutted Gamon.

Dusit squeezed his hand tighter around Gamon's.

Gamon stared at their joined hands. "She said that you broke up with me through her so you wouldn't have to deal with me… that you couldn't stand me anymore."

"And you believed her?" Of course he did. This was his mother.

Shaking his head, Gamon dashed away the single tear that slipped down his cheek. "I'm so sorry. You were too good to be true."

"Me?"

Nodding, Gamon continued, "I never felt like I deserved you. It's not an excuse, but I was young. I certainly didn't expect she was capable of such deceit."

Wow, that realization must cut. Who would think a parent would be so cruel to their own child?

"We were too perfect together," Gamon said. "I felt like I was in a dream waiting to wake up and have you be gone."

The pieces fit Gamon's negative dialogue and his own. "And you woke up, and I was gone."

"Devastation overwhelmed me. I couldn't think clearly. My mother medicated me for a while. I'm not sure how long." Gamon shrugged. "And I didn't object. I needed something to numb the pain."

Dusit's heart broke again. He didn't want to make Gamon feel worse, but he wanted to explain. "Do you want to know what happened that morning?"

"Please tell me." Gamon's voice was barely above a whisper.

"I went to the kitchen to get you your morning coffee, and your mother was waiting for me. She told me you wanted to break up with me."

"Why did you believe her?" Gamon put his other hand on top of their paired grasp and held on to him as if Dusit were trying to escape.

Dusit moved closer to Gamon. "You weren't the only one who didn't believe he deserved what we had. Remember where I came from? I had been working maintenance a few months earlier. I didn't study theater. I didn't go to college. I wasn't there to be an actor. And there you were, so talented and beautiful. You were starring in a series, and your voice—I knew you were going places. Places that I didn't belong."

Gamon used his whole body to stop a sob. He leaned toward Dusit.

Taking a deep breath, Dusit continued, "I never thought I was good enough for you. When she said as much, it confirmed what I thought."

"Why didn't you—"

"I was in your bed, so she had access to my room and packed all my stuff in suitcases, which she put at the door. She had two big guys there to escort me out." Dusit felt waves of that past humiliation flow over him.

Gamon covered his mouth, but a gasp came out.

Dusit ignored his need to get away from the hurt, but he didn't share how he'd tried to rush back into the bedroom and those men held him back. Or how he had been dragged out the door. "I was locked outside of the building within a couple of minutes."

"Oh God. I'm sorry." Gamon looked at him with glistening eyes.

Dusit tried to give him a reassuring smile but couldn't. Emotions he had tried to bury were swimming to the surface. "I was so confused. Especially after the night we had spent together, so I called you."

"I had lost my phone."

Dusit squeezed his eyes shut for a moment and swallowed. He needed to get the right words, but Gamon's mother was a horrid person. He went with the basics of what happened. "Your mother answered."

"My phone? How did—" He choked on the words and his eyes widened. "I didn't lose my phone. She took it."

Nodding, Dusit laid it out. "Probably."

Gamon swallowed a sob and asked, "What did she say?"

"That you wanted nothing more to do with me."

"And you believed her." Pain was laced through Gamon's words and whipped Dusit's heart.

"I called dozens of times," Dusit said, "and each time I'd leave a message for you. But you never responded—"

"I never got those messages." Gamon spoke through clenched teeth as another tear ran down his face.

Even after all these years, it was important for Dusit to make Gamon understand why he did the things he did.

"But I didn't know that. Not being able to speak to you only reinforced what she told me when she answered."

"Which was?"

"You no longer wanted me in your life and that I was embarrassing myself. She threatened to call the police for harassment if I didn't stop calling you."

"And you believed her?" Gamon closed his eyes as if he hoped to avoid the truth.

"You weren't calling me back or emailing me or even posting on social media, and it all pointed to her telling the truth." The time that had passed made the event sound crazy, but when he was going through the situation, he couldn't think beyond the rejection.

"My mother had taken my computer in for repairs… which, looking back, there probably was no need to do that. She didn't want me online." Gamon groaned. "And it took weeks to replace my phone. She blamed it on the phone company. She cut off all the ways I could reach out to you."

"Why didn't you buy another phone? Or get another computer?" Dusit wanted to understand, and as he unraveled each level, he tore open the old wound.

"At that time, I had no access to my money. She kept a close eye on me. And, well, I wasn't in the best headspace to think clearly." A silent sob jerked Gamon's body, but he didn't let the sound out. "Loss consumed me, and she medicated me, so I wasn't thinking clearly. I didn't get out of bed because I'd be admitting that there would be no hope of you coming back."

His poor Gamon suffered. Dusit knew the despair he described all too well.

Gamon took a shaky breath and released it. "Then when I finally got access to a new phone, she convinced me that if you wanted to contact me you would have before then."

Dusit squeezed his eyes shut for a moment, and then he swallowed past the regret. "Eventually your number was disconnected. I tried to go back to the condo, and the doorman informed me you had left to go abroad."

"She said that I had received a last-minute hosting job on a popular show, and that I had been invited to two designer fashion shows for potential brand ambassador deals. I didn't want to go, but she insisted I couldn't let anything ruin my career. My mother said if I was going to be miserable, I could be dramatically sad in Paris. Everything in Bangkok reminded me of you and of us, so leaving seemed to be the only answer." Gamon put his hand over his heart. "Thinking about it, she must have had everything planned and set in advance."

Dusit gave a low whistle. "That's some high-class manipulation." She was a bitch, but she was clever.

"How could she have done that?" Gamon's eyes glistened, and he pressed his lips together.

Was he looking for answers from Dusit? Dusit had none. "I don't know. She had a strong focus on ensuring your success, so she probably justified—"

"To the point of it costing me everything that mattered." Gamon caressed Dusit's jawline. Then his hand turned into a fist and dropped away, and his face took on a scowl. "I should have known. I feel like such a fool. Why didn't I track you down?"

"I wish you had." Though within a couple months after, Dusit was on his downward spiral.

"Somehow, she knew every time I was preparing to reach out to you, and she derailed me each time. She kept telling me not to humiliate myself. That you left me because you were done. That if I had any feelings for you, I'd respect your needs and leave you alone. I was dumb enough to believe her."

The anguish in Gamon's words echoed the pain Dusit felt. He wished he could dull the pain. "I did the same thing. I believed the lies."

Her lies.

Gamon's fists clenched, and his head dropped forward. "I should have known."

How could he have? What kind of mother does that to her son?

Dusit could feel pointless rage rising, so he tried to cool the emotion with logic. He turned Gamon toward him.

Using his thumb, Dusit gently swiped away Gamon's tears. "Look at me." When Gamon opened his eyes, Dusit said, "We need to remember neither one of us had any experience with relationships, so what did we know?"

"Thinking of all the time we lost fills me with rage." Gamon's voice was rough with sadness. "I'm furious at myself for not having the confidence to go after what I wanted."

Dusit stared into the eyes he could truly see happiness and forever in, but he needed to hear the words. "And that is…."

"You. I've always wanted you since the moment I first saw you. I knew."

"Knew what?"

"That I needed you in my life and you gave my heart a love song." Gamon pulled his hands back. "Is that too much? Am I going too fast?"

"Not at all." Dusit couldn't help but focus on Gamon's plump lips. and how sexy it was when Gamon swiped his tongue out to wet his lips, leaving them glistening.

Gamon leaned back, breaking the spell. "We should agree."

Dusit tried to make his brain work and catch up. "A pact… a pact? About?"

"We won't consider ourselves broken up unless we hear it directly from the other person."

That sounded reasonable and—wait! "Does that mean we're together?"

Gamon's gaze dropped to Dusit's mouth and whispered, "Does it?"

Dusit wasn't above using everything he had at his disposal for the best outcome. Gamon had told him he was always helpless against Dusit's mouth.

He traced his tongue over his lips, leaving them wet. "Yes, it does. Isn't that what you meant?"

"Um, uh, I meant if we were together—in the future… and yes."

With another swipe of his tongue, Dusit leaned into Gamon.

Gamon groaned, "We're together."

“Absolutely.” Dusit couldn’t stop his smile of victory. Ever so slowly, he skimmed his hand up Gamon’s arm and behind his neck. He fisted the hair at the nape of Gamon’s neck and secured him. “Bed.”

Without waiting for a response, he pulled Gamon off the couch and backed into the bedroom, never breaking his gaze from Gamon’s eyes until the backs of his legs hit the bed.

His eyes went wide as Gamon gasped, and then his lips parted in invitation.

Dusit’s mouth was on his before there was time to think. The soft glide of Gamon’s lips on his felt perfect. The kiss didn’t make the past evaporate, but it reminded them of the here and now.

He lifted his arms to allow Gamon to pull off his shirt. “Wait. Are you okay? Before, when he—”

“I want you all over me. I want you to erase everything.” Gamon wasn’t slowing down. His shirt was off, and he was unzipping Dusit’s pants.

“And no breaking up for the good of the other person. None of that drama series bullshit.” Dusit worked on opening Gamon’s pants. After some shifting, they simply got out of their own pants.

“Yeah, I hate that romance trope.” Gamon was hard and ready to go.

Dusit nibbled at Gamon’s neck.

“Definitely. This time around—” Gamon pushed him back onto the bed and crawled over him. “Even if I’m bad for you, I’m going to be selfish enough to stay with you.” His smooth skin slid across Dusit’s as their bodies tangled.

Dusit rolled then over until he was on top of Gamon.

He pulled Gamon’s arms above his head, positioning him. No clue who started the kissing, but Dusit didn’t care, not if their mouths continued to touch.

Kissing Gamon was better than any full-on sex he’d had with anyone else. Each kiss held an invitation for more. It was love wrapped up in desperate want.

Gamon rocked against Dusit. The slide of their erections drove Dusit mad, but he couldn't stop kissing Gamon. He'd lost a lot of kisses, and he was determined to reclaim each one… with interest.

Between kisses Dusit got out a response to Gamon's pledge. "Me too. I'll keep you even if I'm dragging you down."

Practically purring, Gamon said, "I enjoy going down."

Yes! Dusit liked where this was going. "Do you?"

Gamon's arms flexed, and he rolled over so he was on top.

Damn, Gamon had gotten stronger, and that was hot.

Doing a slow slide down Dusit's body until his face was at dick level, Gamon smiled and gave him a stroke. "As a matter of fact, I love going down on you."

"Really?" Dusit forced himself to keep his eyes open. He was an adult; coming from two strokes shouldn't be possible, but right then the impossible seemed probable.

Gamon ducked down and used his tongue to give Dusit one long wet lick up his cock. At the tip, Gamon glanced at him with an angelic expression, making everything that much more powerful. "Really."

Breath whispered over Dusit's dick, which was now fully ready to take part in every and all activities on Gamon's agenda.

Dusit loved being at Gamon's mercy. Not sure what to say to make things continue, he simply nodded.

Gamon wasted no more time and took him into his hot, wet mouth. He held him there as if savoring the moment and smiled up at him.

Dusit threw a hand over his eyes to block out that image. No way he'd last any length of time watching his beautiful man suck his cock.

Then Gamon's tongue did a slow slide down to Dusit's balls, and he licked them, all while still holding Dusit in his mouth.

Dusit groaned at the incredible sensation. "Gamon…."

Gamon started bobbing his head.

"Gamon. Gamon. Gamon." Dusit began to chant, as if saying Gamon's name could extend his will not to come.

Dusit was incredibly turned on, and he longed to orgasm in Gamon's mouth immediately, but simultaneously he desired additional time to savor the experience of being enveloped in the wet heat emanating from Gamon's mouth. He wanted everything all at once.

But Gamon added a hand to stroke him as he sucked, and that did him in.

"Gamon," Dusit called out one more time, and then helplessly, he came. He filled Gamon's mouth until a few drops seeped out of the corners of his lips.

So sexy. Dusit throbbed once more.

He was done.

Gamon moaned as he licked Dusit clean. He shifted restlessly on the bed as if seeking sensation.

"Take my mouth." Dusit demanded—more for himself than for Gamon, although Gamon had always liked to come after Dusit, which worked well for Dusit. After giving head, Gamon would come almost immediately so Dusit could swallow his pleasure as he shivered through his own aftershocks.

Not having to be asked twice, Gamon straddled Dusit's neck.

No teasing necessary. Dusit grabbed Gamon's cock and sucked.

Gamon put two hands against the wall and moaned. He held himself still.

Adding suction, Dusit bobbed his head as much as he could in his current position, which wasn't much. He loved driving Gamon insane.

But in short order Gamon obliviously got what he needed, because he grunted and filled Dusit's mouth.

Dusit had been starved for Gamon's taste and shivered as he swallowed once, twice, and then once more.

"Mm," Gamon sighed as he lay down next to Dusit. He kissed Dusit's lips with a soft tenderness.

The kiss melted Dusit's heart. This was what perfect happiness felt like. Gamon snuggled against him with a satisfied smile on his face.

Love for this man consumed all Dusit's heart. Love for this man had become impossible for Dusit to bury, hide, or deny. He loved him completely, now and forever. It was simply a fact. Something he should share with—

Dusit's phone rang.

The caller ID said it was Achara.

Gamon grinned. "Get it. Maybe there's been a schedule change allowing us to go in later tomorrow."

He loved the idea of keeping Gamon in bed longer. "Mm, that would be nice."

"Hey, Achara, what's going on?" Dusit said into the phone as he stared at Gamon's angelic face. How could he be so lucky?

"Dara Boome?" Achara asked.

"Huh? Who?"

"Do you know a Dara Boome?" Achara's tone was hurried and sharper than usual.

"No. Who is that?"

Gamon's eyes opened.

"The girl who is claiming you impregnated her." Achara's words were like missiles aimed at blowing up their happiness.

"I what?" No way.

Achara sighed. "Check your email."

"My email." Dusit didn't mean to keep repeating everything, but his brain was trying to keep up. He put Achara on speaker and scrolled through his emails. "There's about half a dozen from someone by that name."

"Open one and be sure not to delete it."

"Okay." Dusit held his phone so Gamon could read the message too.

"Oh my," Gamon gasped. "Achara, she's accusing him not only of making her pregnant, but of forcing himself on her."

"I was afraid of that." Achara didn't seem surprised that Gamon was right next to Dusit. She continued, "Right now, I'm getting her posts taken down, but she appears determined."

Dusit hated feeling helpless. "What do I do?"

"Do not engage with her at all. Print out all the emails. Save them to several files. Those are evidence. Change all your passwords on your online accounts. I've already reached out to the production house's lawyer." Achara's advice was sound.

Here we go again. He couldn't believe it. "Another crisis that I'm causing."

Achara *tsk*ed. "You're not causing anything… unless you know her?"

"No, I don't." He really didn't.

"Have you been to Phuket recently?" she asked, referencing the city where the young woman apparently lived.

"Not since I was seven. We visited my mother's brother."

"Good. We will see what we can do to prove that. It will help."

Dusit knew the answer but asked anyway, "What about the investors? Will that be enough to appease them?"

"They only recognize two kinds of news: One that makes them money and one that doesn't. Which one do you think the investors want? And which do you think this is?"

"Why does this keep happening?" Dusit asked no one in particular.

Gamon threw an arm around him as if he could protect him from his irresponsibility. If he hadn't been so out of control the past few years, these accusations wouldn't seem possible.

"Reach out to Rose to make sure they know. But I'd bet Kanawat Anwar already has people on it."

"Will do. Thank you." Dusit ended the call. He didn't want to look at Gamon.

"Hey, we'll get through this together." Gamon's arm tightened around him.

"Together?"

"Didn't we agree we are now together, or are you dumping me already?" Gamon joked, but his eyes held the shadow of past worries.

"That would be unthinkable. We are together."

"Good. We will weather this storm too. Call Rose and let's see what he has to say."

CHAPTER 16

GAMON'S PHONE buzzed, and one look showed they were texts from his mother. He shouldn't read her toxic messages, but he couldn't seem to stop himself.

Dusit was discussing the current accusations leveled against him with Rose.

Gamon had no clue what the girl thought she would get out of accusing Dusit of rape resulting in a pregnancy, but here they were.

Dusit gestured to the balcony, so Gamon stepped outside. A blast of humid heat greeted him. The joke of there being only one season in Thailand was true. To Gamon the weather was always hot, and in summer it was hotter with more rain.

He sat in a patio chair, hoping for a breeze that wouldn't come.

While he tried to get air into his shirt, his phone buzzed again. He steeled himself. Gamon was an adult and didn't have to read her criticism, insults, and nastiness, but he did. He was still compelled to check because maybe one day she'd stop being abusive—today was not that day.

Her first text read: *See, I told you so. That boy cannot be trusted.*

Then: *Forcing himself on that poor girl like an animal.*

Gamon wasn't in the habit of denying a victim's reality, but there was no way Dusit would have done such a thing drunk and certainly not when sober, along with the fact he hadn't been to Phuket as an adult. The pieces didn't add up.

Peeking through the sliding glass door, Gamon watched as Dusit paced and shook his head.

Gamon's phone buzzed again. This time his mother texted him an I-told-you-so with a link to one post about Dusit's supposed fatherhood.

Gamon had had enough and did what he should have done before now. Better late than never. He took a deep breath and blocked his mother's number with his exhale.

Blocking her didn't feel good—having to take such measures made him sad—but he needed to protect himself from her. She had proved time and time again that given the chance, she would hurt him.

He slumped in a chair and stared at his phone. The noise of the traffic below drifted to the balcony, but everything seemed to be at a distance. He had blocked his mother from contacting him.

A hand on his shoulder made Gamon jump. "Oh, I didn't hear you come outside."

"Yeah, you were deep in thought. Is there anything I can do?" Dusit squeezed Gamon's shoulder for a moment before sitting next to him.

"With everything that's going on for you, and you still worry about me…," Gamon mused aloud.

"Of course. You are my everything." Dusit knelt in front of him. "Is there anything I can say or do to make you feel better? I'm terribly sorry about having another situation. I don't want to drag you down. If you want—"

"Dusit Sitwat, do not continue your sentence. We are together in all of this." Nope, Gamon was not having Dusit say foolish things.

"But you're not the one causing—"

"Should I plug my ears and hum off-key?" Gamon threatened as his fingers hovered over his ears.

Dusit groaned. "But—"

"I'm the reason. I cost both of us way too much." Gamon gulped back an unsteady inhale. "I'm not making the same mistake ever again. Stop the nonsense."

Dusit's head dropped. He sighed and then chuckled as he smiled at him.

"What?" Gamon didn't mean to snap, but he wanted to know what was so amusing. He was serious.

Leaning back, Dusit put his hands out in front of him palms first. “Remind me never to make you mad.”

Gamon tried his best to glare but failed as he softened his expression with a smile. “What did Rose say?”

“He suggested”—Dusit added air quotes—“it would be best if I went to stay with Charong and his sisters.”

Gamon wanted to deny the logic in that, but the optics of a family setting would help lower the flame. “I’ll help you pack.”

Doing something would feel good. Gamon went into Dusit’s bedroom and gathered a couple of days’ worth of clothing. “You shouldn’t need more than this.”

Dusit leaned against the doorframe. “You’re so calm. I can’t believe you’re not even mad at me.”

“Why would I be mad at you?” Gamon added Dusit’s toiletries. “You did nothing wrong.”

“How are you so sure when no one else is?”

Gamon slipped his arms around Dusit. “I know you. If the only issue was that you got someone pregnant, that might be possible, because I know you’ve had sex with women. I’d help you pick out a name if she were keeping it… but you… forcing someone—”

Dusit straightened. “I could have been drunk.”

A laugh broke from Gamon.

“What?” Dusit folded his arms in front of his chest.

“Drunk or sober, you wouldn’t have done that. It’s not in your nature.” He wanted to be Dusit’s rock. The person he could depend on.

Dusit fell into him. Gamon yanked Dusit back into his arms.

Gamon steadied him and gave him a warm hug infused with love. “We will get through this together. You’re packed. My guess is Rose wants to meet with me.”

“Yeah, he said he’d call and probably stop by in a few.” Dusit kissed him on the nose and stepped back.

Zipping Dusit’s duffel bag, Gamon said, “It’s only for a couple of days. And if the meeting ends at a reasonable time, we’ll do another sleepover at Charong’s… if you think he wouldn’t mind.”

"Definitely come over if you can." Dusit grabbed the bag off the bed and trudged to the door.

"We've got this… together." Gamon trailed after him and set Dusit's shoes in front of him.

Dusit stepped into his sneakers, gave Gamon a gentle kiss on the mouth, and then left.

Gamon wanted to see him off downstairs, but he didn't want to make this harder on Dusit.

He called Achara. She hadn't found out any more information.

ROSE ARRIVED at the condo armed with the first round of coffees. "I brought copies of both of your contracts. Kanawat is having a lawyer go over the wording, but he suggested we do the same."

Gamon was glad he had signed on to the Kanawat agency when they'd come to him with the second season contract. But how was Gamon going to find something a lawyer couldn't? He didn't know, but he'd try. "Of course."

"The investors want a meeting with you tomorrow," Rose informed him.

"I'm sure they do." Gamon understood them logically. They wanted to make money off their investment in the series, and right now this scandal wasn't helping. "They plan to force Dusit out, right?"

"In short, yes." Rose shrugged and rifled through his bag. "Only two investors understand how that would affect the show. The rest don't understand fandoms and how the series needs both of you to succeed. That's why we need to look at your contract with nonlegal eyes."

Gamon took the two pages held together with a staple from Rose. He reached over to a box on the coffee table and pulled out a pair of reading glasses.

Smiling, Rose pulled his own stylish readers out.

"You wear glasses too?" Gamon sat at the dining table and draped the granny chain attached to them around his neck.

Rose turned on all the overhead lights. "I'm old, but I thought you only wore them in the show as part of your character."

"When I'm going to do a lot of reading, it is easier on my eyes." Gamon stared at the contract. "You do believe we can overcome this, right?"

"Yeah, I do, especially if you're on Dusit's side. Investors would have an easy time taking down Dusit, but not so you."

"No way anyone is taking Dusit away from me again." Gamon's anger bled through his tone as he enunciated each word to ensure there was no mistake.

Rose put his hands in front of him in surrender and feigned being afraid of Gamon. "And I thought Dusit had anger issues I needed to manage."

"Ha, ha." Gamon tried to dial his emotions down. "I only got Dusit back, and everyone and everything seems to be determined to ruin things. Nothing is pulling us apart this time."

"There's definitely a story there."

"Let's save my 'too much drama' to be a BL tale of woe for another time. Right now…." Gamon waved his contract and started combing through it. He didn't know what he was looking for, but he had to find it.

The minutes turned into hours. Rose and he took turns going downstairs to get coffee at the twenty-four-hour shop. During his midnight run, Gamon texted Dusit and told him he wouldn't be doing a sleepover.

His cell rang, making him smile. He answered the FaceTime call.

Dusit stared at the screen. He finally asked, "Is everything all right?"

"Yes, Rose and I are still combing through the contracts."

"Your contract too? Why? Oh, I mean, if you've changed your mind I can back out of—"

Gamon growled. "Dusit, don't make me mad. Apparently even Rose finds my wrath worrisome, so consider yourself warned."

Dusit smiled into the screen and put a hand out in front of him in surrender. "I'm simply saying even if we aren't a working ship, we are still together. I don't want you to—"

Something tickled Gamon's brain. It seemed to be a piece of the puzzle, but it was frustratingly out of reach.

Gamon snapped, "What did you say?"

Moving the phone away from his face, Dusit stage-whispered, "Rose is right. You are scary."

Yes, that was it. Gamon grinned into the screen. "No, ships. We are a ship."

"Um, yes. Fans put us together."

"That's it!" Gamon left the coffee and started running back to the apartment.

"What's it?" As Gamon took the steps to the lobby two at a time, Dusit warned, "Be careful."

"I will. I've got to go." Excitement flooded him, making him run faster.

"Okay?" Dusit made it sound more like a question, but he ended the call.

Gamon bounced into the elevator and hit the button for his floor. He shifted from foot to foot. He'd never noticed that this elevator went at a snail's pace. Pushing the button a few more times didn't make it go faster, but Gamon couldn't help himself.

He burst into the apartment. "Yes. It is so obvious I missed it. I didn't see it because it's so straightforward."

Rose ended his call, probably with Nok or maybe Kanawat. "What did we miss?"

Grabbing the contract, Gamon double-checked. "I'm right. Look, right here."

Rose's lips slowly turned up into a grin as he read. "I've got a better feeling about tomorrow's meeting. I'm heading home. I'll let Kanawat know what you found, and I will meet you at the studio office tomorrow."

GAMON GOT a few hours of sleep and then dressed himself for battle. He gathered all the brands that were negotiating to sign him and Dusit to be brand ambassadors and all the brands he was currently or in the past promoted.

Looking in the mirror, he adjusted the red suit. He wasn't wearing any shirt under it, which made the suit hit differently. He added bracelets, necklaces, and a single gold hoop to his ear from the luxury brands that had signed them.

The clothes made the man. Stylish, elegant, and successful rolled off him. He grabbed his designer bag, put on his famous-brand shoes, and strutted to the car with his fuck-you-I'm-a-star attitude on full display.

As they got closer to the studio, his bravado faded a bit, so he scrolled through pictures of him and Dusit. Seeing Dusit's face reminded him what this fight was about.

He swaggered into the studio's office like he owned the place. Even though he was playing a role, he'd earned this level of respect, and to save Dusit, he'd use whatever he could.

Everyone, regardless of their gender identity or orientation, stopped to stare as he passed them. His aura demanded everyone's attention. He was usually low key, but when triggered, he could bring out the haughty prince who was aware of his value and power.

Achara stood outside the conference room where the investors were meeting with him. "Well, damn. You look—"

"Thank you." Gamon didn't believe in false modesty. He was sexy, and his "it" factor blazed through. "Are they in there?"

She gestured toward the door. "Good luck."

"I don't need luck. I've got my contract." He grinned but left her with unanswered questions.

He knocked twice but didn't wait for permission to enter. As he stepped into the room, all conversation stopped. He paused at the door to give them a good look as he surveyed the investors.

There were six of them. The two women appeared friendly, along with the older gentleman who smiled at him. Two young guys and a portly middle-aged fellow stared at him with pinched faces and frowns. Prem paced the perimeter, and Rose grinned at him.

Slowly, he removed his designer sunglasses. All the attention he had captured remained on him.

Rose stood. "Good morning, Mr. Chaisit."

Gamon schooled his face to have no expression. He kept his tone even and matter-of-fact. "Is it? I guess that will depend on how this meeting goes."

"Yes, Mr. Chaisit. I'm sure it will go well, Mr. Chaisit." Rose played his role of worried agent with an out-of-control client to perfection. He made introductions with a quiet voice.

Some of the investors stood.

Gamon politely greeted each investor, but he spared them no smiles. They needed to earn those. They were the people in this room who were trying to take Dusit away from him, and Gamon wasn't having it.

Pulling out a chair for him, Rose said, "Please have a seat."

Gamon put his sunglasses in their case, displaying the brand as if he were already doing product placement for them, and then put the case in his luxury bag.

The wide eyes of some of the investors meant they recognized the extremely limited-edition bag he held.

"Thank you, Rose." Gamon didn't hurry into action. He opened his bag and attached the pocketbook hook to the table so his bag wouldn't touch the floor. Finally he sat in the chair Rose had offered.

Making them wait was a power move his mother had taught him. He'd never used it in this way before, but it was quite effective.

He interlaced his fingers and put them on the table in front of him. His luxury bracelets jingled, hopefully reminding them of the brand ambassadorships he represented and could represent… and their cut of the payments. "I appreciate everyone coming. I wanted to meet with you."

The investors looked at each other as they sat down, then at Rose, and then back at each other.

Gamon ignored his inclination to soothe their discomfort. His deadpan stare probably increased the awkwardness.

One of the younger guys started the conversation. "I'm sure you've seen the reports of the latest scandal Dusit—"

"You mean Mr. Sitwat?" Rose corrected him, reminding them to respect his clients.

"Er, yes. Mr. Sitwat has caused another scandal. He—"

"Excuse me, but I need to correct you. Dusit didn't cause this scandal. Someone decided to fabricate lies." Gamon refused to allow the negative narrative to continue unchecked.

The middle-aged man set down his coffee cup harder than necessary. "We can't be sure they are lies, and—"

"I can be. Dusit would never have forced himself on anyone." Gamon would not let what they were implying stand.

Another investor sneered. "Maybe you don't know Dusit as well as you think you do. Several years have passed since—"

"Dusit Sitwat forced no one. Furthermore, he's not been to Phuket since he was seven." By naming the place where the event was supposed to have taken place, the fan had given them a way to prove Dusit's innocence.

The other young guy scoffed. "How do you know he isn't lying about that?"

Rose leaned forward. "Because our office has searched the records of all the airlines flying in and out of the Thai airport and all the ferry and private boat services. We also made sure he didn't use the train to go through Krabi to get to Phuket. The Kanawat agency can say with certainty that Dusit Sitwat has not traveled to Phuket in the last ten years… and yes, we went back that far."

The women and the older man each acknowledged the information with a smile.

Three of the investors muttered their doubts.

Rose added, "Kanawat doesn't make mistakes. Therefore, I will repeat: Our agency can state with confidence that Dusit Sitwat has not been to Phuket as an adult."

"Well, maybe she got the place wrong," the younger investor pointed out.

Gamon's bitter chuckle escaped his mouth. Were they serious? "An island versus a city on the mainland? That seems unlikely."

Rose put a calming hand on Gamon's knee, probably warning him not to be snappish. "I always believe victims, unless the details aren't credible, and in this case—"

"Still, this is another scandal connected to Dusit. He's trouble. We can't have—"

"I will tell you what you can't have." Gamon's words pelted them like jagged rocks.

The middle-aged man pointed at Gamon. "We need to change the actor. It's as simple as that." Then he picked up a donut.

Gamon simply said, "No."

Another investor gasped, "What?"

"I said no, as in no one will remove Dusit Sitwat from this series." Gamon articulated each word as if he were in a language class.

Shaking his head, the investor slapped the table; others nodded along with him. "Don't you see you're not in control here?" he insisted. "You are simply an actor."

Prem covered his mouth. Gamon was aware of how careful he was with the actors he directed.

Here we go. Fingers crossed.

"I might only be an actor, but I have the power here." Gamon pulled out a copy of his contract and set it on the table.

Pointing to the pages, one of the younger guys said, "You're making our case for us. You signed this contract. We have the right to recast as we see fit."

"Have you read my contract?" Gamon tilted his head as he looked around the group.

The middle-aged man frowned. "Of course. My lawyer drew it up."

"Well then, you should be familiar with it. The contract clearly states if any action or inaction harms the ship of Gamon Chaisit & Dusit Sitwat, that is a breach of contract. Therefore, the contract will be invalidated. And fines will be levied."

The younger men laughed, and someone added, "Yes, so? That means what he has done—"

"No, that means what you are proposing to do. Breaking up our ship violates our contract. I respectfully ask you to stop going down this path." There was nothing respectful in the tone Gamon used, but he simply didn't care. They needed to understand he'd fight them and would quit acting before he agreed to another actor replacing Dusit.

Several of the investors looked like fish out of water with their mouths open, gasping for air, or in this case words to defend their position. All the while the women and the older gentleman grinned.

Finally, the middle-aged guy found his words. "Dusit Sitwat is a disaster and needs to be removed."

"The fandom won't allow such a thing." Rose's voice was calm, the voice of reason.

The investor slapped his hand on the table again. "I don't care what the fans think."

The oldest investor grinned. "You should. Have you seen the fan mail these two have gotten when the second season hasn't even aired? The fans buy everything these actors sponsor. Y-series and their fandoms are not soft power—they are power."

"Do you understand their fans do community service in their names?" one of the young women added. "We… I mean, the fans are funding schools throughout some of the harshest neighborhoods."

Nothing anyone offered seemed to touch the negative investors. One reiterated, "Dusit Sitwat needs to be removed from this role. That is my final assessment."

Gamon tilted his head and studied the man as if he were nothing but a mosquito. "Your final assessment goes against my contract—our contracts. He has done nothing, and what you are proposing I do will harm our ship. And I am under contract not to do so, therefore I will not be working on this series unless my co-star is Dusit Sitwat."

A smiling investor spoke up. "Understood. So how can we combat this situation?"

Gamon liked how she included herself with the use of "we." She appeared ready for the more productive conversation of what the next move to resolve the issue should be.

Giving her a nod of thanks, Gamon looked over at Rose.

Rose replied, "Mr. Sitwat is working with the Kanawat agency's lawyer to resolve this matter."

The director added, "I put the production on hold a few days. It's at a place in the schedule where I'd normally give a few days' break anyway, so this delay won't affect production."

Rose cleared his throat. "Gamon will also do a live stream to address fandom concerns."

One of the pinch-faced younger investors asked, "Will Dusit—I mean Mr. Sitwat—be a part of that?"

After a quick glance at Gamon, Rose must have picked up the telegraphic message Gamon was sending him, because he said, "Maybe not the initial one, but he needs to be seen from now on."

"Agreed. I want people, especially our fans, to know how much I support Dusit. Without him, I would not have agreed to do this series." Gamon wanted to impress upon them how instrumental Dusit was in making this series happen at all, let alone making it a success.

"You'd really walk away from this series, even with the penalties?" One investor was trying to understand why Gamon would choose to do that. "Every clip that's been released of behind the scenes of this series has gone viral and has been made into memes."

"If you sink our ship, we go down together." Gamon put his sunglasses on and stood. "We understand each other, right?"

The youngest woman grinned with happiness. "Completely. This group understands and will not remove Dusit Sitwat from this series."

The other investors, whether with folded arms or smiling, all nodded their agreement.

Gamon didn't let them see him sag in relief. "Thank you for your time."

Rose gave him a small smile and inclined his head.

Turning on the heels of his designer boots, Gamon left the room. He glided through the hallways with purpose.

It wasn't until he got back in his car that he collapsed in relief.

His driver said nothing but seemed to assess him. Being discreet, he'd never ask what he wanted to know.

Gamon smiled at him and gave him a thumbs-up to answer his unasked questions.

The man grinned back and said, "Well done, sir."

Chapter 17

Charong sat down at the dining table next to Dusit with a meaningful look that said the interrogation would begin.

Dusit had been grateful no one had pressured him to talk last night, but this morning was another matter.

Lyric sat across from him with her feet on the chair and her arms wrapped around her knees. She frowned in his general direction but didn't appear to be registering him.

"Everything's almost ready." Chat hurried in and out of the kitchen carrying enough food to feed a large crew on the series set.

"What more could you have cooked?" Charong stared after her, shaking his head.

"Are you sure I can't help?" Dusit always hated feeling like he was being waited on, but Chat was a caretaker, and when under stress she clung fiercely to her role. Heaven help anyone who stood in her way of taking care of those around her with food. You did so at your own peril.

"I've got it," Chat called out as she glided through the door with two more dishes. She set the plates of food on the table and surveyed the spread. Smiling, she sat down.

Charong snapped his fingers in front of Lyric's face. "Feet down."

Lyric gave her brother a glare but did as requested. "So how did it happen?"

Chat waved her hands toward the table filled with dishes. "We are having breakfast now, and—"

"It's okay, Chat. I've never met her." Dusit stated that fact and hoped his chosen Bangkok family believed him.

"I knew it," Chat claimed. "None of her story made sense to me."

"No?" Dusit truly saw Chat as a sister, so he was relieved she didn't buy into the negative narrative floating around about him.

Chat grimaced. "I mean, you're Dusit Sitwat. Who would you have to force to have—I'm sorry."

Charong's mouth dropped open as he stared at her while Lyric nodded.

Dusit snorted. "Thank you, I think."

Her cheeks tinted pink, and Chat covered her mouth. "No, I mean…."

Charong reached across the table to squeeze her hand, which acted as the switch for her mouth, and then he stared at Dusit. "What I don't get is how anyone can simply say whatever they want about you."

"He's an actor. His private life isn't his own." Lyric summed up the curse of the entertainment industry.

"It's still not right. Real fans want their actors and idols happy. He deserves peace like everyone else." Chat claimed it as if it were his right.

Peace? Ha, that's the one thing he couldn't ever seem to have.

Chat put some vegetables on his plate. "Eat."

Dusit smiled. Gone was the fangirl and back in place was his adopted sister, so he ate the greens and smiled. She always cooked at least one of his favorite dishes at every meal he attended. "Delicious."

She straightened and grinned back. Her smirk said "of course it's great," but her lips said, "Family recipe."

He continued to eat, but then the curious stares began again. They couldn't help themselves. Maybe if he gave them more details. "I'm meeting with the lawyer today. She's trying to arrange a meeting with this person."

Chat gasped.

"You're going to meet her?" Lyric demanded, folding her arms over her chest. "That's probably why the idiot did it. To meet Dusit Sitwat. Don't be a twit and give her what she wanted."

What was the big deal? "I'd rather not, but I need to have a sit-down with her and her lawyer."

"Really?" Charong leaned toward him with a puzzled expression.

"If my lawyer thinks it's a good idea, why wouldn't I?" Dusit trusted Rose's agency lawyer wouldn't steer him wrong.

Charong got confirmation from his sisters, so he said what they had been thinking. "This person is harming you. She's hurting your reputation."

Dusit sighed. That was all true. "I know. Honestly, I want to know why. You know? Why me? Why would she say this about me?"

Wiping a hand over his face, Charong said, "Last night she posted a picture of her ultrasound, and—"

"No," Lyric said. "The fandom provided evidence that the picture was altered using Photoshop."

Charong added, "Your fans must be crazy talented with all things technical."

"Most fandoms have fans that are internet savvy, computer literate, and would make fine detectives," Dusit corrected.

"There's no excuse for what she is doing, but my guess is she's young." Chat wrung her hands.

"That's what Rose believes too." Dusit wasn't sure, but he was stuck on not understanding why. Young or old, why would she do this to him? He checked the time. "I'll be meeting with my lawyer soon."

Charong leaned toward him. "Who is covering the cost of that?"

"My agency has a lawyer on retainer." Dusit hoped it wouldn't cost him any money, but if it did, it did. No choice in it.

"Good. But if you need money or something, let me know." Charong slapped him on the back.

"There's no need." Dusit could handle what came his way. He always had.

Charong grabbed his arm for a moment and made sure Dusit looked him in the eyes. "That's fine. But if there is, we've got money saved for family emergencies."

For family. Dusit loved his mother and father, but he could only get home once or twice a year. So being part of this family was….

Dusit swallowed and blinked quickly. "Thank you. Truly."

"Don't mention it." Lyric tossed a bun at him, which hit his nose and fell onto the plate.

"Lyric!" Both Chat and Charong shouted.

Picking up the bun, Dusit saluted her with the baked good and took a bite. "Thanks."

"Anytime." She clearly knew what he was thanking her for—derailing him from getting overly emotional. Lyric was not one for sentimentality.

When the meal was winding down, he stood and grabbed his plate. "Thank you for accepting me into your family."

Charong slapped him on the back again as he passed by.

"Ow," Dusit pretended to be injured and deliberately stumbled toward the kitchen.

Chat swatted Charong in the head. "Don't hurt him. He's been through enough."

Dusit mouthed "Ha, ha, ha" at Charong but then widened his eyes to the realm of innocence as he smiled at Chat. "Thank you for protecting me."

Charong growled and then sighed.

"You're no match for your sisters." Dusit carried his dish to the sink and rinsed it.

Charong followed him into the kitchen. "But then neither are you."

Dusit pointed out their reality. "That's why I never go up against them. It's easier to do what they want me to."

Lyric waltzed behind them. "And that's why Dusit is my favorite brother."

Chat waved them all out of the kitchen. "Lyric, go to school. Char, rest up, the bar is open late tonight. And Dusit, good luck today."

"Thanks." He had a feeling he'd need it. A text from Gamon had an emoji of a thumb pointed up, along with *Achara is taking me shopping.*

He hoped everything went okay. But he knew better than to question Gamon at that time, so he sent a smiley face emoji with hearts for eyes and *Have fun. I'll see you later.*

ROSE MET Dusit outside of Charong's in a car. He held the door for him and then slid in beside him. "The lawyer's office is thirty minutes away without traffic, but even so we will get there in plenty of time."

Lacking patience, Dusit asked, "Did the meeting with the investors go well? How is Gamon… really?"

"He's great, and he did an excellent job. Even the best Y-series screenwriters couldn't have written a better character for him. He arrived dripping in every luxury brand he represented and whom we are working with right now. His star power as he reminded them of your loyal fans and all the money he could mean to them was off the charts. When pressed he let them know if they didn't make the right decision, he'd happily go down with your ship and walk away from everything."

Guilt started to wash over Dusit. "I'm sorry he had to do that. I never wanted—"

"Don't, man. You'd have done the same for him." Rose tapped him on the knee. "Right now, your job is to deal with this nonsense so you can get back to work."

"Yeah." Dusit stared out of the window, watching the buildings go by until the traffic ground the car to a halt. He sighed.

Rose glanced at him. "New suit?"

Peering down at his dark blue suit and the flashy tie more fit for his character than for him, Dusit said, "Gamon packed for me."

"Looks good on you, and if this clothing line wants you to be their spokesperson, I can investigate it for you. You'd look great on the runway. I hear their fashion shows are well attended."

"Me? A model?"

Rose laughed. "Yes. You. A. Model."

Dusit didn't know if he was kidding or not.

"Lots of designer brands do crossovers with actors and idols. It would be good exposure for you and could open future opportunities."

"So lots of freebies?" Dusit wasn't much for fancy clothing, but he did like to dress for Gamon. Did Gamon still like to do the couple-clothing matchy-matchy thing? This time around, he'd do it without complaint.

Rose chuckled. "Yes, and from working with these brands, I know they typically give their brand ambassadors the clothes they wear to walk the runway."

"Interesting." Dusit shrugged. He'd never understood the fascination with the promenade up and down the catwalk.

"Their show is in Paris," Rose added.

"Paris? Well, it would be nice to see where Gamon had lived." The city of lights was more accepting, so Dusit could easily imagine holding Gamon's hand as they strolled through the streets and over the bridges of the Seine.

Rose seemed to miss nothing. "So how things going with you two?"

Dusit couldn't help but smile. "Good." But then frowning, he added, "Minus one scandal after another."

"We will get through this. The two of you are going to get through this, and it will become one single line in Wikipedia."

Rose's confidence might be misplaced. Dusit didn't know, but he hoped Rose was right.

Returning to the original topic, Rose said, "I'll reach out to the brand to gauge their interest. We are here." Then he got out of the car.

ENTERING THE production house's office building through the garage would have been fine, except for the three actresses getting into their cars who whispered furiously while scowling at Dusit and the security guard who gave him a suspicious stare.

Rose cleared his throat. "Good morning."

The security guard stopped glaring. "Oh, um, good morning, Mr. Thongsi." He begrudgingly added, "Mr. Sitwat."

Dusit offered a bright smile, as if someone hadn't spread vicious rumors about him.

As they got into the elevator, Dusit couldn't help but to acknowledge, "Guilty until proven innocent."

Shaking his head, Rose said, "You know how the verdict of public opinion works and how fast attitudes can go from negative to positive in one well-worded tweet."

Rose held the meeting room door open for Dusit to step through and then followed.

Sitting at the table were his lawyer and two other people he didn't know. The one with her head down seemed young and scared. She appeared to be in her mid-teens.

Everyone stood and exchanged greetings.

Dusit's lawyer said, "Mr. Sitwat, it's very nice to meet you. Thank you for foregoing our initial private meeting. Because of this situation, Ms. Boome's lawyer wanted to meet immediately to rectify this issue."

He bobbed his head, wanting to end this situation as soon as he could.

Everyone returned to their seats as he and Rose sat.

Even though he already knew, he asked, "And Ms. Boome is....?"

His lawyer glared at the young woman. "Ms. Boome is the person who decided accusing you of rape was the best way to meet you."

The young woman jumped in her seat and shook her head. "No, I'm sorry. I didn't mean for it to sound like that. I didn't mean to write those posts about... you."

Rose pointed out, "But you did."

"I tried to take it back and to stop, but people kept questioning me and...." She dropped her head into her hands. Her body trembled until her lawyer handed her a packet of tissues.

The anger Dusit felt dissipated around the edges. She really was only an inexperienced kid. Though his curiosity became stronger. "Why did you do it?"

It was a simple enough question.

She glanced at him, tears cascading down her cheeks. "I... I wanted to meet you, and then, well... it kept getting worse."

Dusit's lawyer adjusted her suit jacket. "Because you kept making it worse, Ms. Boome. Isn't that correct?"

"I really wanted to meet him." Shaking her head, she sniffled into the tissue she clutched. "I didn't mean to.... But I didn't know what to do."

His lawyer, with way too much snark, asked, "Have you never heard of fan meets?"

Ms. Boome's lawyer cleared his throat. "Dara—Ms. Boome—didn't mean for it to get out of hand. It is a transgression of youthful exuberance."

Dusit's lawyer pinned him with a look. "Youthful exuberance?"

"Yes, she was under the misguided impression it was a way to meet Mr. Sitwat."

His lawyer focused on straightening the pad of paper in front of her. Then she picked up her silver pen and twirled it through her fingers. She stopped and stared at Ms. Boome.

"Well, Ms. Boome, you are meeting Dusit Sitwat after you slandered him, causing him and his reputation great harm. You are such a fan you put the filming of his current series on hold. Investors are threatening to pull their funding."

"I'm sorry. I really am." She put her hand to over her heart. "I didn't mean to hurt you."

His lawyer took a law book out of her bag. She pointed at the large volume. "Under section 326-333 of the Thai Criminal Code, we can not only sue for damages, but you can go to prison."

Ms. Boome's hand covered her mouth as she gasped, and more tears dripped down her cheeks. "I could go to jail?"

Dusit gave his lawyer a time-to-dial-back look.

"I'm Rose Thongsi, Mr. Sitwat's agent," Rose said.

She gave him a starstruck look until her lawyer tapped the table in front of her. "Yes, I know who you are."

Rose leaned forward toward Ms. Boome. "Are you pregnant?"

Ms. Boome sat back as if she'd been pushed and frowned. "No." She wiped her face with a tissue.

Dusit's lawyer's eyes narrowed in on her. "Did you Photoshop the ultrasound picture?"

"Yeah," Ms. Boome whimpered. "Please don't send me to jail."

Ms. Boome's lawyer interjected, "She will publicly retract her statement and apologize on all social media platforms until Mr. Sitwat and the Kanawat agency are satisfied."

Shaking his head, Rose sighed. "A lot of damage has been done to my client."

"I'm really sorry." Ms. Boome finally looked at Dusit. "I'll do whatever you want me to do, but don't send me to jail."

Dusit followed the instructions to remain silent, but he couldn't help feeling sympathy for her. She was just a kid.

His lawyer stood. "I'd like to discuss this with my client."

"Please review the retraction and apology Ms. Boome has written." Her lawyer handed over two pages to Dusit's lawyer.

Once they were in another conference room, Dusit didn't sit down with his lawyer and Rose. He paced back and forth.

Rose and his lawyer read the retraction twice.

His lawyer said, "I'd add this." She handed Rose a page from her briefcase.

Rose scanned the page and then said, "Agreed, connecting this situation and the production house's need to believe victims in the cases of rape frames everything in terms of how they reacted. It firmly places Dusit as the victim. And points out how generous he is by not prosecuting her. The wording also protects our agency and the production house from the criticism of not taking care of our actors."

She sighed. "Yes, I'm aware fans are quite protective, and this neutralizes any possibility that they might attack the agency or production house."

Dusit rubbed his hands together and stopped pacing. "I don't want to send her to jail. I don't even want to sue her. I need to get this behind me."

The lawyer slid the pages in front of a chair. "Read the retraction and apology, along with our additions."

Dusit sat down and read the letter. Ms. Boome's words got straight to the point and admitted she lied. She stated she had never met Dusit in Phuket or anywhere else. She confessed she wasn't pregnant and had simply wanted to meet him.

Raking his fingers through his hair, Dusit knew this wouldn't be over that simply. "Some people will say I paid her off."

His lawyer sighed. "Yes, but most will understand you were the victim of vicious slander."

He longed for this to be over and to get back to Gamon.

She twirled her pen between her fingers again. “I still think we should prosecute this case.”

Glancing over at Rose, Dusit knew he would implement what he wanted if it wasn’t harming anyone else’s reputation. “I don’t want to make an example out of the kid.”

The lawyer exhaled hard and tilted her head. “But we don’t want the next teenager who watches too many dramas and *lakorns* to cast themselves in the lead role of the fantasy they’ve written in their head.”

Rose tapped his fingertips on the table. “I agree with you. We need to discourage other fans from pulling the same stunt, but I must weigh the optics of Dusit going after a teenager for a stupid choice.”

She folded her arms over her chest and exhaled hard. “I represent Kanawat’s agency and your actors, but you have the final say on litigation.”

“Don’t go after her.” Dusit didn’t want to ruin her life with prison and debt.

Nodding his head, Rose added, “Let’s get her posts up. The agency will drop a second memo of support for Dusit. We also will include the fact that we have cleared your name. We will blast her apology and admission of guilt, along with the news of her not being pregnant, across all social media platforms.”

Dusit was all about moving forward, because that brought him closer to being with Gamon. “What should I be doing?”

“The agency has drafted several posts for you. In a couple of hours, you can post one every twenty minutes. I’ll email them to you. We will try to get you trending. Then Gamon will do a live later.”

“It’s not exactly what I wanted to trend for, but #DusitNeverMetHer sounds good.” No one laughed. Everyone was already on their phone executing the plan.

“And it’s #DusitIsInnocent.” The lawyer stood. “I apologize for meeting under such circumstances, but I’m glad we can rectify the situation. I’m sure your agency will monitor her future posts to ensure this is the last of Ms. Boome’s nonsense.”

Rose talked directly to the lawyer. “We let the kid sweat enough. Let’s go back in there.”

"Should I go back into the room with you?" Dusit didn't want to see her again, but he'd follow the lawyer's advice.

"No. Again, we don't want to reinforce this behavior for how to meet a BL actor." She left the room.

Dusit jumped to his feet. "I can't wait to go home."

"Um, could you wait one more night before you do?" Rose's expression said he knew what he was asking. "Let's get public opinion turned around. Then tomorrow you and Gamon can do a live stream from the condo."

"If I stay at Charong's again tonight, any issue if Gamon visits?" Dusit couldn't help but to push the boundaries when it came to Gamon.

Rose chuckled. "Could I stop you?"

Dusit smirked at him. "Nope. We will keep it quiet. I promise."

DUSIT LET Gamon in.

Gamon glanced around. "Where is everyone?"

Grinning as he led Gamon to the guest bedroom, he said, "Chat had a late study group. Lyric is sleeping at her friend's house, and Charong works late tonight."

"It's only us?"

"Yup." Dusit shut the door.

Dusit yanked off his restricting tie and started to unbutton his dress shirt. "Chat filled the refrigerator with meals to reheat. You hungry?"

"Yes." Gamon stared at him.

Dusit didn't feel like food, but he'd get whatever Gamon wanted. "What are you hungry for?"

"You." Gamon's voice was husky. His eyes narrowed in on Dusit.

As he pulled his shirt off roughly, Dusit felt the fabric give and tear. He tossed it to the floor and smiled. "Here I am."

Gamon made to tear off his jacket, but the cuffs got caught on his wrists. He flapped his arms as if he were a flightless bird trying to fly. "Help, please."

They'd only been apart for one night, but Gamon's desperation bled through his uncoordinated movements. He jerked this way and that, trying to defeat the demon coat.

Dusit chuckled. "Stop moving."

"I'm trying." Gamon pouted and kept squirming around.

Finally Dusit stilled him and wrangled the jacket off of him. "There."

Gamon's hands lacked their usual grace, so Dusit took over. "I'll get your shirt off."

"Thanks." Gamon let Dusit take care of him… which was all Dusit wanted.

Mm, Dusit needed to possess all of Gamon. He wanted to tease him until Gamon could think of nothing but Dusit giving him an orgasm. But these types of thoughts were going to make him lose control way quicker than he'd like.

Dusit needed to focus on something and slow Gamon down or this would be over before they started. "You want to play a game?"

Gamon pulled his mouth off Dusit's neck long enough to mutter, "What game?"

"I promised Rose we'd be quiet," Dusit whispered, sharing Rose's request.

Looking toward the door, Gamon said, "Okay, but you said no one was home."

"But let's pretend we're not alone."

Gamon gasped, and Dusit knew he had tapped into one of Gamon's turn-ons.

He teased, "What if we were on set and an intern heard your needy moans?"

Gamon took a quick inhale and put his hand over his mouth, his cheeks turning pink. "No, I—"

"Or you begging to come as an investor listens to the wonderful sounds you make." Dusit slowed his words and dropped his voice to a deeper range.

"I… um, I—"

"I'm going to stroke you once for every two strokes you give me, and you are going to try to be silent." Adjusting his pants, Dusit was pleased he was back in control—at least of Gamon.

Gamon stared at him with dreamy eyes that said he would agree to anything Dusit wanted. Nearly breathless, he asked, "And how do you win?"

"Whoever doesn't come wins?" Like either of them wouldn't finish the other off.

Gamon gave him a small smile, his cheeks tinting to a darker shade of pink. To be so experienced but still blushing was both endearing and hot. Dusit didn't know how that was possible, but it was Gamon. "Unless it's a ruined orgasm, I'd think it's who *does* come who wins."

Aroused as he was, Dusit couldn't argue with that logic. "Isn't the idea of waiting and edging exciting too?"

A strangled "Yes" came out of Gamon's mouth.

Got him. Dusit licked his lips and asked, "You want to play… my way?"

Gamon unzipped Dusit's pants and fished out his cock, which was happy to report for duty. He licked his hand and without even a kiss, stroked Dusit's cock twice.

Dusit caressed the length of Gamon's shaft, protected by his pants, and glided a single finger down Gamon's zipper.

"That doesn't count." Gamon frowned.

"I love how you get so desperate." Dusit didn't hold back the smirk, because Gamon was too cute. He unzipped Gamon's pants and swirled a finger around Gamon's wet tip.

Shivering, Gamon gasped and closed his eyes. "I can't seem to control myself."

"That's why I'll keep you in check." Dusit nuzzled Gamon's neck, sinking his teeth in and gently sucking.

Gamon shoved his own pants past his ass and thrust his freed cock through Dusit's fist. He moaned, "Mm."

"Shh, otherwise the crew might hear you. It's late, but there's always someone around." Dusit continued to pretend they were at the studio.

The tremble that rolled through Gamon spoke volumes. He huffed out a breath of frustration. "Right. Forgot." He stroked Dusit twice.

Taking his time, Dusit let Gamon's foreskin ride up his shaft right over the tip on the upstroke and then slowly slid his fist all the way down.

Opening his mouth, Gamon gave a soft moan.

"Do you want people to hear you? You want everyone to know the graceful, composed Gamon Chaisit loves to be teased and touched?" Dusit taunted while giving him a quick stroke.

Gamon shivered. "Only by you."

"I think you like it. I think you want people to know all you want. All you need is me to keep stroking you off."

Gamon breathed out a "No." He stroked Dusit twice at exactly the right speed.

Dusit closed his eyes; if he saw Gamon bite his lower lip it would be game over. And this pretend play was too good not to continue. He opened his eyes and gave Gamon a tauntingly slow twist stroke.

Gamon's toes cracked. He must have curled them. "So good," he panted as he pushed Dusit's pants down and stroked his cock twice.

Trying not to thrust, Dusit forced his attention onto Gamon. "You want me to give you your stroke?"

"Please." Gamon angled his hips as to give Dusit more space to work.

Dusit licked his palm with long, wet, slow licks while he stared into Gamon's enormous eyes.

Gamon moaned. "Dusit, please."

He rubbed Gamon's erection. "But what if you get noisy?"

"I won't." Gamon made promises there was no way he could keep.

"If you get loud, the crew will know what we're doing in here. Maybe I should stop." Dusit started to move his hand away.

Gamon grabbed his arm and held it. "No. No, you shouldn't stop, please."

Biting back his smile, Dusit whispered. “They will know that I’ve got my fist wrapped around you and I’m going to make you come… eventually.”

Gamon gave a shaky inhale and squeezed his eyes shut. As he thrust, he asked, “Eventually?”

“Yes, eventually you’ll come. Though I’m not sure when that will be.” Dusit was into controlling Gamon more than he realized.

Gamon spit in his palm and caressed the wetness along Dusit’s shaft.

Pressing his lips together, Dusit avoided making a sound, but it was touch and go, because this game of “don’t come” was so delicious. He wanted to have it all at once, but he wanted to savor the moment.

Dusit gave Gamon a slow stroke, and Gamon shuddered. He was getting close to his limit, and remaining standing was taking its toll.

How he wanted to throw Gamon down on the bed and make him lose total control, but he didn’t. Gamon always craved mental play along with the physical.

Dusit remained still. His hand around Gamon’s shaft tightened, and he felt the dick throb with need.

“Please.” Gamon shifted.

Dusit shouldn’t love Gamon’s desperation as much as he did, but there was something about being longed for on such a base level that triggered things in him. “Beg.”

Gamon squeezed his eyes shut and pressed his lips together.

Dusit startled him with an unexpected stroke.

A strangled moan sounded. “Dusit, please make me come.”

Sliding his fist along Gamon’s shaft at an achingly slow pace teased them both. “What, you want me to make you come?”

Gamon’s mouth dropped open, but nothing came out but a gasp.

“I didn’t hear you.” Dusit was dying, but Gamon was way into this game.

“Want you to make me come.” Gamon articulated his words between pants.

“Do you?” Dusit gasped and continued stroking him, forgetting all about one stroke for two.

"Please, Dusit." Gamon rested his nonstroking hand on Dusit's shoulder. In a silent plea, he arched his lower half toward Dusit.

Hard to say no to that. Dusit instructed, "Faster."

Gamon moaned and frowned. "You said faster. So why are you going slower on me?"

"Are you close?" Dusit's control over Gamon excited him.

"Yes. You know I am." Gamon was trembling.

"I love edging you… forcing you to savor… to need… to want me." The longing to come was doing Dusit in.

Whimpering, Gamon exhaled hard. "I do. I crave you."

Dusit was getting so close.

Gamon trembled.

"Come with me." Dusit stroked Gamon at the speed that always brought him off.

Gamon threw his head back and hissed out a "Yes" as he came.

Ribbons of come hit Dusit, arousing him to the point of no return. He'd done that. He'd made Gamon lose control.

But Gamon didn't stop jerking Dusit off as he exploded, so Dusit came too.

Dusit squeezed a last drop out of Gamon as Gamon finished him with perfection. He rested his forehead on Gamon's shoulder and tried to catch his breath.

"Well, that was spectacular," Dusit said. The orgasm, the control, Gamon's surrender to him—all of it.

"Truly a miracle." Gamon chuckled.

"Miracle?" That might be an understatement.

"Yup, but I was quiet." Remaining naked, Gamon strutted to the bathroom like he was on a runway, but then he turned. "Coming?"

"I just did, but we can try again…." Dusit hurried to follow him.

CHAPTER 18

GAMON DID not want to get out of bed. He snuggled against Dusit's warm body.

"Mm," Dusit nuzzled his neck.

Their alarm went off.

Leave it to Dusit to be with it enough after last night's second time to set a clock. As he turned off the phone alarm, Gamon wasn't as grateful as he should have been. "We should get up."

Dusit grinned. "Looks like you already are."

"True, but I meant out of bed." Gamon constantly got hard or was getting hard whenever he was around Dusit. It was no longer embarrassing, simply a fact. Should he be concerned about this much lack of blood flow to his brain? "We should shower."

"Great idea." Dusit jumped out of bed, caressed Gamon, and then led him to the bathroom.

Gamon had meant alone, but… he would not argue.

AFTER QUITE the satisfying shower, Gamon sat at the dining room table. Each of Dusit's family by choice surveyed him.

Dusit put some omelet on Gamon's rice. "So—"

Chat leaned over and whispered, "Is everything taken care of?"

"If you mean—"

"Yes, she means the stalker fan," Lyric added for clarity.

"Didn't Charong forward the text message?" Dusit glanced over at Charong, who ducked his head.

Chat threw eye daggers at Charong while Lyric swatted him.

"I'm sorry, it got busy. I got slammed." Charong steepled his hands in apology as if formalizing the sorry would get him forgiveness.

Lyric folded her arms. "Why didn't you use the family chat?"

Gamon's "Aw" escaped as he placed his hand over his heart. He was so happy that Dusit had found people who supported him here in Bangkok.

Chat smiled. "Dusit should share our contact information with you in case you need to get in touch with us."

Why would he—

Continuing, Chat added, "If you need anything, let us know. You are Dusit's person, so you are ours as well."

Lyric put her hands in front of her as if to gentle his nerves. "In a nonstalker, noninsane way."

"Thank you." Gamon blinked his eyes quickly because letting tears escape would make Dusit concerned. "I'm honored."

Conversation flowed between the siblings as Dusit shared the details.

Gamon allowed himself to sink into the feelings of belonging and family, wishing he had a different family.... Then he looked around the table and realized his wish had been granted.

Dusit pressed his knee against Gamon's. "The driver texted. He's outside."

Gamon tried to take his plate and glass into the kitchen, but Chat stopped him and took the items from him. "You go. Take care of yourself and Dusit."

He knew enough not to fight as an unfamiliar tightness clenched his heart. "Thank you, I will."

Chat tapped Dusit on the shoulder. "I know you have to film right through until late tonight, but when are you and Gamon coming for dinner?"

"No pressure. We know you're super busy." Charong gathered the plates.

Dusit grinned. "Let me text you next week's schedule so we can figure something out."

Family that you wanted to spend time with… what a revolutionary concept.

THE ACTOR Gamon was doing a scene with stopped. There was screaming in the hallway, and the words were becoming louder… and more recognizable.

Gamon groaned. To the actor, crew, and Prem he said, "I'm sorry. I need to—"

Prem waved him off. "Cut. Set up in five."

The sharp tone of his mother's voice cut through the intern who was attempting to keep her away. Her scathing voice echoed off the walls. "I don't care that he's busy. I may not be his manager, but I'm still his mother."

He didn't want to see her, but she didn't give him a choice.

Why did she think this was okay?

Stalking over to her, he managed his anger as he focused on putting one foot in front of the other. "Please lower your voice."

She stopped for a moment, and a small smile stole across her face. Then she growled, "I will not lower my voice. You need me loud so perhaps you can hear me."

The crew and other actors stopped, openly staring as they pretended to do things but didn't leave the area.

"Mother, please come with me." Gamon hurried down the hallway and into a small conference room. He didn't look back or wait for her.

Would she follow him?

She did and sat down at the table.

He shut the door and leaned against it, not saying a word.

Her usual censure-filled stare didn't force the words out of his mouth. She'd taught him the person who speaks first has less power in the negotiation.

Folding his arms over his chest, he narrowed his gaze on her and waited.

When two long minutes had passed, he shrugged and reached for the doorknob.

"Stop. Where are you going?" She sounded panicked.

"Leaving. You aren't saying anything, and I'm at work." Did he need to point out the obvious?

She waved her hands about and said, "I don't like this at all."

He wanted to ask why he should care, but instead he asked, "What don't you like?"

"You."

His bitter laughter barked out. No kidding.

"No, I don't mean you. I mean this." She gestured to him. "This aggression doesn't suit you at all."

He was hurt, but he couldn't continue tolerating her gaslighting. "I'm not being aggressive, but I'm no longer going to tolerate you treating me poorly."

"I'm your mother." She held her title like a shield.

"And?"

She gasped and put a hand over her heart as she sputtered, "You can't ignore me."

"I'm not ignoring you. I'm simply not going to see you until you stop being abusive."

"I'm not abusive. I just—don't like that boy at all. Even if you are gay, why must you choose him? He's so… so base."

Gamon pushed his hands into his pockets. He shared a truth that had been true for years. "I love Dusit."

"But look at all the trouble he's in." She waved her cell phone around as if it were evidence in a court case.

Shaking his head, Gamon reminded her, "He's not in any trouble."

"If anyone finds out that your relationship is more than fan service, your career is over," she warned him.

He didn't care. If he had a choice between career and Dusit, hands down the decision wouldn't take long. Dusit was always the answer, and the person he'd side with. "And?"

Her mouth dropped open. There was satisfaction in leaving her speechless. "What do you mean and? Your career—"

"Dusit is more important to me than anything."

Her hand went to her head as she gasped. "How can you say that?"

"It's true. He is everything to me." Serenity came over him. It was a truth he could blanket himself in.

"But I'm your mother." Her voice was rising and entering the indignant range.

"Then you need to act like it." Gamon sighed. He wished that felt better to say.

"What's that supposed to mean?" In the past, the tone she used would have cut him in two.

This time… he wasn't having it.

He gestured for her to lower her voice. "You can start by respecting my need for space. When I'm able to, I will reach out and—"

She put her hand on her hip. "When is that going to be?"

"We need time apart." Gamon needed to be in a place where he could set and keep boundaries with her.

"Is that what he told you to do?" The word "he" came out of her mouth like poison.

"Dusit would never say that… even after everything you did to us. But I need some time. I'm furious."

"I only did what I thought was best." She pouted. Ah, denying and attacking him hadn't worked, so now she was donning the cloak of victimhood, and she would be throwing blame on him any minute.

"You threw away the only person I'll ever love. You made me feel hopeless and alone… for years." It had been a horrible time for him.

She gave him her look of unappreciated sacrifice. "You weren't alone. I was with you every step of the way."

Why was he debating this? This wasn't an argument; this was a restatement of boundaries. "Please do not show up at the set. And don't drop by the condo. I'm going to inform security in both places you do not have permission to approach me."

He witnessed a mix of emotions cross her face. First there was surprise. His mother didn't think he had this in him. Was that a flash of pride? He wasn't sure because her expression changed to sadness, and her body slumped for a moment before she morphed into anger.

"You will regret this." She stood rigidly.

He opened the door and held it for her.

Her heels clicked down the hallway.

Sagging against the doorframe, he sighed. Why was setting and keeping boundaries so hard? Couldn't she be like the loving mothers from TV dramas?

He smelled coffee and glanced down at the cup that appeared under his nose. "Thank you."

"Do you need a hug?" Leave it to Dusit to know what he needed.

"Yeah." He eased into Dusit's arms and felt safe as they tightened around him—allowing him to lean into Dusit for a moment.

"Was it difficult?" Dusit asked.

He rested his head on Dusit's shoulder. "Did someone tell you she was here, or did you hear her?"

"The intern. I think their name was Laurie." Dusit released him and handed him the coffee.

Gamon took the cup and sipped. The coffee was prepared exactly as he liked it. "Ah, perfect. Thanks."

"You feel okay?"

"Putting boundaries on people is hard for me, but I can't let her walk on me… or you. What she did and how she continues to act has consequences."

Dusit frowned. "But she's your mother."

Gamon stepped back and used his word of the day. "And?"

"I mean…." Dusit's words ground to a halt.

"What she took from me—from us—that time cannot be replaced. I refuse to let her continue to mistreat me." Her lashing out at Dusit is what woke him from his place of tolerance.

Dusit sighed. "You're right. I'm here however you need to me to be."

Gamon needed a subject change.

Sliding a hand into Dusit's back pocket, he teased, "I'll give you specific details about those needs a bit later."

Understanding, Dusit smiled bigger than usual to allow Gamon the shift in topics. "Deal."

DUSIT READ a question from their live stream without filtering. "Why are Gamon's lips swollen compared to the pictures he posted this morning?"

Looking shocked, Gamon parted his apparently damaged lips, but nothing came out.

Dusit gave the camera one of his sexy smiles that always melted Gamon. "We shot some scenes and… well, you know my character adores kissing his character's mouth."

Dusit appeared to be having fun playing coy.

Relaxing a bit, Gamon smiled at him and then at the camera. "My character is rather irresistible."

Dusit stared at the screen, pressed his lips together, and stated, "And my character isn't known for resisting."

Despite their efforts to shift the narrative, the only comments scrolling past were about Dusit's lips wearing Gamon's lip gloss.

Oops!

Dusit cleared his throat. "We haven't even eaten or taken off all our makeup yet."

True, but Dusit was wearing Gamon's gloss because he'd kept on kissing him long after filming stopped.

Gamon did his best to deflect. He held up the bottle of makeup remover he was planning on using before Dusit's lips distracted him. "We are hoping this skin-care company reaches out about a collaboration. I love their line."

What was he doing? Was this Product Placement 101 or Advanced Fan Redirection?

Dusit added, "It's a product that doesn't irritate my skin, and it smells nice."

Gamon opened the bottle and passed it under Dusit's nose, then his own. "Mm, yum. The remover smells floral but very fresh."

Still, some commenters continued to play detectives—their questions focused on Gamon's mouth and kissing.

Finally Gamon found a question he wanted to answer. "When will filming wrap up?"

"The director says next week or the week after."

Dusit rubbed his hands together. "Yes, and then we will do fan meets. Gamon, this one is asking about your music."

"I recorded a couple of songs for the last episode, so they haven't been released yet." Gamon remembered he needed to speak to someone about when they wanted him in the studio for any redos. He automatically kept a smile on his face, but he was ready for this live to be over. "We have some early scenes in the morning. So we should end this here."

Dusit waved. "Rest well. Behave or not… until next time."

Gamon blew a kiss at the screen and ended the live. He fell back onto the couch.

"How bad do you think that was?" Dusit slipped an arm around his shoulders.

Probably bad. "Let's not jump to conclusions until we check out the other social platforms."

One peek made Gamon's heart sink. "I shouldn't have posted those pictures this morning. I should know better. No same-day photos."

Dusit pulled out his phone, and after scrolling a bit, he said, "I swear if I ever need to find someone, I'm calling on our fans. They are the best detectives."

"If the police put some of these fans on cold cases, they could surely close them."

"Why do they care?" Dusit asked a question he had to know the answer to.

"You know why. Some people would be thrilled to confirm our relationship outside of our working relationship, while others want to condemn us for not putting the fandom first or because they are homophobic."

Dusit chuckled and showed him his cell phone screen. "Look at this post. The fan is comparing not only today's pictures but also the first series, and our lips are blown up."

Gamon looked down. They were going to be found out. "We can say we were workshopping a scene or doing fan service."

"Fan service is being done less and less. Plus we haven't been around any fans to pretend to be our characters," Dusit said, pointing out the quick turn the industry was making on forcing working partners to pretend they were together beyond the series. The international audience shouted until investors heard them, and the production houses did too.

Gamon felt the weight of not wanting to bomb Dusit's acting career. "I know, but I want to navigate this properly."

"Want to call Rose?"

Dusit always had good ideas when Gamon couldn't see beyond his panic. "I think that makes sense."

Rose answered on the first ring. "Been expecting you to call. Gamon is also there?"

"Right next to me."

"I figured. Nok caught the live and told me about the comments."

"They are going to find out." Gamon accepted that, though he didn't want to create a stressful situation that pushed Dusit back to drinking. "But I don't want it to ruin Dusit's career."

"My career? What about yours?" Dusit's need to protect was triggered.

Gamon wanted to stay on track but needed to backpedal to keep Dusit's head in the game. "Rose, if it were to come out that we are together in real life, how would that affect our careers?"

Rose waited a moment before answering. "You two have a strong international fan base that is very gay-relationship friendly. To the point where some would prefer only queer people play these types of roles."

"That's true. Gamon speaking in English and French has really helped make more fans feel connected to us."

Gamon remembered the praise and adoration Dusit had expressed for his learning to say several things in English and French. "The fans also loved you for practicing greetings."

Rose cleared his throat. "*Don't Break My Heart* won't have a third season because the plan is to stop at two seasons. Your fanbase reception will direct how the investors feel about casting you in more series."

A bit of confidence wove through Gamon. "Having talked to a bunch of the daughters of *Don't Break My Heart*'s current investors, I think we can still get support… if we wanted that."

"Also while coming out might turn some people away, same-sex marriage is legal in Thailand," Rose added with a definitive nod. "Outing yourselves might bring in investors we never had. Kanawat calls that possibility the honesty bump."

Dusit patted Gamon's knee. "See, it's not that bad."

"I think you two need to think about it and what it could mean. You have several modeling gigs and three ironclad brand-ambassador deals." Rose, having experienced what they were going through, made sure that if their orientation came out, the company could not drop them without paying a huge fine.

"That's good."

"Meanwhile, let me talk to the production house and some investors. You might find yourself very much in demand." Rose frowned. "But we still need to be prepared for things to not go how we want."

Why had he been so stupid? He'd been so happy. "I'm sorry, Rose. I know I shouldn't have—"

"Hey, it is what it is. I understand how tough it is to be under a microscope all the time. We need to navigate this situation." Rose smiled into the screen as if he were trying to give Gamon confidence. "I'll be in touch soon. Try not to obsess. Night."

Sighing, Gamon acknowledged, "That was for my benefit."

Dusit hugged him for a moment. "It's going to work out."

"What if it doesn't? What if everything is ruined?" Gamon frowned. Images of their careers crashing flashed through his mind. Dusit had been through so much all ready.

After grabbing Gamon's hand, Dusit kissed his knuckles. "It's already worked out as far as I'm concerned. We are in this together, and whether we continue acting or singing or raise chickens, we won."

Leave it to Dusit to put things in perspective. Gamon snorted and then raised his hand. "Do these hands look like they should farm chickens?"

"No, not at all. Although I know of a job your hands are great for…." Dusit gave him a cocky smirk as he toyed with the zipper on his jeans.

"Do you? When should I start?" Gamon grinned. "I guess you're not going to let me obsess, huh?"

Dusit unzipped his jeans. "Nope, and if I have to use my body to remind you what's important, it's a sacrifice I will gladly make."

Gamon shoved Dusit's jeans and boxers to his knees. "Are your hands good at this job too?"

"Probably not as good as yours, but my mouth is." Dusit undid Gamon's pants.

There was definitely no brain space left for negative thoughts or worry.

THE NEXT day, Achara circled Dusit, heels clicking.

Dusit was deep in his character and struggled against the ropes that secured him to a chair.

Gamon had tried to keep himself in check while he was lashing Dusit to the chair, but he failed. He couldn't maintain a steady inhale and exhale—each breath was shaky—and his hands trembled. Gamon shouldn't be this excited. This was only a scene… from his wishes-and-dreams list!

Achara cleared her throat, and Gamon glanced away from Dusit. She smirked at him. "Somehow, I don't think we need to workshop this kidnapping rescue. But let's please the director."

Gamon tried not to react, but how he wished he hadn't gotten tipsy with her that time and confessed how much bondage turned him on. Or that his number-one fantasy was Dusit tied down. He avoided her too-pleased-with-herself smile and busied himself rechecking the ropes.

Dusit cursed his imaginary captor and pulled against the ropes. His frustration and anger were on point.

The more he struggled, the hotter Gamon became. This was neither the time nor the place, but there was something about having control over Dusit that gave him a charge. The ultimate would be having him trust Gamon enough to surrender.

This is just acting… just pretending. This was a bondage scene right out of Gamon's fantasies.

Gamon never had trouble remembering his lines, but with less blood going to his brain, he tripped over his scripted rants at the invisible captors.

Achara was no help. She stood there with a hand covering her mouth, her body shaking. It appeared she was trying to hold in her laugh… and failing.

He was glad no one else was there to witness how unprofessional they were both being. Dusit was the only one enveloped in the scene.

Gamon got his head back into the scene and fake-punched the imaginary kidnapper but then stumbled over his lines yet again. What was meant to be pithy banter came out as oddly stated questions.

He needed to get a grip, so he covered his face with his hands and did a breathing exercise.

Dusit broke character and asked, "Gamon, you, okay?"

"I'll be fine." All he wanted to do was—

Glancing down at Gamon's pants, a slight smile turned up the corners of Dusit's beautiful lips. "Achara, can we take our lunch break early?"

She put a hand on her hip and stared at the two of them like they had done something bad. Sighing, she rolled her eyes. "I guess we will not get anything accomplished with Gamon like this."

Gamon wanted to feel insulted, but he was a hot basket of lust. "Like what? I'm—"

Achara narrowed her stare to gaze directly below Gamon's belt. "Dusit, I'm trusting since you asked that you'd like to get him sorted?"

"Correct. I'd very much love to sort him out." Dusit leaned away from Achara when she bent to untie him. "Leave me tied up."

Gamon swallowed hard. He didn't know which was sexier, Dusit understanding him or allowing Gamon to have him in this way.

"Keep in mind you only have an hour and a half." Achara locked the door as she left.

Dusit chuckled.

"What?" Gamon demanded, half embarrassed but totally excited.

"Hour and a half. I estimate I need about five minutes." Dusit smirked with well-earned confidence.

Gamon huffed. He was being teased. "For…?"

"To sort you out." Dusit grinned. "And that's with my hands tied behind my back."

"Five minutes, huh?" Gamon was shaking with excitement and was close to the edge of insanity but would do his best to meet that challenge. He could hold out. "We shall see about that."

"Please." Dusit seemed to morph into an innocent captive. "I'm totally at your mercy… sir."

Crazy sexy aside, safety first. Gamon ran his fingers over the places on Dusit's wrists and ankles that secured him to the chair. "Any pain?"

Dusit smiled at him with patience and affection. "Not where the ropes are tied."

Gamon dropped to his knees and ran his hands all over Dusit's body. "I love you tied up."

"Glad you—"

Loving that Dusit had lost his words, Gamon continued to rub him through his pants. "Are you in pain here? You're all swollen."

Dusit struggled against the ropes and tried to thrust against Gamon's hands.

Gamon smiled up at him. "Who will not last five minutes?"

Dusit shook his head. “Don’t know.”

As if in slow motion, Gamon teased down Dusit’s zipper. He adjusted Dusit’s pants and underwear to let his beautiful erection out. Gamon breathed over it.

Thrusting toward Gamon’s mouth, Dusit closed his eyes.

Gamon’s heart was pounding hard with anticipation, and his own dick was jealous of Dusit’s freedom, but he moved his face out of the way and waited.

Dusit opened his eyes one at a time and strangled out, “Gamon.”

Gamon’s answer was to run his tongue along all the exposed parts of Dusit. Once Dusit’s cock shone with spit, Gamon got to the tip and whispered, “What?”

Tugging at the ropes, Dusit only seemed capable of moaning.

Gamon gave him long licks, and then on the fourth pass, he covered Dusit’s tip with his mouth and gently sucked.

“Gamon.” Dusit struggled breathlessly against the ropes.

Unable to resist, Gamon bobbed his mouth a few times. So good.

He stood, pulled off his pants, and then grabbed a condom and packet of lube out of his pocket before it could fall to the floor with his clothing.

Dusit’s eyes widened, and then he smirked as if he could read Gamon without even looking at him. “One might think you planned this. You look… delicious.”

“Should I use a condom?” They had discussed testing before, but Gamon felt it was responsible to ask what Dusit wanted in this moment.

“Nothing showed on the latest physical for me.” The investors had been unwilling to accept Dusit’s own latest results and demanded he be put through every test available… again.

“And I told you my tests revealed no issues.” Gamon gave his own dick a stroke, but only one. Any more and he wouldn’t be able to stop. “So we are good without this?” he asked again, waving the condom and hoping the answer was yes.

Dusit groaned out a “Yeah.”

Gamon dropped the condom to the floor and opened the packet of lube with his teeth. Then he used the cool gel to open himself up. When he could take two fingers with ease, Gamon glanced at Dusit.

Dusit appeared enthralled. If Gamon hadn't been so aroused, he might have found the intense interest embarrassing, but at that moment Dusit's stare excited him. Gamon wanted Dusit to see him preparing himself.

He swung his leg over Dusit and straddled him. His erection tapped against Dusit's torso.

"Gamon, what are you—"

But he didn't bother to answer. Gamon simply took Dusit inside with one long sensuous slide.

Dusit threw his head back and groaned. He strained against the ropes.

The stretch burn allowed Gamon to step back from the edge he'd been teetering on. "Hey, hey, hey… you're all tied up. You can't do anything, can you?"

"No." Dusit shook his head. "I need—"

"You are totally dependent on me."

Dusit choked out a "Yes."

"Does that bother you?" Gamon would stop if it did.

Dusit smiled and then chuckled a bit. "Are you kidding? I've got the hottest person I've ever met threatening me with a good time—*Oh no, he's going to ride my dick.* Please. Don't. Stop. And I do mean *don't* stop."

Gamon laughed, which squeezed Dusit's length, making him very aware of how deep he was inside. His laughter turned into a groan. Dusit belonged inside him.

Dusit rested his head on Gamon's chest and bit Gamon's nipple. "Move."

He did. Why did Dusit feel so good? It had always been like this between them. The years of their separation melted away, and it felt like no time had passed since the last time they had done this. Gamon found their rhythm with ease.

"Tell me." Gamon wasn't sure what he wanted to hear, but he needed Dusit's voice. The slow slide of his body up and down on Dusit's lap was making him pant.

"I'm helpless and in your control. I'm giving you everything… always." Dusit's struggle to get the words out ramped up Gamon even more. Then Dusit looked up into Gamon's eyes.

If Gamon hadn't already been completely in love with him, that would have been the moment he fell.

Gamon touched his forehead to Dusit, and said, "Mine."

Dusit shifted restlessly, so Gamon rode him harder, savoring the increased burn and friction.

"Going to come." Dusit sounded surprised.

"I'm going to make you come." Gamon twined his fingers in Dusit's hair and tugged his head back. He kissed his mouth as he focused his energy on sliding up and down.

A strangled gasp preceded warmth spreading through him.

Dusit came.

Gamon's slide was easier now, so he tried to take Dusit at the perfect speed and depth. He loved the feeling of Dusit's cum inside him and loved how, if he tilted his hips a bit, Dusit was hitting all the hot spots in Gamon.

Dusit panted and shivered. The look of complete satisfaction Dusit gave him charged parts of Gamon.

Gamon stopped sliding up and down. He wiggled and felt all of Dusit inside him.

He wasn't sure why he relished this kind of control so much. Maybe it was the trust Dusit put in him, or possibly his own need after so many years of feeling trapped and helpless to experience being in control—and now he was.

Right now, he was in total control, and he could do whatever he wanted.

Per usual, one thing was on his mind. "I'm going to come."

Dusit seemed to be out of words and simply nodded.

Gamon rocked his hips from side to side on Dusit's fading erection. He had done that. Sitting down hard and still rocking, Gamon stroked his dick.

"All yours. I'm all tied up and helpless. You made me come, and I couldn't stop you." Dusit gave him a small smile that sang of his knowing he was throwing fuel on the fire burning in Gamon's filthy brain. "Not that I wanted to stop you. But you were in control of the speed, the depth, the—"

Gamon couldn't hear beyond the roar of pleasure that rocked his core. He swayed and stroked and came all over Dusit like he was marking his territory. "Mine," he said again.

When Gamon was done, peace overtook him from deep inside. He placed tiny kisses all over Dusit's face, pausing once or twice to untie the ropes that had held Dusit a willing captive.

"Yes. Yes. Yes," Dusit murmured as he nuzzled into Gamon's face.

Dusit's erection was now completely gone, which caused his dick to slip out of Gamon. His cum soon followed.

They had marked each other.

After a while, Gamon couldn't stand the slow drip of cum, so he said, "Let's take showers and we can change into what we will need to wear for our scene."

Frowning, Dusit said, "Are you sure? I enjoy wearing you."

Gamon glanced down at Dusit's shirt, which was frosted by him, and chuckled. He scrunched his face as more of Dusit's cum dripped out. "Positive… and that was over five minutes."

Dusit looked at his watch. He patted Gamon on the back. "Right. Six minutes is over five."

"What? No, that was at least…." Gamon looked at the wall clock and then at Dusit.

All he could do was laugh.

CHAPTER 19

DUSIT COULDN'T help but to hold his breath. Interviews with Chaow could go downhill fast. This vlogger was too smart to miss anything, and he always went right for the scoop.

Maybe having Monyakul Tham-boon on as a guest would distract Chaow. Monyakul sat across from Chaow. One of his legs crossed over the other, and his arms folded over his muscular chest. The man worked out. Gamon had said he had done several lakorns, but Dusit knew him from all the action-hero movies he did.

Or maybe Chaow would ask Dusit about his character. He'd really paid attention this time to his character's arc and growth. His character went from a toxic red flag to husband material in a few episodes.

Chaow leaned forward. "It's been about three weeks since the last episode of *Don't Break My Heart 2* aired… and that was around the same time you two shared some important news with us."

No such luck.

Monyakul leaned toward Gamon with a big grin. "What news?"

Even though Monyakul was exploring the BL genre—if the number of Y-series–focused vlogs he'd been on proved anything—he and the entire Y-series industry of Thailand had to know every detail of him and Gamon admitting they were together.

"I've been abroad on location, so I must have missed it. What news?" Monyakul was a damned excellent actor. The only thing that gave him away was the twinkle in his eyes that only Dusit seemed to register.

"You've missed exciting news…. Ready for it?" Chaow smiled into the camera. "Gamon and Dusit…? Dusit and Gamon are together."

There it was. Everyone already knew, but every interviewer wanted their own show to announce it on the off chance someone in the Y-series or BL industry missed the news.

Dusit had already informed his parents, and although they weren't thrilled since they'd never considered having a son-in-law, they genuinely liked Gamon. They said they were glad Dusit had found someone to love him since he lived so far away.

Monyakul clapped once. "Congratulations."

Gamon gave him his patented superstar smile and grabbed Dusit's hand.

Chaow asked, "So tell. How did this come about?"

They had agreed to keep how they started private. Neither one of them needed folks sifting through timelines and piecing together private details based on social media history.

Gamon turned his delightful charm onto Chaow with a smiling head tilt and eyelashes fluttering. "How could I not love Dusit?"

Chaow fanned himself. "Love him. Tell us how the whole thing between you two started."

While keeping the official start date vague, Gamon wanted to let the fans know that they had been building their love for years.

Dusit grinned at Gamon. "Do you want to me to begin, or do you want to—"

"Before *Don't Break My Heart the Series* started filming, Dusit first stepped into the studio to stand in for the actor who bailed." Gamon's face and voice took on a dreamy quality.

Dusit saluted the screen. "I don't remember his name, but if he's out there, I'm extremely grateful you did."

Chaow chuckled. "I bet that man has got regrets."

Not their problem. Dusit squeezed Gamon's hand.

"Were the feelings immediate for you, Gamon?" Chaow rocked in his chair.

Gamon grinned at the interviewer, then at the audience, and then he stared at Dusit. "Without a doubt, but we had a job to do."

Dusit held out his hand with his index finger elevated and reminded the audience, "It was the first time I had acted. We… I needed long hours in the workshop."

"Was it actually true that you hadn't seen each other since the last fan meet you had?" Chaow didn't bother to keep the suspicion out of his voice.

Exhaling hard, Gamon said, "The first episode of the second season captured the moment I saw Dusit again for the first time."

"I can't imagine. What was that like?" Monyakul touched his heart and appeared to be engrossed in their love story.

Gamon put his hand to his own chest. "My heart was racing, my hands were sweating, and I wanted to jump out of my skin. I was excited, scared, worried, but I truly longed to see him. The poor intern who was tasked to stay with me tried her best, but I was a mess because I didn't know how he would feel about me."

That seemed crazy. Of course Dusit would still be in love with Gamon. Dusit was scared Gamon's opinion of him would have changed. He'd been the one to screw up everything he touched during their years apart.

Dusit tilted his head. "I still can't believe you were worried."

Gamon barked out an unexpected laugh. "Worried, excited, confused, terrified.... I was every emotion all at once. I was afraid you wouldn't like me anymore."

"How could I not like you?" Dusit hadn't meant for his voice to break as he lowered it. "I've always loved you."

"Always." Chaow covered his mouth and gasped. "You two are the sweetest. Aren't they, Monyakul?"

The action-hero star cleared his throat and shifted in his chair. "Um, yeah. Yeah, they are. Real cute."

Dusit didn't know Monyakul well but wanted to know what that odd expression on his face meant.

"There's someone for everyone," Gamon chirped.

Chaow waved a hand in front of his face. "Yes, I can see how nerve-racking that must have been for you. What did you do?"

"When it was finally time to open the door, I could barely breathe. I kept my eyes down until I said my line, and that was it." Gamon gave Dusit a small smile.

"Aw," Chaow patted Gamon on the knee. "And what about you, Dusit? What was happening on your side of the door?"

Shrugging, Dusit smiled. He didn't want to play it cool. "As I said, I was a wreck. I needed to see him. The fact we were doing it as part of the show was crazy-making. I mean, it was cruel. I didn't know if Gamon was going to punch or hug me. But I decided either would have been fine as long as it was Gamon."

Gamon nudged Dusit's foot ever so slightly. Oops, got it. A bit too harsh for the investors who demanded the condition: Always be gracious if you wanted to keep working. "Though after seeing the first scene, I understood why that needed to be captured. I could never have acted that well."

Chaow grinned. "You seemed overwhelmed."

Dusit leaned into Gamon, and he was comforted. "Completely. It had been so long since we'd seen each other. I… I didn't know what to expect."

"Well, your fans knew they would get another huge hit series—" Chaow gestured between Dusit and Gamon. "—even more important, you've got each other."

Monyakul sighed.

"Makes you wishful, huh?" Chaow asked Monyakul.

Monyakul bobbled his head between a nod and a shake. "I've just never seen real life echo a series before."

"Well, we have some couples that have come from meeting on a Y-series, right?" Chaow smiled and gestured to them. "You two are the most recent to give us all hope. Now Gamon, tell me, did you know as soon as you saw him again?"

Gamon squeezed Dusit's hand again. "I've always known. Dusit is my person."

"And you're mine." Without a doubt, Dusit mouthed the last sentiment.

"So why did you come out now?" Chaow's detective hat was set on raining water on his love session with Gamon.

They had struggled with what they wanted to say and how they wanted to say it. Gamon had been fielding this question, but it was his turn so the fans didn't think it was only Gamon's reasons.

Here goes nothing. Dusit took a deep breath. "We know our true fans want us to be happy, and I can only be happy if I'm with Gamon. He's my heart, and I didn't want to hide that from the world."

Gamon pressed his lips to Dusit's knuckles and smiled into the camera. "Love is beautiful. And two men can love each other beyond a series. I want people to know these relationships are not only a fantasy. With the right person, it is real."

"And same-sex marriage is now legal in Thailand. Any announcements?"

"Not just yet." Gamon grinned at Dusit.

Dusit wanted to be engaged immediately, but Gamon suggested they wait a little and enjoy each other. Engaged or not, as long as he was with Gamon, Dusit was satisfied.

"Let's look at this spicy snippet." Chaow pointed to the computer. The clip would be shown in a smaller box on the screen.

Gamon was on-screen. He said, "I'd be happy to show you." Within a heartbeat Dusit spun and pushed Gamon against the wall. A shiver ran through him. He yanked Gamon's hands above his head and said, "You mean like this?"

The clip ended.

Chaow fanned his face. "Wow. Monyakul, what do you think of these two?"

Monyakul swallowed hard and shifted in his seat. He opened his mouth, but nothing came out.

"Speechless, Monyakul?" Chaow teased.

Monyakul slapped his knee, appearing to break the hold the scene had on him. "It's wonderful. I've always fully supported LGBTQIA+ rights." Leaning forward, he batted his long eyelashes as he gave everyone his star-studded smile laced with sex.

Dusit wished he'd tone it down a bit. Gamon was his.

Monyakul continued, "Perhaps I need to do a Y-series."

"What? Really?" Chaow bounced in his seat. "Is that a request?"

Grinning, Monyakul gestured over at Gamon and Dusit. "If that can be the result… where do I sign?"

"Oh my." Chaow fanned himself. "You must be teasing." He turned to Gamon and Dusit. "What is next for you two?"

"After we do the fan meets and tours, we have some runway work in Paris next spring."

"I heard it is for Fashion Week? Oh, how exciting! So many BL actors are also successful models. The luxury brands love you two. I see you're wearing some of your sponsors' brands."

Gamon showed off the bag he had slung over his shoulder and shifted so the camera could see his shirt.

Dusit held out one of his wrists to reveal the watch and then put the other one out to present a row of bracelets, which annoyed the hell out of him with their constant clanging.

"But how about another show?" Chaow asked what everyone had been asking since the last episode aired.

"Maybe…." Grinning at Gamon, Dusit tipped his head in question.

After Gamon signaled he was ready, Dusit took a deep breath and gave voice to their plan. "We are thinking of doing something behind the camera."

"What? Directing?" Monyakul seemed to go on alert.

"More like producing our own show." Dusit couldn't believe they were going to do this. Gamon had done a bunch of research and planning before shooting *Don't Break My Heart 2*. Otherwise, he'd never feel confident enough to pull off a producing role.

"Your own show? A series?" Chaow leaned forward. Excitement sparkled in his eyes as he knew this was fresh news.

Dusit shrugged.

Gamon gave his million-baht smile. "Perhaps… that and a bit more."

"More? Wait. Are you two going to start a production house?" Chaow put everything together.

Monyakul leaned forward. "Ah, that's smart. Then you can have control over what shows you make."

Chaow straightened as if he sensed even more possible bombshells. "That's all the rage. Actors understand what's lacking in the industry, and those who have branched out into producing have received a positive response."

Gamon shifted in his seat. "We are still considering moving in that direction, though we have a lot of things scheduled before making such a big change."

Dusit hid his grin. Gamon was honest but wasn't an oversharer. He didn't have to admit to the hours of research, the gathering of resources and people, and collecting names of investors who were very interested in being part of this new venture. He added, "We are simply considering all our options."

"I don't enjoy depending on others. I want to make our own breaks. I crave independence, and this type of project ensures it." Gamon's voice remained even, but Dusit knew all too well why Gamon longed for independence.

Gamon wanted to guarantee he'd never depend on anyone again like he had his mother.

It was a good thing, but Dusit was angry that Gamon's mother had made him need to go this far to protect himself.

"So there is a project?" Chaow wanted the scoop.

"I'm not ready to confirm or deny." Gamon batted his eyelashes as a distraction.

Chaow remained undeterred. "You're not making any official announcements?"

Dusit jumped in. "Not yet."

Sighing, Chaow frowned and then turned to Monyakul. "What about you?"

Monyakul stopped staring at them and grinned at Chaow. "Sounds like I know where I want to apply for a role in a Y-series. I'd love to work with Gamon and Dusit."

Gamon put his hands in front of him and waved him off. "We're nowhere near that stage… if we even do it."

Crossing his arms over his chest, Monyakul smirked. "So how does one get a ship partner? Do I wait for one to sail by? Or is there, like, a game show where I can win one?"

Chaow's eyes widened. "Oh, that would be fun. I love the idol survival shows where they put together an idol group."

"I've seen those. I never understood how the audience and fans make such a huge decision about who gets a space in the group." Dusit mused, "Though it would be interesting to see an actor seeking his ship partner."

Clapping his hands, Chaow rocked in his chair. "That's a perfect name. *Seeking a Ship* rolls off the tongue."

"Well, let me know when I can start auditioning my potential ship partners." Monyakul's tone suggested he was only half joking.

Dusit glanced at Gamon, his wheels spinning fast. "I enjoy those shows too."

Chaow asked, "Who would be a good ship partner with you? Any thoughts?"

Monyakul ran his fingers through his hair. "Someone unexpected. I noticed many of the Y-series have one bigger guy and one smaller. I don't want to have to worry constantly about breaking my partner, so I need someone who is sturdy."

Dusit chuckled. "Sturdy?" Monyakul looking for a sturdy actor for a ship partner… and possibly more? Did he think all Y-series were like a dating game?

Monyakul continued, "What? I think if I were to look at men that way, I'd want someone as big as me. I'd play sports with them and—" He was going all in.

"Not bigger?" Chaow teased.

"Bigger is fine too." Monyakul stared off into space. "Someone who could wrestle me."

"I'm starting to like you," Dusit said without thinking. The guy was amusing.

"Me too," Gamon added.

Monyakul spread his arms wide and then slapped his knees. "Well, great. I'll tell my agent to expect a call from your production house—"

"If we set it up," Gamon added.

"You mean when. I've got a couple movies to finish up, and then I'll be ready." Monyakul smiled and then turned to Chaow and asked, "You'll do my first interviews, won't you?"

Chaow landed a hand over his heart. "Of course. Of course."

"Great." Monyakul turned to Dusit and Gamon. "And I'll be waiting for your phone call."

IN THE car heading to Charong's, Dusit chuckled. "We don't have a production house, but we already have our first actor wanting to work with us."

Gamon grinned. "He was funny… and a talented actor. I really love the idea of a survivor show to find a ship partner."

The excitement was catching. "It would be half *Survivor* and half *The Bachelor*."

"We could—" Gamon was interrupted by a text. He looked at his phone and then said, "Hm."

"What?" Dusit threw an arm around him.

Gamon continued to stare at his phone as if the words would change. "I got a congratulations text from my mother."

"That's nice." Dusit could find peace with Gamon's mother if she was able to act like a real mother to her son. It didn't feel right to be at odds with a parent.

"She wants to have dinner with me." Gamon glanced at him with a confused expression.

"She does? Are you ready for that?" Dusit would don his battle gear and fight the dragon if Gamon needed him to.

"Maybe? She promises to behave. She gave me her word not to speak critically."

"Your mother said that?" That was a surprise. Hard to trust *her*, but Dusit trusted Gamon with his whole heart. "Don't look so worried," he said. "Go if it feels right. She's not going to break us up this time."

CHAPTER 20

THE HOT season was in full swing. Gamon pointed to an outside table at the restaurant called Pride. "Let's sit near that big fan."

Dusit sat down and glanced around. "Still can't believe how much this area has changed. It used to be grubby and sketchy, a place for men to have hookups."

"People are no longer hiding in darkened corners." Gamon gestured to the Pride flags in various sizes hanging over the alleyway and on the buildings.

He'd decided to stop hiding who he was. Not everyone would accept him, but Gamon wanted to live his life in the light not the shadows. Coming out hadn't destroyed their careers; for every path that closed, two alternative routes to success opened.

Yawning, Dusit smiled down at his cell phone screen saver. The picture was of the two of them kissing at the Eiffel Tower. "I still can't believe we were in Paris a few weeks ago."

"I can't believe you walked the runway." His man burned that runway up. Dusit was so confident and sexy strutting down—

"She's a new designer and very talented… and a fan of ours. How could I say no?" Dusit chuckled as if it wasn't his fault he was so sexy. And he was. "Even if Charong hasn't stopped teasing me about it."

"At least Lyric was impressed." Gamon chuckled.

"It really is unbelievable how popular Thai Y-series are worldwide."

"Achara says it's because people crave visibility. Shows that center on gay, bi, or queer characters do that and give others an understanding. She believes the countries that produce these series are guiding the entire society toward understanding, which leads to acceptance."

Dusit glanced around. "Hard to believe. But looking around this area, the change has had an effect."

A man strolled over to their table. "What do you want to drink?"

"I'll have—wait, it's you…." Gamon struggled to find the man's name. "Niran?"

"You remember me?" Niran touched his heart and gave Gamon a big smile.

Gamon stood and waied to one of the men they'd taken to the hotel.

Dusit stared at Gamon, then at Niran. "Oh. Oh, now I know."

Niran laughed.

Looking around, Gamon was almost afraid to ask, but did. "Where's Somchair?"

Gesturing for them to sit, Niran took a chair and leaned toward them. "After that night—you know, with you two—Somchair and I quit and found jobs here."

"That's great." Gamon pressed his lips together. He didn't want to suggest anything negative about sex work. "I mean—"

"I know. The owner also once worked as we did, so she threw in a room upstairs as part of our salary."

"I'm thrilled for both of—" Dusit stared at the door.

Somchair filled most of the doorway.

"Are you checking on me?" Niran grinned at him.

Shrugging, Somchair said, "Making sure you're okay."

Niran jumped out of the chair. "I'm taking drink orders, and you remember—"

"Of course." Somchair stepped onto the patio.

Dusit stood and waied, and Gamon followed.

Somchair returned the greeting. "I have you two to thank."

"Us? Why?" Gamon couldn't imagine.

"After that night, seeing you two like you were—are—I couldn't let him… do that anymore with anyone else." Somchair teared up.

"Why so dramatic? Are you auditioning for a show?" Niran teased as he hurried to his lover and fit his body under Somchair's arm.

Somchair tightened the embrace in a show of possession but also appreciation. "Sorry."

Niran stood on his toes and kissed Somchair's cheek. "I'll take their orders and see you in the kitchen. And when I mean see you, I mean—"

"I know what you mean. Stop." Somchair's ears were red, and his voice was hushed. He growled and then smiled over his shoulder at Niran and disappeared into the restaurant.

Niran smirked. "I do so love embarrassing him. I'm amazed I can still make him blush. Sit."

They took their seats again.

Dusit smiled at Niran. "You two look happy together."

"We are. And I see you two are as well." Niran added, "I saw how you came out. It was impressive."

"It was important to Gamon… and to me. We wanted people to see what the happily ever after looks like." Dusit grabbed Gamon's hands and kissed his knuckles.

"You certainly have with your socials. The pictures you post are great. You two are worthy of #relationshipgoals."

Gamon made sure they posted not perfection but reality. He gave Dusit a look. "Though perhaps too real."

"That time you tried to cook was priceless and needed to be shared."

Niran laughed. "Oh yes. The fire. That was—"

"Adorable," Dusit inserted as he patted Gamon's hand.

Shaking his head, Gamon muttered, "It's impossible to stay cross at you."

Niran got his pen and paper out. "Tell me what you want to drink."

Dusit tilted his head at Gamon, asking silently what he wanted.

Gamon gave him a head bob to indicate he'd have his usual.

"Two mango juices," Dusit ordered. "And, um, take your time so you can *see* Somchair."

"Thanks." Niran hurried into the restaurant.

There was a clatter of pots.

Dusit glanced at Gamon with big eyes.

Gamon covered his mouth, but that didn't stop him from joining in with Dusit's laugh.

"I think they might be a while," Dusit smirked.

Dusit's cell phone buzzed. "Let me see who texted."

He stared at his phone for a long time.

Curiosity finally got the better of Gamon. "Who is it?"

"Your mother." Dusit turned the phone so Gamon could see he wasn't joking.

"Texting you?"

"Yeah, she wanted to make sure I join you for dinner the next time you see her." Dusit sounded worried but pleased.

Gamon sighed. "You don't need to see her." He had agreed to meet her once a month, and she had been biting her tongue more as promised. He felt less attacked. But to put Dusit through that….

"We should go."

Gamon grimaced. "I'm not sure. It's only been a few months since I've come to a better place with her." Not great, not even safe, but one where every minute wasn't a lecture or a cutting bite.

"I think we should try it. We can ask Achara. She agreed to be our advisor."

"If she has any time, what with seeing her doctor and all." Gamon might be pouting. He hadn't been able to see her the way he had pre-doctor-coupledom.

"You two still get together once a week for lunch." Dusit frowned for a moment, then smiled. "Why don't we invite her and her doctor for dinner? That way you get to see her—"

"And find out more about this doctor person." The guy sounded nice, but Gamon wanted to see if he was worthy of Achara.

"Didn't you encourage her to give him a chance?" Dusit didn't have to point out the obvious.

"Yes, a chance, but they are already living together." Gamon sighed. They did text every day and talked a few times a week in addition to the lunches.

"So are we." Dusit grinned.

"I know I'm being silly. I miss her." Gamon's phone buzzed twice. He glanced at it. Achara was double-checking the day for their lunch date next week. And the other—

"That's Achara, right? See, and you two still text all day long."

"I guess." Gamon turned the phone around to show Dusit. "The other text was from my mother."

Dusit gestured toward the phone. "She's texting you almost exactly what she texted me. She wants us to have dinner."

Gamon frowned at the phone. He didn't want to let her walk all over him. "Yeah, but that's how it starts. I know how it ends."

"Your situation is completely different. You are independent. You stood up to her. She's clearer on the boundaries and knows you will keep them."

"I don't want to be her doormat." Gamon was over that. He was still angry with himself for allowing it to begin with.

"You aren't, and you won't be." Dusit's protective tone eased Gamon's confusion. "You don't need me, but I'll be your backup. If she gets like she used to get because I'm there and you don't leave, I'll help you. I'll carry you if I must…."

Truth was, in some ways Gamon missed her. As terrible and overbearing as she could be, she was also smart and perceptive. Her eye on the entertainment industry was excellent. She studied the industry and understood the nuances. "I do like having somewhat of a normal relationship with her."

"I'll text her back." Dusit looked at their calendar and proposed a couple of evenings to her.

Almost immediately, both his and Dusit's phones buzzed. She confirmed with the names of several restaurants, and a "You choose."

Dusit texted back Gamon's favorite.

Another buzz, and Dusit smiled at his phone.

"What?" Had his mother said something inappropriate?

"She thanked me for looking after you and wants to get to know me better." Dusit glanced over at him. "She appears to be trying."

"I guess." Gamon sighed. She was, and much harder than he'd expected her to. It felt odd… different. Maybe it would be okay.

There was a huge clatter of pots, making Gamon jump and then laugh as Somchair's name drifted out to the patio. "I think getting our drinks will definitely take a while."

"That's fine. We should talk about where we are with everything production-house related."

"I think we are ready." Once again, Dusit wanted to push forward.

"But have we done everything?" There was so much to juggle. How could he do this? He'd never done this before. Did he even know what he was doing?

"You've been preparing for this for ages. All the legal paperwork is in, according to our lawyer. Prem Li put us in touch with a good crew who are ready to go. He even agreed to oversee the new director. And most importantly Chat is ready to start a fandom during her school break."

It was a risk using a new director fresh out of school, but there were too few women directing, and if Gamon could give someone who was talented a break, he should. "She's excited about the opportunity and is ready to go. I've got confirmation for the editor and her team."

Dusit asked, "What did you think of the script?"

They wouldn't need it until early next year, but Gamon didn't want to take chances. "You were right. The final draft is excellent."

"We've got the script. The crew, directors, editors, and even the location has been set. People want to be a part of this because of you." Dusit sung his praises too often.

He was grateful his name helped gather such talented people. "Yes, but most of them want a production house that will take the positive messaging and visibility of the LGBTQIA+ community to the next level."

"I think the reality show is the perfect way for our actor to find a partner, and then the series will tell the next part of the happily ever after." Dusit grinned at him.

"People need to see there's something beyond the meet cute and getting together. Same-sex relationships have difficulties like all relationships. It's important we—"

Dusit gave him a thumbs-up.

"Sorry I'm lecturing again." Gamon shrugged. "I know I've said it before, but I really believe these series help promote understanding and acceptance of queer people."

"Numerous fans have shared how these novels and shows gave them hope growing up. To get the message that being different wasn't a bad thing."

Niran stumbled out onto the patio. His hair looked messy, and by his grin Gamon was pretty sure he knew how it got that way. "Sorry it took me so long. First I had to grow the mangos and then let them ripen and—"

Dusit's laugh barked out. "Are we talking about our juices or…."

"I'll never tell." Niran asked, "May I take your orders?"

Dusit ordered, "A burger, well done. He'll have a burger rare, with cheese."

"Got it." Niran stopped at the door and said, "I don't have to find the cow, so your food should be out quicker."

"He really is a character." Dusit smiled after him.

Toying with his phone, Gamon asked, "Do you really think I should?"

"Make the call." Dusit gestured to his phone.

Gamon took a deep breath. "This is the beginning of everything." He scrolled through his contacts and placed the call.

"Hello?"

"This is Gamon Chaisit with Rainbow Productions. Is this Monyakul Tham-boon?"

"It is."

Gamon shouldn't jump right into business, so he asked, "How have you been?"

Monyakul chuckled. "Waiting for this call."

Keep reading for an excerpt from
Not Another Boy Band
by Z. Allora!

CHAPTER 1

IKEDA DAIKI tugged his fox hat down on his head. Shutting the window, he hoped to block out the noise of Tokyo waking up.

He stared at the sketch pad. The first character he ever drew—his nameless love—smiled back at him in a way that still turned him inside out. Daiki had been drawing him since he was twelve years old.

No one else had ever laid eyes on him. He was Daiki's precious secret. Daiki had a treasure trove of pages and pads filled with sketches, all for himself.

The bookcases that lined one wall of the main space of his apartment were filled with the creations he shared with the world—mangas, from his one-offs to his series to his weekly serials—all neat and tidy on the shelves.

He had turned his living room and dining room into a working manga studio that fit him and his four assistants. Daiki was living his artist fantasy. All the things he'd ever wanted had come to pass.

Gently, he traced his finger over the lines that depicted the character's sexy half smile, the one that haunted his dreams… well, haunted almost everything.

If only he could chase away the loneliness with someone a little more three-dimensional, but deadlines gave him little time or opportunity to meet anyone.

His cell phone buzzed, reminding him his assistants would be here in another two hours.

Daiki needed to put away his special one, but doing so was always hard. Easing himself past the loss, he flipped through one of the sketchbooks. He hesitated on the picture of him holding his beloved tight.

The background of the sketch was a simple black sky with a huge moon. They hugged on the roof while looking at the stars. He caressed the dark hair made by his pencils as he imagined they were talking about the future and what plans they wanted to make. All the big things, like where they would live or what vacations they would take, and the small things too, like what to have for dinner.

To share his life with someone....

He flipped through the pages, drawing after drawing, and he needed to stop.

"I'm Pygmalion," he mused, tracing a finger once more over the full lips he'd drawn. He must be crazy to have fallen in love with a picture based on someone who didn't exist.

It probably wasn't healthy, but like many twentysomethings, he hadn't found his special someone... outside of two dimensions. To get to where he was in his career, he'd needed to stay laser-focused, so dating wasn't drawn into his storyboard. Though even the people he did meet, no one could compare—maybe he didn't want them to.

Letting his finger follow the gentle wave of the image's hair, he imagined this man would be smart, kind, and eager to change the world. Help Daiki explore things he'd only drawn, things like—

Work!

He gathered his drawing supplies and put them all away, then slipped the sketch pad back into the locked fireproof drawer of his desk on top of over thirty would-be mangas.

Switching to digital mode, he turned on his computer and morphed from fantasy to real life—make that as real as a *mangaka* could get.

The first of his four assistants walked in. Kobayashi Hikari was always early. She bowed and greeted him, "Good morning, Sensei," then disappeared into the second bedroom. He had designed the room for his assistants. There were bunk beds for napping or late nights, privacy to change clothing, and a closet to store their things.

She reappeared in a ninja costume.

"Morning." Since Daiki wore his fox hat to work, he could hardly criticize anyone else's method for sinking into their artistic zone.

"Who are you working on?" she asked.

"Hironori."

"Oh, I love him. I'm partial to the enemies-to-lovers trope anyway. Tie that in with a big boss falling in love with the head of a rival company… I'm all in." Her soft tone suggested she was smitten completely. His character certainly lived up to his name, which meant "benevolent ruler." Daiki had leaned into that in last month's manga.

Daiki chuckled. He couldn't deny his wish to be more like this character. Taking what he wanted in business and having no problem demanding more in love.

Hikari sighed. "You've got to love Hironori's bold ways and determination that always gets him what he wants. Though this month it looks like *who* he wants."

Brave Hironori accepted who he was, took risks, and was never lonely. "He does. You want to—"

"Yes, please." She jumped at any chance to work on this manga.

"It's just the dialogue." He needed to work on delegating, but it was hard for him not to do everything.

Hikari laughed and made grabby hands, so he sent her the files.

He scrolled through the storyboards on the screen and started to work on his edits.

His assistant Ito Rei, who seemed to have no interest in anything other than drawing, strolled in with Takahashi Ichiro, a new graduate who wanted to burn down the manga world one storyboard at a time. Sounded like they were still debating *sekkusu-banare.*

"But sekkusu-banare literally means drifting away from sex, so if that happens—" Rei interrupted herself to greet them. "Morning, Sensei. Hikari."

Ichiro followed suit and then trailed after Rei. "But how can the impact be negative on manga?"

"Later." Rei rushed to her seat and started to work.

Sighing, Ichiro gave Rei a pointed stare, but she ignored him, so he sat down.

"Greetings, Sensei. I picked up tea and soda." Last to arrive was Sato Akihiro, Daiki's high school pal, who usually worked far into the night. He should have his own studio, but their friendship caused neither to discuss it.

"Morning, Akihiro. Thank you. I forgot." Thankfully, one of Daiki's assistants always remembered.

"No problem, Sensei." Akihiro gave him a nod before ducking into the assistants' room.

Hikari popped up from behind her monitor. "I'll set up a delivery with the market down the street so the staples Sensei generously keeps on hand for us will arrive on Wednesday afternoons. Everyone get your lists to me after lunch."

"Sounds great." Less time on the day-to-day and more time to focus on drawing. His assistants really were outstanding.

Wearing his favorite maid's costume from Daiki's first spy manga series, Akihiro took his seat. He said her character was powerful and understated, exactly the way he wanted to draw, conveying much with little.

Glancing at the schedule, Daiki reminded the group, "We still have twelve days before the *ne-mu* is due on the monthly series, but it's Tuesday, so the final sketches are due on the weekly serials."

"Yes, Sensei," they each muttered.

Luckily, he didn't cut things close. He had storylines and rough sketches months in advance, and in some cases years. Whole series were just waiting for an editor's markups and a publisher's go-ahead.

He had two editors with different publishers catering to his distinctive brands and vastly unique audiences. The editors knew of each other and of his immense catalogue of unseen work that, unless he died an untimely death, he would bring forward at a slow but consistent pace. To flood the readership would overfeed them and then leave them wanting. Plus Daiki liked to imagine having time off. If he had something to do with free time, he might actually take it.

Drawing had always been his go-to. Even back when he was living with his grandfather in Inari. His grandfather ran one of the souvenir tea shops, so growing up meant every Monday began before dawn. He helped haul the supplies up the mountain, and then he'd run down the steps to get to school on time. When Daiki was old enough, his grandfather would usually stay the week. Daiki had been lonely until he found drawing and an entire world opened to him.

He adjusted his fox hat to cover his ears and allowed himself to sink deeper into the storyboards.

BEEP! BEEP! Beep!

It couldn't be time already. How was that possible? The day had flown by.

Daiki stopped the alarm and gathered his things. "I'm off to meet with the editor. Tonight at dinner, please order without me."

"Don't forget this." Akihiro rushed to the door, and handed Daiki his brand-new electronic drawing pad.

Daiki slipped the device into his messenger bag, next to other drawing supplies. "The train ride would have been long without a drawing app on a screen larger than my phone. Thank you."

When Daiki caught the train, the car wasn't crowded, so he sat down. He had made this trip many times over the last decade, but what if the publisher was meeting to tell him they were cancelling his series? Storyboards of how the event would play out flashed before him. The end scene was him leaving the meeting and walking home in the rain.

Then before he wrote *The End*, an imaginary Hironori leaned against the wall of his mental storyboard. His dialogue bubble said, "Let them. There's a ton of other publishers and editors who want you."

In the next story window, Hironori took a long drag on a cigarette. The cut of his chin was a bit too sharp, but the cigarette dangling from his lips gave the image a hazy sexual look. Lower on the page, Daiki envisioned Hironori staring at him. The dialogue bubble said, "Business is business. Your mangas sell." The final picture read, "But check your investment and savings accounts."

He shook himself. His life was not a manga, but somehow that's how he saw it… and someone else was drawing his story.

The train arrived at the station. As he passed the station restaurants and food shops, his stomach growled. Did he forget to have lunch? He turned at the newspaper stand and zigzagged up the steps to the street level, avoiding people.

The bustling road was filled with people hurrying home from their long day.

Daiki made the quick trip down the street, past the shopping center and an office building. He ducked his head as he entered a restaurant, then headed straight to the back room where the editor held her meetings. The only thing that changed was the prices on the menu. Now that he was a brand, each of his publishers treated him to nicer meals when they met.

"Nice to see you," he greeted her.

Saito Azami, who liked cats more than people, welcomed him with her attempt at a friendly smile. "And you."

He acknowledged her assistant, who gestured to the far chair. "Please."

After sliding past both of them to get around the table, he sat down. He'd had hundreds of these meetings over the last decade, but each time worry skittered through him.

After they ate, Azami-san held out her hand. "Let's see this week's work."

He pulled out his final sketches.

She skimmed through the pages with her red pen and gave him a few comments. Her assistant took a pass and asked a question or two. The editing ended with him having about an hour of additional work to do.

When he didn't move to leave, she asked, "Is there something else?"

"Yes. We've talked before about the direction I want to take."

Her quiet sigh indicated her frustration at his insistence. "It's almost the start of the new year."

Not for weeks, but he couldn't give up on this. "All the more reason to clear the slate. I want to move away from outdated tropes. Drawing past the titillation of a gay romance to what it means to be gay in Japan. I want to use my stories to give validation and visibility to those who need it."

She stood. "Give me some time. Let me see what's out there."

Standing, he gave her a more formal goodbye than usual or necessary.

It had started to drizzle, but at least the air wasn't cold enough to turn the sidewalks into ice. He tightened his scarf and meandered back through the crowds and neon.

Should he have been firmer? No, he'd been clear, and she did say she'd look for something. That wasn't a guarantee, but this exchange was the furthest he'd gone.

On the way to the train, he passed a semicrowded bar. People were smiling and laughing; he was tempted to stop in. Maybe he could.... But his assistants were waiting for him.

He hurried to enter the station and jogged down the stairs to the underground.

CHAPTER 2

WANT VISITORS? Sage got a text from the twins.

After editing his video, he was ready for a break, so he typed, *Yeah.*

Buzz us up.

Ryley Griffin—or Lee as they liked to be called—and Ryder Cage, aka the twins, were already outside. The twins, so nicknamed in high school because they were always together, had decided Sage was their best friend back in ninth grade, and he didn't disagree.

Sage opened the door. With Lee in his leather skirt and band shirt and Ryder in their layers of black lace, they were polar opposites today, but they always fit together. "Lee, he/him pronouns today?"

"Well done, buddy. How did you know my pronouns are maleish today? My skirt or my lack of shaving?" Lee was gender fluid, and their pronouns changed with their presentation.

Sage rolled his eyes. "Combination."

Ryder glided across Sage's living room—slash bedroom slash dining room slash anything else he needed to live—and eased onto the sofa like the model they were and with far too much grace for the tiny apartment. Ryder was nonbinary and used them/they, though he/him pronouns didn't bother them. "As much love as I have for you, Lee, your adherence to the binary to counter the binary doesn't earn you points."

Elbowing Lee, Sage added, "Or blowjobs."

Lee simply shrugged and sighed.

"When are you going to move out of this place?" Ryder folded the sheets Sage had left rumpled under the cushions.

"What? I love my place." He'd moved in right after high school. The microapartment wasn't fancy, but the place was clean and safe.

"You sleep on the sofa," Ryder pointed out the obvious.

"Because I turned the bedroom into my work studio." Sage often repeated himself on this topic.

"It's not like you couldn't afford something with a second bedroom." Ryder grimaced and scratched at a stain on the sofa's armrest.

"You sound like my mother. I have what I need. I'm comfortable." Sage didn't want uber luxe to be comfortable. His apartment was what he as a studio drummer could afford, and he was good with that. It wasn't that Sage had been untouched by the wealth and privilege he'd grown up with; he acknowledged his head start in life. But he wanted to make it on his own.

Lee shrugged and plopped down next to Ryder, who fussed with Lee's leather skirt until it lay properly. "Are you done with your latest video?"

Frowning, Sage admitted, "Yeah. Still have to edit it, though."

Ryder grinned. "What's the topic?"

"Visibility or lack thereof."

"Again…? Seems like you have a theme going. What is this, the third in as many weeks?" Lee pointed out the obvious.

Sage paced from the galley kitchen to his favorite chair and crashed into the softness. "Fourth, but who is counting?"

"Look, had you not raised the issue, we wouldn't have known how tenuous the situation can be for gay/queer idols in Asia, or anywhere for that matter." Ryder gave Sage's knee a squeeze.

Sage sighed. "There's still so much to say about how being queer shouldn't limit what you're able to accomplish in your career. Your band shouldn't dissolve like sugar in water just because someone is brave enough to be themselves."

"Amen," Ryder said without irony.

Lee gave him a nod. "Preach."

Sage couldn't stop himself. "Something needs to be done about this. I don't have all the answers, but wouldn't it be exceptional to see some openly queer people in a band and not have the labels ditch them? Having their fans stand by them and support them? This isn't an Asian issue, a music issue, a writing issue, or even a gay issue. It's a human issue. We all deserve respect."

"Yup, we do." Ryder smiled at him.

"The first step is visibility. Seeing and understanding leads to acceptance. I want to see real musicians with more talent than looks giving me music and lyrics from their very soul. I want those people to be both on and off the rainbow. I believe the fans are ready to embrace people on various stripes of the rainbow… because they themselves might very well be on the yellow brick road."

Lee crossed his arms and turned to Sage. "So I guess you'll be putting your trust fund where your mouth is."

"Oh yes, of course he will. What should he wear?" Ryder waved the finger of judgment at him. "Certainly something better than this if you plan on being seen."

"What's wrong with jeans and a T-shirt? You told me they are fashion staples." Not that he gave a shit, but Sage was all about taking less flak from the fashionista turned model. "And wait. Why am I putting my trust fund in my mouth?"

Grinning, Lee pointed at him. "You threw down a challenge with these vlogs. Are you telling me you will not pick it up?"

"Forming a band isn't on my agenda. I live a comfortable life as a studio drummer." Sage's rock-and-roll dreams were a mere buzz in the back of his mind, one he'd shelved a long time ago.

Lee gathered up one of the stacks of books he'd piled on the coffee table. "These are new. *Music Business for Dummies*, *Music Business 101*, and why, look, all of these books appear to be about how to start a band. Imagine that."

All Sage was doing was imagining, strolling down the "would never happen but if it did" path.

Ryder reached over and felt Sage's forehead. "Are you sick? Didn't you say on your vlog there should be more bands who were open and accepting?"

"How would I—what? You two think I *could* start a band?" That was ridiculous enough to make him chuckle, but the serious expressions on their faces stopped him.

"You are a drummer." Ryder pointed to Sage's hands, which were currently twirling drumsticks.

Excitement coursed through Sage, making the sticks spin faster. No, he couldn't start a band. He tucked the drumsticks back under the cushion. "Studio drummer. Big difference from performer."

Lee shrugged. "A drummer drums."

Granted, he made a decent living off his studio gigs—and the bigger names were requesting him—but he'd never performed live.

"If you're interested, we know someone who could help make this happen." Lee was suggesting they could tap into their global network of friends.

Sage tamped down the excitement. It was a crazy risk. Besides, what did he know about starting a band—aside from a fuckton of research?

Caressing a hand down Lee's arm, Ryder asked, "Are you thinking of—"

"Who else?" Lee smirked.

Ryder strutted to the fridge and grabbed a water, showing why every designer clambered for them to be on their runway. Freezing as if a photographer had given the order, Ryder tilted their head, making their long hair slip over their shoulder, and then asked, "Would he help? We didn't exit on the best of terms."

Patting the space next to him, Lee said, "It wasn't the worst either."

Ryder rejoined Lee on the sofa.

"Who are you two talking about?" Sage needed to take back the reins of this runaway conversation.

"We know someone who could help you launch your band." They spoke in unison. It used to spook Sage when they did that, but he'd gotten used to it.

"Um, there is no band." And why did stating that fact feel wrong?

Ryder laughed. "You keep saying that, but there is. There has to be. Otherwise how do you get visibility?"

Knotting his hair on top of his head, Lee said, "Sato, from the Miszuka photoshoot I did last year, can help set you on the right path."

"Wait, didn't you two date him?" His friends had an interesting dating philosophy, and as for sex, well, no need to go into their business.

"No, his brother. Let me text him." Ryder's thumbs were flying across his phone.

Lee nodded. "It's all about creating a total platform so there's a built-in fan base to follow."

"I'm aware of how a platform works." Sage rolled his eyes. He'd had to—wait, was he really doing this?

Ryder added, "You're talking manga, anime, recording, then live shows?"

Chuckling, Sage tapped out a beat on his leg. He allowed himself to imagine his band giving validation for those who needed it. Nah. "You two are insane."

Ignoring him, Ryder continued, "Also a social media presence, commercial spots, perhaps a game show or six. Japan loves game shows. A bit of light humiliation is always a turn-on."

Lee arched an eyebrow. "Good to know."

Wait, what? Dare he ask? "Japan?"

"Where else? Both your parents are from Japan. You know the language. Why would you start your band somewhere else?"

"I have no band." How come the word "yet" was fighting to get out of his mouth?

"No, because first there should be a manga and maybe videos of the band forming." Ryder giggled and waved Sage off with purple nails.

"I'll shoot the videos, but which artist?" Lee asked as if clearing his intense photography schedule would be easy.

Sage argued, "You act like it's that simple."

Lee and Ryder studied him for a long moment. Then they shook him off like yesterday.

"Band name?" Ryder asked.

Snapping his fingers, Sage had that answer. "There's only one name for my band."

"And that is…?" Ryder asked.

"Kashi-sei. It means visibility in Japanese."

"Perfect." Giving him a kiss on either cheek, Ryder glided over to the door. "We'll come up with some artists for you to consider in a few days and start the wheels turning on all the ins and outs of starting a successful band."

Lee waved to him and followed Ryder.

How could he possibly start a band… and in Japan, no less?

Kashi-sei.

SCAN THE QR CODE BELOW TO ORDER!

Z. ALLORA is nonbinary. They didn't always believe in romance, but before giving up on happily ever afters, Z. took out a personal ad in a college newspaper. On October 20, 1987, at 5:08 p.m., Z. found what they didn't think existed—their other half. Five years later, Z. married their best friend and true love.

Z. spent much of their adult life traveling the world and has visited thirty-five countries. Z. also lived in Southeast Asia, Israel, the UK, and China.

During the pandemic when Z. couldn't travel, they studied the changes in Asian BLs/Yaoi and dramas. Many of these shows evolved from basic visibility to exploring Pride events, homophobia, sexual orientation, gender identity, and same-sex marriage at a level that was never seen before. These Asian BLs are no longer simple romances about same-sex couples in love but have become the soft power that is changing hearts and minds about LGBTQIA+ issues and people throughout Asia and the world.

Z. holds the opinion that every single one of us deserves to be happy forever. Regardless of where we are on the infinite spectrum of gender identity or orientation, our differences and similarities should be both respected and celebrated.

Email: Z.AlloraHappyEndings@gmail.com
X: @ZAllora
Blue Sky: @zallora.bsky.social
Instagram: @z.allora
Facebook: Z Allora Allora (and join Z.'s Yaoified Love group for fun, character chatter, giveaways, and silliness!)
Website: www.zallorabooks.com
Blog: zallora.blogspot.com

Z. Allora

Kulap Rose Thongsi rode the rollercoaster of the Thai Y-series industry for almost ten years until a scandal sidelined him. Starring in My Reality the Series is his last hope. His agent reminds him regularly that if Rose doesn't succeed or violates his contract, he won't get the balloon payment Picture Perfect owes him.

Noknoi Ayutthaya never wanted the pressure of being the lead in a drama. His agent has given him an opportunity he can't in good conscience refuse when his family is in debt and his sister's school payment is due. He doesn't expect to get the part, but he's going to give it his best shot.

Falling in love was not part of Rose's life script, but with Nok he can't help himself. Will they be able to succeed in the Thai Y-series industry while keeping their love a secret? Because the industry might accept same-sex romance in drama, but in real life it could destroy careers… and lives.

Scan the QR Code Below to Order!

ROCKING THIN ICE

Z. ALLORA

Can a sexy rock star show a relationship-phobic ice skater that there's more to life than gold medals?

When ice-skating's bad boy Blaze first glimpses Drake, every fantasy he's ever had flares to life. Not only is rock star Drake sexy as sin, his songs awaken a longing in Blaze that he's denied for years. But Blaze Parker doesn't believe in relationships—at least not those that last more than twenty minutes.

Drake Keys has dreamed about the sensual ice skater for years. When Drake is kicked out of his band because of his bisexuality, he drives across the country to finally see the man he's had a crush on skate live.

Though the attraction is instant and intense, both Blaze and Drake have baggage that puts any relationship on thin ice. Blaze is driven by a long-ago betrayal to prove himself a champion, and Drake, uncertain about the future, hopes to resurrect his music career. As they take a road trip together, Drake romances Blaze, hoping to melt his heart and show him that love is possible… but not without some tough decisions.

Scan the QR Code Below to Order!

The Great Wall
Z. Allora

Made In China: Book One

Destiny will be decided by a battle between heart and mind....

Jun Tai "Styx" Wong loves two things: playing the drums, and his best friend, Jin. But being a good Chinese son means he can't have either—he'll have to marry a girl of his parents' choosing and settle into a traditional job. His move to the bigger city of Suzhou is both a blessing and curse, as living with Jin makes it harder for Styx to suppress his desires. Nearly dying while trying to eradicate his feelings serves as a wake-up call for Jin, who takes extreme measures to keep Styx safe from harm.

When given a second chance at life and happiness, will Styx be able to claim the future he wants with Jin, his bandmates, and his music? Can love and hope grow with the constantly looming threat of Styx's parents ordering him home? Great things await—if Styx finds the courage to break down the wall that stands between him and everything he wants.

SCAN THE QR CODE BELOW TO ORDER!

The Temple of Heaven
Z. Allora

Made In China: Book Two

Music is Tian Di's life and his love, and he's made plenty of sacrifices. His career is finally taking off with his band, Made in China, and he'll continue to put music first… until he meets Jordon. Then insta-lust becomes insta-love and a commitment to the future—no matter how difficult it might be.

Jordon lives in a bubble constructed by his overprotective older brothers, who are so controlling that they've kept him from dating. A talented artist, Jordon managed to keep his success with a Japanese manga publisher a secret from his family, but now he fears discovery. It's easier to let his brothers handle everything, but Jordon has reached his limit. He's ready to draw some boundaries so he can be his own man and face all the challenges that come with that.

Their families and careers aren't the only obstacles. Jordon must accept his identity as a gay man who doesn't top or bottom. Fortunately, Tian Di—and his special talents—helps Jordon open up to his sexuality in an erotic adventure that spans Japan and China, and with love, luck, hard work, and open minds, will end in a happily ever after.

SCAN THE QR CODE

BELOW TO ORDER!

Z. ALLORA

Illusions & Dreams

THAILAND'S #1 LADYBOY SHOW

After Randy Camster failed at marriage, his life centered around work, TV sports, and listening to his friend Jake complain about how Randy's lack of a sex life will be the downfall of mankind. Not true! Well, not totally. Randy has just never understood the fascination with sex… until ladyboy performer Lalana Dulyarat shimmies into his world via an Internet ad for Thailand tourism. After that, it doesn't take much for Jake to convince Randy to take a Bang Cock vacation.

Finding an adorable little imp named Boon-nam wasn't on Jake O'Neil's itinerary. Gay, straight, and undecided, Jake has had 'em all, but never a virgin aching to explore her new body after successful affirmation surgery. Talk about pressure. And what's with everyone warning him not to break Boon-nam's heart? His is the one in danger.

Jake's openness about sexuality has always made Randy wonder if he is too focused on gender. Lalana is even more beautiful in real life than he'd hoped, but she's keeping her "male parts" and has no intention of ever having surgery. Does it really matter? A return ticket to reality awaits. The clock is ticking on the two couples' hopes for love, unless they can find a way to span gender, culture, and half a world.

SCAN THE QR CODE
BELOW TO ORDER!

FOR
MORE
OF THE
BEST
GAY
ROMANCE

www.ingramcontent.com/pod-product-compliance
Lightning Source LLC
LaVergne TN
LVHW091119080826
845145LV00008B/1977

* 9 7 8 1 6 4 1 0 8 8 8 3 1 *